CROOKED BRANCHES ON THE FAMILY TREE

Also by Judith Barnard:

The Past and Present of Solomon Sorge

As Judith Michael (with Michael Fain)

Deceptions
Possessions
Private Affairs
Inheritance
A Ruling Passion
Sleeping Beauty
A Tangled Web
Acts of Love
Pot of Gold
A Certain Smile
The Real Mother

CROOKED BRANCHES ON THE FAMILY TREE

Selected Stories

Judith Barnard

With best wishes —
Joseph Burnard

MILL CITY PRESS | MINNEAPOLIS, MN

Copyright © 2015 by JM Productions Ltd.

Mill City Press, Inc.
322 First Avenue N, 5th floor
Minneapolis, MN 55401
612.455.2293
www.millcitypublishing.com

All rights reserved. No part of this publication may be reproduced, stored in a retrieval system, or transmitted, in any form or by any means, electronic, mechanical, photocopying, recording, or otherwise, without the prior written permission of the author.

"Her Striped Socks" appeared first in Printer's Row.
Cover photograph © Michael Fain, JM Productions Ltd.

ISBN-13: 978-1-63413-855-0
LCCN: 2015917308

Cover Design by M. K. Ross
Typeset by B. Cook

Printed in the United States of America

For Michael

CONTENTS

Crooked Branches on the Family Tree 1

She Walks Like an Old Woman 30

Eleanor's Room 54

The Specialty of the House 80

The Theory of Unquestioned Beginnings 110

A Few Friends for New Year's Eve 131

Mrs. Ellington Falls from Grace 137

An Ordinary House for Extraordinary People 174

Her Striped Socks 203

His Scheherazade 228

What Happens after Shoplifting 269

Crooked Branches on the Family Tree

FOR SIXTEEN YEARS we made love six or seven nights a week, and often on awakening, especially on dark, snow-muffled mornings.

And then we stopped.

We didn't taper off, we didn't sputter in fits and starts over several months or a year. We certainly didn't discuss it, did not ponder whether we had discovered more tantalizing pastimes, or, for deep and profound though unknown reasons, had simply gotten bored.

None of that. We just stopped, cold turkey, as if we'd made a vow and determinedly hewed to it.

Of course only one of us had made the vow, had the determination, but she held to it with an implacability that brooked no questions or demands. And I went along. Inexplicably, I did not remark on the suddenness and completeness of it; did not comment on her seeming serenity; did not dwell on the fact that neither of us exchanged a single look of wide-eyed wonder, or frowning glances of curiosity, or challenge about the transformed partner with whom we shared a transformed life.

My thoughts those days were more tumultuous than my behavior. My wife more than once through the years had accused me of lacking insight, into myself and others, but those accusations were in moments of pique, probably because I was not being sufficiently sympathetic to something she said, and I knew accusations made in such a state, flung like snowballs and equally evanescent, were not to be taken seriously. During this current difficult time, I did have one or two thoughts that, within my shell of silence, might be fear, or even—to exaggerate—terror at the incomprehensible and the darkness that underlay it, but I dismissed it. In an untroubled life, I had never experienced terror, and if there had been occasions of fear, will and intellect had conquered them. Or, another thought: oddly and for the first time, I was following rules set by my wife, absurd though they were, and it was powerfully disorienting to hew to her line without having the faintest idea why I was allowing myself to do that. Perhaps simply to placate her, to help her banish whatever demons held her fast. Or not. I had no clue. She had put herself beyond the bounds of reason.

Whatever the explanation, not a ripple gave visible evidence that something was wrong. It was as if we had rearranged the living room furniture and, without comment on the strangeness of it, taken up residence, making it our new reality. And I was a partner in it—the only partnership, it seemed, we now shared.

We'd known each other since eighth grade, dated since our second year of high school after experimenting with a few others, more on my side than hers, but by the time we slept together, in our junior year, and discovered the brilliance of what we achieved in bed, we were firmly coupled, and we married two days after our college graduation. In that time we established boundaries that made it possible for us to ignore, or make light of, our differences. They were significant, but heat is a powerful mask, and for years we commented only occasionally, and then with amusement, on how little we shared. Our politics differed, our ideas of the perfect society, our preferences in friends, books, films, music, theater, sports. None of that was important; what mattered, what we built our life on, was our sex life: the stuff of fantasy. Our separate lives required their own kinds of focus and perseverance, but, when we came together, ardor and intensity kindled a different vocabulary altogether.

I went to law school and joined an international firm with high-profile clients, while my wife helped her father run his three neighborhood hardware stores. I thought it her new hobby, frivolous but harmless, hardly deserving of the time she devoted to it, but I congratulated her heartily when she opened a fourth and then a fifth store, and was truly astonished when, after her father died, she brought to bear her intelligence and drive and in fifteen years metamorphosed that handful of stores into one of the largest chains in the country.

So we became wealthy and provided for ourselves everything we wanted. We had not taken time off to have children, though we had discussed it. My wife originally wanted a child, perhaps two, no more than that, but I was opposed, and when I pointed out to her the contrast between the time and sacrifices entailed in child rearing and our sublime sexual life, plus, of course, our careers, she ultimately saw the wisdom of that and gave way. And it was a full life that we created. We bought a spacious penthouse in the city; we hired a team of experts to remodel a four-story chalet clinging to a Colorado ski mountain; we spent weekends and vacations in bed.

"Once upon a time, I had everything, too," Aunt Stella said brightly. "Given the basics, most of us do, you know, because 'everything' is a gem of fluidity."

Aunt Stella, my mother's older sister, nearing her ninetieth birthday, was given to sweeping, debatable pronouncements I accepted with a smile, recognizing that, with those who are opinionated to begin with, age seems to give license to declarations carved in stone, and to a self-satisfaction that would be intolerable in those even a few years younger.

"My sister and I married brothers," she said as we sat in her library. "Of course you knew that; who didn't? It entertained the whole family and led to feeble humor and dreadful poems on birthdays and such. I married Leon, and my little sister Rosie, your mother, married his older brother Joe. Even then—"

"Wait." Absorbed though I was in my own affairs, I knew a discrepancy when I heard it, and, for the first time, thought perhaps Aunt Stella was losing the stiletto mind that had held us in awe for so many years. "Backward," I said, trying to be gentle. "You know perfectly well who you married—"

"Whom," snapped Aunt Stella. "And you know perfectly well I do not appreciate being interrupted. As I was saying, Rosie married his older brother Joe. Even then I thought Joe was too old for her, but she didn't want to hear that; she was young and believed his serious demeanor meant he was the perfect man to take care of her. We were happy, so I shut up. Our wedding gifts had cards spouting inanities like 'beautiful symmetry' and 'forever four' and 'perfect balance.' The relatives, even the friends, kept it up for anniversary cards, though you'd think, after awhile, at least one of them would have hit upon something original. But then, originality doesn't happen often in families, does it? Originality needs more space than most families provide."

"We've wandered . . . ," I began, and stopped beneath my aunt's hard look. She was old, I reminded myself, and losing touch with reality, but still she should have recognized my need to talk about my problem, which was, stated baldly, not only had my wife and I stopped fucking, not only had we inconceivably taken it in stride, but after a couple of months of this cataclysm, my wife had decided she'd had enough—of our life, of our marriage, of me—and sent me packing so she could embrace the totality of her new existence... perfectly natural, she pointed out, abundant examples being acquaintances in their fifties who were seizing new careers, fresh outlooks, expanded horizons, unveiled visions. Oh, how the clichés did flow that day. Even when I pointed out that, although several had indeed turned to second careers, none had kicked out a spouse. Only to be told that that would come, that she was in the vanguard, that others would follow when they realized the wonders of discovering the most expansive horizon of all.

"Wandered?" Aunt Stella echoed icily, a tone of voice she has favored as appropriate for a woman eighty-nine years old and in a wheelchair. "No one has wandered away from you or your situation. I am aware of both. It is difficult not to be aware of you, as I'm sure you know. But a little patience seems a modest request since I have a story I wish to tell.

"So, we married on a Sunday evening, our two couples, with a crowd of friends and family looking on, so pleased. And we were pleased. In fact, we were so excited we couldn't stand still; we rocked back and forth or shuffled side to side; we jiggled. We all felt we'd pulled off a great coup, done something wondrous. We were in love, though how much was the novelty of our foursome, or something with depth, I can't recall after all this time. Perhaps I never knew, not even then. Probably none of us ever knew; we were ignorant of so much, including our own ignorance.

"We wore white, Rosie and I, and the boys wore tuxedos, rented. I remember how tall they looked, like picture-book men, even Leon at eighteen and Joe at twenty-six, a greenhorn just arrived the year before from Russia, learning English by taping new words all over the apartment he shared with Leon, and repeating them out loud hour after hour, driving everybody crazy. And Rosie and I, eighteen and nineteen, stood beside them, as fresh-faced as they, as giddy with excitement, getting married on our day off from work at the shirt factory, the boys given a holiday from their uncle's pharmacy where they were learning to mix things. Oh, we were ready for anything that day: marriage, families, work, all the beckoning promises of an unknown future. Eighteen ninety-seven that was, three years short of a new century, a modern century, with freedom from everything the 1800s stank of: serfs and Cossacks, pogroms, poverty, ignorance. The dark. America was different. America was the light.

"The candles were tall, too, like the boys, with dancing flames that made the rabbi's face waver so he looked sly. I knew he was annoyed with me because I wasn't listening; maybe he somehow knew I was thinking of Leon and his hand on my breast the night before, and how close we were to tumbling into bed . . . though of course there was no bed, just the kitchen floor and my parents asleep—or more likely listening—on the other side of the wall, so Leon coughed to cover up his loud breathing and I started humming *Yerushalayim shel zahav,* and then we were laughing and then he went home."

At any other time I would have found it interesting to pursue this mention of sex, a subject Aunt Stella was not given to discussing. But there was no room for any other subject in my overwhelming need for her attention, her sympathy, her rage at my wife's betrayal. Plus a plan for me to follow, what steps I should take, and in what sequence. Old as she was, she had been sharp and clear-eyed all my life, and certainly would give me advice, at least some of which was bound to be useful. She always had advised all of us. As far back as I could remember, it had been Aunt Stella who came up with remedies, with plans and goals; since childhood, we had called her the Wise One, and her house was our Delphi, my cousins and I, and often our friends, bringing dilemmas to be sorted out and solved with edicts delivered firmly and inarguably. Even now, when her confusion of which brother she had married was disturbing, I trusted her to tell me what to do and how to do it.

Perhaps. It occurred to me that she might be far too absorbed in herself to give me her full attention, and that, too, was disturbing: a sign of warped thinking, perhaps of dementia. And yet, now, trapped in a situation foreign and alarming, I had to believe in her; she was all I had. We had always gotten along, and I knew if I could ease her out of her preoccupation with herself, she could at least point me in the right direction.

It was true that Aunt Stella had not approved of our marriage, any more than did my future wife's parents. But when she saw that nothing would stop us, she softened. "You're going to need someone, and I'm here; you can call me any time. But the heavy lifting is up to you; nobody else can shape your life so it works. For each of you and both of you. You think all your differences aren't important, that you can handle them, that it will be easy. Of course it won't be, but you don't believe that now. I hope you figure it all out."

We knew she was wrong. We knew what was important, what satisfied us, and what were our priorities. Everything— my law practice, my wife's growing chain of stores, the few friends with whom we dined now and then—everything was secondary to what our bodies created together. That was the core of our life. But we had no intention of discussing that with Aunt Stella, and so, if her advice in those days was flawed, it was not her fault. On most subjects, she was uncannily right.

Except when she wasn't. There was the time she ordered me to end a casual affair I'd barely begun and had mentioned to her, lightly, as part of another discussion. She did not treat it lightly. "Roaming leads to getting lost," she snapped at me. "Until you know exactly where you're going, stay put." Insulted at being treated like an errant child, I asked her how she would know anything about it. "I know what I need to know," she said dismissively. "Just do what I say." And I did. The affair had meant nothing—how could it, when I had my wife waiting at home while I was on a brief business trip?—and it was easily ended. And of course I told Aunt Stella. When possible, it was politic to keep her happy.

She pointed at her empty wine glass, and I refilled it.

"The wedding seemed endless," she said, "though I'm sure it was no longer than most. It was just that we were impatient." She smiled to herself. "When the boys stomped on the wine glasses, two of them of course, one for each couple, Rosie edged close to me. 'Now I'm your sister and your sister-in-law,' she whispered. 'We just doubled ourselves.' And we began giggling, and the rabbi gave us such a look that I whispered to Rosie, 'You'd think we were dancing naked in front of the golden calf,' and that made us giggle even louder, and of course that made the boys laugh. They'd been grinning anyway because they'd just committed mayhem in this solemn ceremony, stomping with unceremonial energy on two wine glasses in velvet bags lying side by side, as we soon would be— it could not be soon enough—and when I choked out 'dancing naked ... golden calf," their grins burst into laughter. Even Joe, who mostly just smiled, caught the contagion and soon was howling with the rest of us. We couldn't stop; our laughter grew louder, bending the candle flames, bringing shock and dismay to our parents' faces, and twitching lips and outright laughter to the rest of the congregation. It was an epidemic of laughing and sputtering and heaving, while we tried to still our bodies and reshape our faces into adulthood as if we truly were grown-ups taking sacred lifetime vows."

My wife and I liked making love. We were consumed by making love. Once some wag described a couple coupling as a two-humped beast, but that was not us: we were an art form, a lean, beautiful piece of work. We talked about sex, we thought about sex, we fantasized about sex. It filled the crevices that otherwise would have gaped between us, enmeshed as we otherwise were in separate lives, thoughts, preferences, activities. We phoned each other during the day with edgy lasciviousness: driving to work, at our desks, driving home. We'd push back from the dinner table to dash upstairs, frenzied with veal-piccata-induced passion. When we traveled for vacations, we spent most of them in bed, leaving churches and other landmarks to less passionate tourists while we consumed newspapers and coffee between bouts of—as some nineteenth-century authors might have put it—ecstatic sexual congress.

My business trips to Europe and Asia were difficult; we suffered. Unfamiliar scents and vistas, vocabularies and timbres pitched me into a delirium of longing; every nerve aching for my wife's fingers, toes, tongue, throat, while, for her, the tedium of home and work was smothering, offering no distractions from thoughts of our lovemaking, or rather the absence of it.

I had distractions; I will say that. But it was not from desire. Necessity was what drove me: without relief there was no way I could concentrate on my work and return home earlier than scheduled. But none of the women who filled my nights had my wife's energy, her creativity, her intuition and laughter. This is not to say some were not extraordinary—it was unimaginable that, in all that time, in so many countries, at least a few would not be extraordinary—and those women I remembered with pleasure. But I never returned to any of them. That was a rule kept faithfully for my wife. She, in her abstinence, deserved no less.

Once again, Aunt Stella's wine glass was empty. One did not tell an aunt of advanced age how much to drink, so I refilled it, and mine as well. It was a Sancerre, and a fine one; she had given up red wines about five years earlier because, she said, they gave her headaches and reminded her of times past when she had not behaved well.

With 'sacred lifetime vows,' Aunt Stella had paused in her narration, and I leaped in. "You once told me that roaming leads to getting lost. But now I have a problem—"

"And so it does, and so it did, for you. Look at you, where you've landed. You married for the wrong reason and then made that reason your raison d'etre. It didn't matter whether it was at home with your wife or in beds all over Europe. You lost your way years ago and kept compounding it. Stupid, you know. And of course adolescent."

I confess I was stunned. My mouth hung open, idiotically.

"Oh, how naive you are," Aunt Stella sighed. "We all knew. You—"

"All?"

"—preened. Visibly. Annoyingly. Men do, generally. When

women do it, they have better reasons: accomplishments, managed upheavals, successful rearrangements. Rosie and I did, a year and a half after our wedding, a time when most couples would have begun coasting on the automatic pilot of familiarity and habit. But we weren't 'most people,' Rosie and I; we didn't believe in automatic anything. So, you could say we were happy in our married lives, but something wasn't right, and we knew it.

"In the first place, we weren't having babies. We should have been; everyone expected it, including us. But the months went by, our families wondered, we wondered. In all other ways, they'd decided we didn't need their attention: we were normal young married couples, nothing to titillate them into gossip and knowing glances. So, they looked elsewhere, which was fortunate, sparing us the spotlight when we decided to alter our lives.

"We had set a pattern by then: our two couples lived a block apart, the four of us ate dinner together once a week, the men bowled together twice a week, winning trophies that crowded our mantles, and every day Rosie and I had a four o'clock glass of wine. And one day, as I said, we decided to rearrange our lives.

"Rosie was sipping wine that day and mending a rip in her best Paul Poiret evening gown . . . amazing, isn't it, the details we remember? The dress was black, lace over silk, with long sleeves, and even though it was decorated with pink roses I thought it made her look severe, older than her age. Of course I never said so because Joe had bought the dress for her; Joe didn't like girlish-looking women, and I must say that was the way Rosie looked. She was gorgeous, more so as she got older, but she never lost that wide-eyed look of wonder, like a girl on the cusp of a great adventure.

"Well, there we sat in the peaceful sunshine in what seemed like a peaceful, perfect world. It wasn't that we were ignorant of the rest of the planet: we knew there was a war in Africa with people called the Boers, but it was safely distant from us. Joe had brought home a new book by a doctor named Freud, and I borrowed it, and he and I talked about it every chance we had. And there were odd flying things in Germany called Zeppelins and a tower in Paris taller than any in the world, but what did all of that have to do with us? The world's scandals and wars weren't ours, our parents had turned their backs on all that when they chose the safe port of America, and we grew up blessed with the ignorance of the sheltered.

"So, Rosie and I drank our wine and talked as usual about our small world, until, not as usual, up popped Joe's age. Joe had become very American, well, we'd all become American, but Joe had the drive, the satisfaction in business that was the essence of capitalism, and what was more American than that? By then he had designed and built a small house in a neighborhood that was beginning to improve and put on it a price tag so low it seemed crazy, but of course it wasn't, because he sold it within a week and built a couple more and sold them, and soon others took notice: men who bet he'd make money for them. And he did. They provided the financing, and he designed and built houses and began hiring, beginning with an architect who gave him lessons at night and became his partner, and they hired assistants, and all of a sudden they were building apartment buildings as well as homes, in poor neighborhoods and classy ones. Whatever they built, they sold, and soon there were stories in the newspapers, and people began calling him to build them a special house or maybe a shopping mall or an apartment building higher, better-quality than any in the neighborhood. It was wonderful to watch, like babies being born, one house becoming two and three and then a community, and Joe was the happiest he'd ever been. He got in the habit of coming over for breakfast and telling me everything he and his partner were doing; Rosie liked to sleep late. Joe did love to talk when he had a good listener, but working all day and taking lessons from his architect partner every night, he didn't see much of Rosie, and I knew his fierceness for success was bothering her, but I didn't know how much until that day, while we drank our wine and talked.

"'Things aren't good with Joe,' Rosie said gloomily. 'I don't know what to do anymore. You'd know; you're stronger than me. Smarter, too. You'd know how to handle him, make him come home in time for dinner, go to shows, go dancing. You could probably even get him to bed before he's so tired he just collapses. He's too wrapped up in work and he's getting . . . he's acting old.'

"'He just goes to sleep?' I asked. 'Every night?'

"'Every night.'

"That was a shock; she'd never mentioned it, kept it locked inside herself for God knows how long. 'Maybe a whip . . .' I said and smiled, but Rosie looked like she was going to cry—Rosie cried easily—so I said something else, something about a vacation, getting away from work and the house, that sort of thing. I talked for a while to keep from saying what I really thought, which was that they'd never been right for each other, I'd known that from the start. And finally Rosie said, 'You go. Take him somewhere. I'm so tired of knowing I'm not what he wants. I'm so tired of . . . well, actually . . . I'm tired of him.'

"Had I tried to get Rosie to say that? I can't remember. I may have. I really and truly can't remember."

I did try to bring my wife home; my focus had narrowed to that. She had moved out, and my bed was wide and cold; my enormous house offered only absence. My days were as busy as ever, but empty, depleted of libidinous phone calls and snatches of colorful fantasy between meetings and conference calls. I had nothing from the previous night to recall with satisfaction, nothing to anticipate for the evening ahead, though I could recall in detail past afternoons when desire built to a heated frenzy that propelled me into our house at the end of the day where she would be waiting, in the living room with its ample couch, or the kitchen with its long trestle table, or the garden where the grass was soft and lush, or the bedroom with its capacious bed, or carpet, if we didn't manage to make it that far.

In the living room of her new apartment, as yet only partially furnished, I stood, not having been invited to sit down, and unfurled a long line of irrefutable arguments for her coming home, but she refused even the courtesy of considering them. "I'm here," she said, as if something so simple should be equally simple for even a simpleton to grasp. "This is where I live now. This is my home."

"You have a home," I said, my simplicity equal to hers, pointing out something too obvious to need repeating. Still, I repeated it. "You have a home, a place in the world, a husband who wants you. Everything women strive for, work for, commit crimes for . . . you have it all, waiting for you, ready with open arms to welcome you back."

She shrugged. I could not believe it. After eloquence, she offered a shrug. I waited for her to say more, to undo the damage done by that shrug. When none came, I left, I admit it, in a rage, slamming her front door behind me.

It was after the fourth encounter in her apartment, the fourth variation on that conversation whose conclusion was always the same, that I—this is extremely difficult to say, something I have not told even Aunt Stella—I fell apart. Fell to pieces. Fell on my wife, forcing her to her knees, my hand on the back of her neck, pushing her head down. I flung her skirt over her head, yanked down her underpants, and took her from behind, ripping into her with a demented energy that, I must admit, brought an astonishingly explosive release but, as with a cooler head I might have expected, not the kind of satisfaction I was used to.

She never made a sound. I'd known for years that she hated it; she'd told me, long ago, after we tried it a few times, but still she was silent throughout, and remained silent and unmoving. I lay there until my breathing quieted, then pulled out of her. I leaned forward and kissed her pale, perfect buttocks, inhaling the metallic scent of the blood that seeped between them, willing her to sob or to show anger, rage, hatred, renewed passion, an upsurge of love, whatever she might offer that would propel us past this moment.

She said nothing. She remained exactly where I had forced her, buttocks in the air, head hanging straight down between tight shoulders. Her eyes were wide open, which was unnerving, her lips a tight line. And then, with a barely perceptible movement, she shrugged.

My throat closed with a surge of rage, and I made some kind of a sound. A lesser man would have howled, would have allowed savagery free rein, but I stayed where I was, my entire body taut as a wire, until I was able to breathe again.

Then, with admirable composure, I stood, zipped my pants and buckled my belt, adjusted my tie, my shirt, my suit jacket, and left her apartment without a word. I would not go back. When she wanted me, she would call. I would not go back for anything less.

Instead, I took to visiting Aunt Stella. Who, perhaps because of her dotage, took the wine bottle herself and, ignoring my glass, filled her own with most of what was left, allowing me the last quarter inch. "Did I manipulate Rosie into offering me her husband?" she asked. She settled back and picked up her knitting. "I wouldn't say yes, but I wouldn't say no. I was of course stronger, she was right about that, and smarter, and I'd known for some time that Leon and I weren't any more right for each other than were she and Joe. Every time the four of us were together, I knew it would be better for Joe to be with me. Better for him and better for me, because we could grow together, do more, be more. And I kept imagining Leon with Rosie, a couple. My Leon was as sweet and fun-loving as Rosie, which was delightful for a week or a month, but not a lifetime, not for me, anyway. I loved Leon, but I knew I loved Joe in a different way, a better way for a lifetime together, and I saw perfectly clearly that he needed me as much as I finally knew I needed him. And I have to say that Rosie was right there with me when she said I should take Joe on a vacation, and I said I would, and she came back with, 'And I'll take care of Leon. You'd like that.'

"We started giggling, the same way we'd giggled at our wedding, and, caught up in that childish laughter, in a moment of pure foolishness, I let myself wonder if Rosie and Joe and Leon and I really had been married. I mean married in that consecrated way that comes from sober ritual. The whole time the rabbi was talking—English, Hebrew, prayers, commands—we'd been jiggling, twitching, about to explode, and afterward none of us could recall a word he'd said. And so, I thought, still fantasizing, when we upended solemnity with underlying hysterics, had we so warped the spirit of the ceremony that, in some peculiar way, the marriage was never consummated?

"'Never consummated,'" I said to Rosie, and that set us off again. Because, as soon as we talked about it, we both saw how obvious it was that she and I were with the wrong brothers, Rosie out of her depth with serious, determined Joe, and me floundering around with the showman Leon—the food maven, the chef, the master bartender, always on stage, always the maestro. I haven't told you about Leon. He'd opened a small grocery store and he ran it alone, mostly to save money, but also because he loved it: schmoozing, serving, wrapping, flying about from customer to customer, the host of an endless party. So of course more and more people, mostly women, came, the atmosphere being contagious, and soon he added an eat-in and take-out delicatessen along one wall of his store, and we were making a nice living. But it wasn't enough for my maven of a husband. He bought the store next door, turned it into a fine restaurant with white tablecloths, silver, crystal, candles, and hired a famous chef. My Leon, the host, would greet people at the door and remember who liked a special burgundy with his sirloin steak and who was on a diet and who had reserved one of the little private rooms at the back because it wasn't his wife he was with that night. Oh, he was so good you can't believe it; he was such a mensch everybody loved him and they all wanted to be close to him.

"So of course pretty soon the place was overflowing, and he built an addition with a stained glass door connecting the dining room and a new nightclub, with a singer and a dance floor, and in time it, too, grew bigger, turning into a cabaret decorated with huge, stained glass windows he found in hotels and homes that were being torn down, and a balcony around three sides looking down on the little stage where the piano was, and the waiters and waitresses put on two shows a night. He named it The Grand Palais Leon, pronouncing it Lay-OHN so overnight people were calling me Mrs. Lay-OHN and sucking up to me, and I didn't have a husband anymore, I had a star performer, and I didn't have friends, I had people who wanted a seat up front.

"But still, it was a fun time, no question. Fun and exciting, at least for a while. We had dinners at the cabaret, good drinks, fancy clothes, sex at home, and it was good sex, wonderful sex, I won't minimize Leon's talents, and of course we were so young . . . good Lord, the energy we had then! Anyway, we had all the good life anybody could want, but it turned out it wasn't the life I wanted. Rosie was the one who never got tired of it, and, more and more, when Joe was working and I was home because I'd had enough nightlife, she'd go to Leon's place when it opened at six in the evening, and sit with him, and soon the two of them were the hosts. They were there until long after midnight, dancing and chatting up all the customers, and when she woke up about noon the next day she'd call to tell me all I'd missed.

"But of course I hadn't missed any of it, except maybe the excellent coq au vin Leon's chef had on the menu. And his crème brulee. But I only thought about them when I was contrasting them with a different kind of life and trying to be sensible. I'd always thought of myself as a sensible person, and here I was stuck between brothers, like some frilly girl in a romance novel. No question, I was having a hard time. When I could put my finger on what I really wanted, it came down to making my life bigger, building something big and lasting, larger and more important than entertainment. And it wasn't long before it became pretty clear what I wanted. It was what Joe had: creating things that were essential. I wanted to be part of it, bricks and mortar, houses and whole neighborhoods, apartments and office buildings, and people making their lives in them, babies being born, trees and gardens planted . . . oh, I did go on and on.

"Some of the time I thought I sounded like a teenager dreaming of leaving a mark on the landscape. I told myself I should be content to make a good home and raise children to be fine people, that that was my career and it was a noble one, I truly believed that. But noble, as good as it was, seemed narrow compared with what Joe was doing. That's where my thinking got stuck.

"So I was muddled and going around and around, until I put into words what I'd known all along but hadn't been willing to admit: I wanted Joe for the man he was, and I wanted to share the life he was making.

"It wasn't that I didn't love Leon; as I said, I did love him, the way I knew I'd love my children, the way I loved Rosie, to tell the truth. I found them amusing and touching and very dear, but not really grown up, at least, not my kind of grown up. So when the time came—and it had to come from Rosie; I couldn't be the one to suggest it—I set them up together, and I took Joe."

I shouted, finally getting a word in, "You didn't! You couldn't—"

But my aunt stopped me with a look and an upraised

hand. "I am talking," she said. "Your job is to listen." She sat back. "Took him on that vacation Rosie suggested—two weeks in New York for vaudeville and Buffalo Bill's Wild West show and museums and long walks—and then, when we came home, Rosie and I took the boys to dinner at a fancy restaurant, not Leon's, somewhere neutral, and told them we'd been thinking about it and had decided we'd all be a lot happier and better off if we switched spouses.

"Of course Joe and I had talked about it in New York, and so had Rosie and Leon, so there wasn't much surprise around the table, though there was a lot of talk about what people would say and would we all be as close as we'd always been, with no second thoughts, jealousies, curiosities, that sort of thing, but we were thinking of objections only so we could tell ourselves later that it hadn't been easy, that we did it reluctantly, from necessity.

"And I did wonder, a little later, if we'd been trying to avoid admitting that Rosie and I were being cruel: manipulating two men for our own needs, ignoring their egos. It's true each of them was desired by one of us, but it was also true that each of them was being discarded by one of us. I did give that a lot of thought. I couldn't talk to Rosie about it because she would not permit a word of caution after we'd made it happen. And soon I stopped worrying about it; there was no way of going back (can you imagine what that would have been like: ping-pong balls whizzing across a table, never sure which side was best?) and the fact was, we settled into our new lives without a stumble. As soon as we'd convinced the relatives we were fine and they shouldn't make a drama out of it—though in fact they never got used to it—not one of us ever looked back or even talked about it.

"And did we preen? Well, of course, but not for long; we were too busy—"

"You traded husbands!" My mouth was working, trying to shape words. I'd seen it coming, she'd actually said it, but I couldn't grasp it until she came out with *we settled into our new lives without a stumble.* How could they? It was not possible to believe they would dream up such a caper, much less carry it out. I knew them; I'd grown up with them. However sharp I'd always thought my aunt, however frivolous my mother, I would have dismissed as inconceivable the idea that either of them, singly or in concert, would stray from what they saw as respectability. They didn't have it in them. They were ordinary, conventional, middle-class women, settled in their ways. It was true that Aunt Stella proved to be amazingly capable at running a corporate office and working on plans with Joe, and my mother was an ideal hostess at late-night parties, even working with Leon in his office, not with numbers, which bored her, but with interior design and planning events, but I knew their limitations: they were not women capable of flights of imagination.

What had happened, how did it happen, that in one flaring moment they found the creativity, the backbone, to devise a scheme and hoodwink two men to carry out this one reckless act before lapsing back into mediocrity? What made them take the chance of sticking out in their social worlds? They were incapable of defying propriety. All the years I was growing up, Aunt Stella and Joe lived a block from us; their kids and my sister and I spent days, weekends together; our families had dinners together, went to concerts and theater, made impromptu picnics, celebrated holidays, attended school functions, took trips, always together, an extended family in which the four of us kids shared parents as comfortably as we shared candy after a night of trick-or-treating. With never a hint that something in our two families might be peculiar.

I couldn't fathom how they'd done it. I glanced at Aunt Stella, smiling as she made her knits and purls in perfect symmetry; I looked around the room, the snug, book-lined library, her retreat for as long as I could remember, and for the first time wondered who she really was.

"—know when something is for the best," Aunt Stella was saying. "A skill, perhaps an art, whatever it is, Rosie and I had it; look at the good lives we made for our two families. Fine children, fine businesses, wonderful marriages. Every day was exciting; every day was an adventure, and we shared all of it, because, as you well know, we spent a good part of our lives together, you remember all that, the dinners and concerts, even the political rallies.

"And you know how happy your mother was. Rosie the hostess, absolutely the best, Leon's partner in the three cabarets they opened and the dinner theater in New York; I'd never seen her as beautiful or as happy. Leon, too, he thrived, and they're still happy, retired and traveling and living in that place in Arizona. They even took up golf; Rosie says it keeps her thin.

"And I was with Joe, my dearest Joe who understood me as no one else ever did; we took every step of our lives together. While the children were in school, I managed the office, and Joe and his partner built and built; eventually we had a company of forty architects and forty, something like that, land planners and designers, engineers and landscapers, everything kept growing. And there were dinners and receptions, benefit events; we were, in a small way, famous and had invitations enough to keep us out every night. But even after more than sixty years, what we most looked forward to were quiet evenings at home, dinners in front of the fire in the library, this library, talking, reading, listening to music. I know to you it sounds tedious, but those were the times we treasured: the world—good, bad, indifferent—beyond the windows, and, inside, the two of us, entire. It's all in the past now, but I remember the fun of it, the wonder: city councils named streets after Joe; he and his partner got awards and gave speeches; people wrote, thanking him for the communities he created, the kind of livable—"

"I know, I've seen them." I was exhausted and bored. "But you know, Aunt Stella, I wanted to talk to you about something else today."

"To talk about yourself, you mean. True, that's why you're here. I remember. You may think I forget things, at my age, but I remember . . . I do remember."

She was thinking of Joe. I knew it and, out of respect, kept silent. Let her mourn; he had been gone less than a year.

"Well," she said at last, "you don't see why I told you about us? This long story? Why do you think I never told you before? Rosie either. None of us told any of you; who would have cared, after all these years? And the relatives never talked about it; we'd embarrassed them, and they were happy to let it fade. But today I had a reason."

I finished my glass of wine. "You always tell me, eventually, what you've decided it's in my interest to know."

She laughed. I had to admit, my aunt had a wonderful laugh, hearty and infectious. There was no fakery in her.

"You were often sweet as a child," she said. "Self-absorbed, of course, that has never changed, but when you were young, you had a nice sense of humor and a willingness to help others who were having difficulties: a school problem, gluing a broken toy, working on a jigsaw puzzle, that sort of thing. We admired you for that. But soon enough your sense of humor vanished, as did your kindness. What was left was solipsism."

I stood up. "I didn't come here for—"

"Oh, sit down. We're now talking about your favorite subject, and you're going to leave?"

I sat down. I would not have scored any points by arguing. My wife called Aunt Stella the high priestess of the family on whose altar we placed burnt offerings for her favor: approbation, admiration, affection, love. "No arguments," said my wife. "If you try, she peels off your words and gets to the heart and eviscerates it. You don't have a chance against her."

Another conundrum: how did my wife know so much about my aunt?

"So," said Aunt Stella. She put her knitting aside. "Why did I put you through our biography? To teach you something. To give you some ideas about other ways to live." She held up her hand, as if I'd been about to object, as, of course, I had been. "Not trading spouses . . . why would I suggest that to anyone, even though for us it was necessary and right? I told you that story because the four of us found something you've never even looked for: lives with depth, with layers of meaning in work and play, with subtleties—a word you would do well to study."

"Oh, for Christ's sake," I said; I couldn't help myself. "This is crap. You two pulled a lousy, cheap trick on your husbands so you could laugh at your joke all these years, and you call that subtlety?"

"Bite your tongue!" My aunt had snapped at me. It was not like her. "Shame on you. Listen to me. Crawl out of your little black hole and pay attention to something besides your own ignorance." She took a breath. That was not like her, either; usually, once begun, she rolled ahead full steam. "What we did was save two marriages and give the four of us space to be the best we could, instead of settling for what was good but not sufficient. What was more than one-dimensional. If you're looking for a measuring stick, Leon and I had a fine time in bed, but we all knew there was more: a lot of life on the other side of the bedroom door."

She looked at me for a long time until, like a teenager, I began to squirm. "Well?"

"There's not a lot to you," said Aunt Stella, and I started to tell her she was crazy; my life was a string of successes. But I stayed silent, reminding myself of her age, her limitations. She was old, her outlook on the world warped by dementia.

"One-dimensional," she went on, almost thoughtfully. "Sex, the big number one: conquest, rush, release . . . until next time. What else do you have? What do you and your wife share, besides sex? What do you do in your spare time together, besides sex or what leads up to it and what follows it, mostly thinking about next time? What have you built together? Where are you now, since she stopped having sex with you?"

I was on my feet again. "I never told you that."

She shook her head, one of her infuriating, woeful headshakes. "Do you think you're the only one who talks to me? Does it ever occur to you there is a very large world out there in which people have relationships without regard for you or your whims?"

"She talked to you," I said.

"Great heavens above, of course she did. We've been friends for years. We like each other."

I felt absurd standing there, looming over my aged, shrunken aunt in her wheelchair, but there seemed no good way to sit down.

"We built our lives, Rosie and Leon and Joe and I, on what we could create together. We made a mistake the first time; we corrected it. In other words—and you would be wise to listen to this; sit down and listen, for heaven's sake, I get dizzy watching you bounce up and down—we took control of our lives in a world where too many people feel helpless: everything is too big, too complicated, too fast moving, scary even, for them to grab hold, at least to slow everything down so they can shape events in ways they need or prefer or just want to try out. The four of us did that. We grabbed our lives and shaped them and shared what we shaped. We grew together, not apart.

"We were four small people in a huge world Joe called irreducible, but on our small stage we gathered all we could, built what we could, and it was, for us, miraculous. Joe and I had wonderful friends and families, wonderful adventures, wonderful love making. Because that's what it was: love, and it never became background; we always were aware of it, of how it grew and changed over the years but never diminished, and every day we were grateful for it. We were joyous. Do you know what that word means, what it feels like?"

"You're lecturing me." I was indeed seated again, but my hands gripped the arms of the chair.

"Of course I am. It's what you came for, isn't it? Well, actually you came so I could tell you what to do to get back to where you were a few months ago." She shook her head again. "All the money you made, the fancy houses, cars, travel, possessions... and what did they all add up to? Can you claim anything but surface? Instant pleasure and then... what? What is it, exactly, you want to go back to? Talk to me about what you've really worked at, what you've searched for and found that's worthwhile, that's important to someone or something beyond yourself. You could have had children, but you were too wrapped up in yourself for that. So what do you have? Do you have a marriage? What have you built, what in your life has depth, dimension, something that will outlast you?"

I said nothing; abstractions never had interested me.

My aunt sighed, one of those long sighs I find condescending and insulting. "You're still young," she said. "Plenty of time to find something to shape your life, to create new layers in it. Look outside yourself, for heaven's sake. Or do you want to tell me I'm wrong about your life? Well, then tell me. But of course you can't. All you can do—" she made a fist, brown-spotted, gnarled, veined, small knobs of glossy knuckles and taut skin—"is come running to me when your little world bursts apart, when your wife wakes up and leaves—late, very late, as she's the first to admit—and when your poor attempts to lure her back with hollow promises of more money, more possessions, fail. Then you turn to the only language you know, and you rape her."

I began to shake, churning with rage I could almost taste. The room, the old woman, blurred; my head was cracking. I lurched forward, trying to breathe, to focus. Wine glasses, bottle, knitting, walls of books wavered, rippled, while Aunt Stella faded in and out, emerging each time clearly enough for me to feel her neck in my hands, hear her bones crack, her animal cries.

I did not touch her. By now I was spinning, a crazy top, toward the door, to get out of there or hurtling toward her, to pound shut her knowing eyes, then careening toward the door again, back and forth, out of control, until, unaccountably and shamefully, I screamed, a short, sharp scream that sliced the air between us.

Aunt Stella cringed in her chair . . . which saved me. I looked down at the little clump of fear that had been my formidable aunt, and my madness cleared. Already half-turned to leave, I kept going, staggering out of the library, across the dining room, living room, and foyer to the hallway, the elevator, the lobby of her building, the grassy stretch before it, and at last came to a dead stop on the sidewalk, taking shuddering breaths of the sharp October air.

I began to walk. I needed to move; the direction was unimportant. My steps were ragged and slow, matching the chaotic mess in my head, but after a time I began to focus my thoughts and little by little my steps, while still slow, were more regular. There are times in our lives when we have no option but to face the truth. My aunt, whom I had honestly loved, was senile, fabricating a narrative pathetic in its adolescent fantasies. I had come to her for advice; she had given me a puerile piece of fiction, concocted, it was obvious, in the long empty nights after her husband died, when no one remained to question her poor end-of-life attempt at titillation (for who would pester Rosie and Leon, shuffling around their geriatric village in the sands of Arizona?). The fact that she thought I would buy it, even admire her for courage and creativity, was insulting. A woman I had loved and admired had become a demented crone, delusional, self-referential, and so uninterested in others' problems she was not even pitiable.

Her hostility to me, who had genuinely loved and admired her, was baffling and would have been discomfiting had I the time to think about it. But I had more important things to do. I had to shape a life. That was a tidbit I did get from her.

I would sell the house—far too big now, in any event; we should have thought of it long ago—and find an apartment in the city, one with a breathtaking view to all points of the compass. I would hire a decorator to furnish it brilliantly in the colors and styles my wife favored. I would buy a few choice pieces by artists she admired, especially sculpture; this was not a time to think of cost. I would buy her a sports car; I remember once she mentioned what fun it would be to own one. And I would lead meaningful discussions with her built around our work, our interests, our lives outside our home. These, plus the great satisfactions we gave each other, which she would be longing for as wrenchingly as I, would inform our renewed life together.

I had no illusions about any of this being easy or quick. But that pleased me (as I knew it would please Aunt Stella if she knew, though of course she would not, until she called; nothing less than her invitation would bring me back to her). My wife and I had made a life built on pleasure. Others have built on far less. We had been artists, and what we had created reached a level of brilliance few ever experience. To recapture that life, perfect until my wife was corrupted by my aunt, was the challenge. It would be a long journey. I would be tested. But therein lay the satisfaction: I knew I was up to it.

She Walks Like an Old Woman

WELL, I AM. Old. And obviously a woman, though, truth be told, that seems not at all obvious or interesting to many, to those, for example, like the young bucks, with or without some nubile lovely clinging to an arm, who look past me or above or to the side, and therefore, if asked when half a block on, whom they had just passed, would look puzzled, would make a quick half-turn to look behind them at my receding figure, and, turning back, would shrug. Somebody old.

I know how I walk: tentatively, cautiously, gingerly. Fearfully. On icy streets, shuffling. My eyes piercing the sidewalk, searching for rigosities, cracks, and crumbling pavement the city hasn't put into its budget, loose pebbles that roll underfoot. Stopping when I need to catch my breath or to admire the scenery: gardens in youthful bloom or drooping from the first frost or hibernating; store windows with pubescent mannequins; homes flaunting their architecture—Gilded Age or Art Deco or those startling, strangely beautiful boxes of glass and steel. And of course, to admire all this, I stop right where I am, so other pedestrians slam into me. And get mad, as well they should, since it's my fault, I admit it—not much chance I'd forget my own anger at their age—and I always apologize, profusely, dramatically, and sometimes I get a smile in return but most often a glare and a stiff back marching into the distance.

But the truth is, I get the same glare and stiff back most of the time, because most of the time, even in motion, I'm an obstacle with my shuffle, or when I take a careful minute to assess height and depth and debris before stepping off the curb, and I know exactly what those stiff backs are flinging back at me: Good Lord, she's so old, why is she afraid of dying?

Because, I might have flung back if they'd had the guts to ask me in person, it isn't time!

Because I'm having a wonderful life. Meaning: not only my mostly delightful great-grandchildren; or the foreign films in the art house a few blocks from my house; or theaters where the dialogue is so good I feel I'm up there with the actors, going through everything they're going through; or because I still can get down on my knees and work in the vegetable garden in my backyard, though those are all pure pleasure and I'm thankful for them. But top of the list is the four months every winter when I click into my cross-country skis on a golf course in Connecticut. The minute I push off in the tracks on that forgiving snow, I'm decades younger, or, better yet, ageless: gliding, floating, flying down the long, gentle hills so beloved of golfers, and of me. (Of course flying is relative, and I do acknowledge that 'flying' doesn't exactly describe the way I ski now, but if it seems that way to me, that's all that matters.)

There's a special freedom in that kind of skiing, being attached to the crystalline landscape, merging into the dazzling white expanse so there's almost no Me anymore, no Irene Bremen with her sad, sagging body that can barely recall the firm curves and easy grace that once drew lingering glances from men and women both, and took her to the top in modeling, especially beloved by Italian designers who spanned her waist with their hands and got excited by her cheekbones.

Those were the years of freedom: Philip and I both working and no children (we waited ten years to settle down; we were having so much fun). Those were the years of hiking with Philip in the Dolomites, biking with Philip in Tuscany and Provence, skiing with Philip down the steepest slopes in

Gstaad and Cortina and Aspen, dinners with Philip at little restaurants where we could always find a quiet corner to talk in low voices about our days, our adventures, our world. Oh, I do miss Philip. Thirty years gone, and they say it gets easier, and of course the ache diminishes, as do the *please* and *I want* tearing me up inside, but what's left behind is a bleak dry patch in the heart where nothing can flourish. I know that's fanciful and I shouldn't try to be a poet, but that's what it feels like, and at my age I say what I feel.

We were well-matched, Philip and I, even though he was fifteen years older, from a family far wealthier than mine and already on his way to becoming wealthy on his own in a way past all my imaginings. We fit together and we lived in absolute harmony for . . . well, that isn't quite true. We did have our differences. He liked the past—a gentler and more embracing time than ours, he liked to say—and so he furnished our home with antiques and traditional styles in furnishings and art that I thought heavy and, truth be told, a little stifling, while I wanted, had always wanted, to experiment, to throw open windows and doors to see whatever was out there that was remaking the world. One time, I cared enough about a Braque collage to argue with him about it—in fact, it exploded into a crazy fight, poor Philip, faced with a termagant, if only for a very bad hour, until finally he said I could spend the huge amount (it seemed huge at the time; I wish he could see where Braque's prices are today) to make it mine as long as I promised to hang it in my dressing room, which I did, and if he ever took a peek in there, I didn't know about it.

But the furnishings were his choice and I'm living with them still, rooms filled with Regency English and other styles chosen by Philip and his various expert decorators who probably told me at the time what period each piece came from, but I truly did not care, so I forgot them five minutes later. My kids—strictly speaking, that's a ridiculous word: they're not kids; unbelievably, they're grandparents themselves, but that's what they are to me—-my kids keep telling me to sell the house. Downsize, they call it, a bizarre word, as if they're urging me to shrink (which I already have, almost three inches, making some of my kitchen shelves unreachable without a step stool, so that's quite enough downsizing, thank you very much).

But they have other arguments about my staying in my fifteen-room house in my familiar neighborhood. "It's not familiar," they say. "It's completely changed: no more young families, no more houses. Look around, for heaven's sake, admit it: this house is a relic, the only one for blocks around, stuck between three-flats and high-rise condos. No next-door-neighbors, no kids on Halloween, no backyard barbecues, no bridge games a few doors down, just you in that huge house with strangers for neighbors. And you know damn well how expensive it looks: it stands out like a sore thumb; do we have to remind you it's been broken into three times in the past few years?"

"Of course not." I bite it off; I'm annoyed and impatient with the same arguments I've heard before. "But they don't try anything when I'm home; it's only when I'm out of town, and even then what did they take? A couple of television sets and a computer; easily replaced."

Matthew, if this time it's Matthew talking, takes a deep breath, as if I'm the one giving him a hard time. "You are not safe there; why can't you see that?" He looks at me; I know my face is flat and I'm turned away from him. "Well, anyway, just in general: what do you want with all that space? How many of those rooms do you even go into these days?"

I turn back to him. "Not many. But I was happy with Philip in all of them for a long, perfect time, and I've found ways to be happy in a few of them since he died. It's a wonderful house, and if you think I'm going to let somebody tear it down to put up some monster building, you've got another think coming. Besides, what would I do with all the furniture? And the art? Except for the Braque; I'd keep that. But all the rest . . . do any of you want it?"

And of course not one of them says Yes. So there you are.

But where was I? I wasn't talking about the house, or Philip, or antique furniture; I was talking about skiing. And walking. And getting on in years, though the few friends I have who are still upright like me are not giving that much thought.

But face it: come November 23, I'll celebrate—if that's the word—birthday number ninety-four, and I am perfectly aware that's a considerable number of years. You'd think I'd be a masterpiece of wisdom with all those years under my belt, and it's true I've learned a lot, but there are still times when I don't feel wise at all, just an ordinary woman floundering for the right decisions in a crazy, complicated world.

"What would you like?" asks my son Matthew. We're at lunch at a quiet restaurant he likes in midtown, and our corner table gives us the privacy I like. "We always go out to dinner on your birthday, but maybe you'd like something different this year. Something more special."

"What don't I have that you could give me?" It's not a hostile question; I'm curious.

"A new apartment at 55 East," he says, and I look to see if he's embarrassed. He ought to be; I'm sure he's been delegated by his brother and sister to be the messenger this week.

But he's not embarrassed; he's aggressive, flinging down a gauntlet, so to speak (though he'd vigorously and righteously deny that). "Just tell me why not," he says when I don't answer.

Well, it's obvious to me, if not to him and his brother and sister. Because, I might say, when you talk about it, you skip the crucial part. You talk about the joys of downsizing to a spiffy apartment in a classy high rise with a doorman and maintenance staff and good restaurants and swimming pool and so on, but you leave out what I call (I know you hate it when I do) the Final Solution: a spiffy apartment in a specific classy high rise called 55 East. And 55 East, in addition to being classy etc. etc., has half its apartments set aside for the mostly able-bodied, and the other half for the decrepit and incompetent: those who graduate or, more accurately, skid, from living on their own to depending on what is euphemistically known as Assisted Living, or, to be realistic, Crutch Living, in which, when you get up in the middle of the night to pee, someone is there to keep you on the seat instead of falling in.

Do I look like that's what I need? When I'm flying—okay, okay, gliding—down a snow-covered slope, do I look decrepit? When I'm walking to the concert hall a mile from my home and finding my own fifth-row center aisle seat, do I look incompetent? Irene Bremer teetering on the edge of the grave or the toilet seat? Bullshit, as my youngest great-grandson likes to say; it's his favorite word these days.

All of which my children should understand, instead of telling me I'm in denial. I'm perfectly aware, without their reminding me, that lots of people even younger than I have gone down that slippery slope. But what does that have to do with me?

So it's left to me to be the mature, understanding one, to

tolerate their whims and to love them in spite of everything: my three beautiful, grown-up children whose lives are in various states from solid to fraying, as I clearly see even when they don't.

"Companionship," Matthew goes on when I sit there thinking instead of coming back with some smart answer. "You're alone there—"

"Maria," I say.

"A housekeeper," he says, it's almost a snort. "You call that companionship?"

"I like Maria," I snap at him. "Even more, I like my own company. If you like my company, why shouldn't I?"

That stops him for a minute. And I'm feeling kindly toward him, so I let him off the hook. "It's not so much that I don't want to move *to*," I tell him. "It's that I don't want to move *from*. I have a house I love, filled with memories of love, and I'm happy when I walk through the rooms and know I'm where I belong. I lock the door at night and it's a satisfying sound, that click of the lock, it makes me feel warm and secure and at home. If you can't understand that, I'm sorry for you."

Matthew, my firstborn, was thirty years old when his father died, and he decided I would need caring for and he was the one to do it. He was married then, with one child and another on the way, but his sister and brother were just beginning to set up their own families, so Matthew saw my solitariness as his challenge, a responsibility he could bear more wisely, charitably, and manfully than anyone else. (Well, that does sound harsh, but it seems never to have occurred to my well-muscled son that I might bear the burden he thought he was assuming by himself.) Who better to be my protector? The fact that I didn't want a protector, didn't need one, had no idea what he'd be doing as a protector (and probably neither did he), was irrelevant as far as he was concerned. He showed up at my house every day at noon to check on me, and on his way home, to invite me to dinner at the apartment he shared with his wife and her two American water spaniels, two of the smartest dogs I've ever been privileged to know, and if I said I was fine, I didn't need to be fed, he would check the refrigerator and oven, even the microwave, to make sure I was telling the truth.

Finally, more annoyed than I should have been—after all, he was doing the best he could—I took to being away from home at noon and five-thirty; a nuisance, but it didn't take long to pay off. Matthew knew what I was doing, and if he felt hurt he never told me. He just stopped dropping by (though, for the first year after my noon and afternoon getaways, he couldn't resist a daily phone call), and, for the rest, we made dates ahead of time and talked on the phone a couple of times a week.

But that's the point: he's never really gotten past the role of protector. He canceled a vacation with his wife once when I was in the hospital for a knee replacement, hardly a life and death crisis. When he and his wife went to Paris he insisted I join them, and I did, I confess it, because I wanted to visit the places Philip and I had loved, and going along prevented yet another argument. When his wife asked him why he invited me . . . well, you can see what's coming. She tries, but she has a devil of a time getting rid of me. God knows I've tried to help her with that, tried to slither away quietly, but Matthew is tenacious; he thinks in some quixotic way he's become my Philip, and I can see, if he doesn't, how it's causing the edges of his marriage to fray.

The waiter brings our lunch, and we don't speak until

he's refilled our wine glasses and left, with that funny little bow French waiters give when they know they've given exemplary service in bringing you an unequaled meal. I start in on my quiche and salad—it's delicious and I'm hungry—and Matthew takes a bite of veal before answering my question about what I don't have that he could give me. "There's nothing you don't have," he says, all earnestness and, I must say, sweetness, "except the things people need more of when they get old."

"Define 'old,' I snap at him. "There's old and there's old, and you know exactly what I am."

"Security," he goes on, as if I hadn't said a word, "safety, emergency help, medical care a few floors from yours, restaurants an elevator ride away, dry cleaning service, mail and packages and groceries delivered to your door, living closer to everything in the city . . . look at you: these aren't just desirable, they're necessary."

"Look at me? And? What do you see?"

"My mother, who is aging and becoming fragile—"

Well, Philip and I did teach them to be honest though not necessarily blunt.

"—in many ways," he finishes, and at that I perk up.

"In many ways? Name one."

"You use a cane when you—"

"When I'm tired, at the end of the day. Is that the best you can do?"

He sits there, my stalwart, handsome son, fork in hand, debating. Finally he gives a little shrug. "Marnie Springer, at Saks. She's working in gloves this month and saw you walk off with a pair last week."

Well, shoot. It's true: I did wander away with the gloves still in my hand, and it's true I dropped them into my purse, the way I always do with gloves, without thinking. And when I got home and found them I didn't think much of it; I just wrote myself a note to bring them back the next day, and that's what I did. When Matthew said Marnie had seen me, I couldn't believe it; she's always so busy with customers. And I couldn't believe she actually gave me away. We've known each other for years and we like each other. Why would she tattle on me, and to Matthew, of all people?

So of course I get indignant. "Shame on her; she should have called me, not you. And did you defend me? Did you tell her your mother wouldn't do such a thing; you know she wouldn't? I'll bet not. I'll bet you just said, 'Well, she's old and failing, I'll take care of her.' Something like that, right? And then what? What happened a couple of days later? She called again . . . yes? To tell you I'd returned them. Were you going to tell me that? Or maybe she didn't call . . . maybe she wasn't watching that time and didn't see me. Fell down as a spy! You hired her, yes? Do you pay her by the hour?"

"Oh cut it out," he says, and now he's riled because he knows I've got him. "Of course I don't pay her, and she did call, a couple of days later. She said you'd put the gloves back."

"Hah!" I say. There is no time in life when it's not totally satisfying to get the better of your children. "Of course I put them back. What else would I do with them?"

"But that's the point," Matthew says. "Why the hell did you do it? You can afford the gloves; you could afford twenty or fifty . . . or the whole goddamn department. Besides, you don't need any more; you've got dozens."

I'm staring at him. I can't believe it. "You think I stole them."

"Well, what the hell, of course I do. You picked them up and dropped them in your purse. Marnie saw you. Obviously you—"

"Obviously nothing." But then I stop. I'm trying to be patient, but I'm only halfway through my marvelous quiche and he's ruining it. But the real problem is, I don't know what to say. If I say I was absentminded, he'll chalk it up to old age. If I say I stole them just for fun, he'll chalk it up to old age. If I say everybody has absentminded moments that get corrected later, he'll chalk it up to denial of old age. Finally I shrug and lie. I don't like to lie, but this time it seems appropriate. "I was thinking of buying them, but someone came up to me, an old friend, and we got to talking and walking."

"A friend? Marnie didn't mention another person; she didn't say anything about you talking to anyone."

"Oh, fuck it," I say, and that stops him cold. I look up from my salad and see that I have shocked my worldly son. And then I think I should apologize, not for shocking him, but for disappointing him, for not being the exemplary lady who makes him proud to be my son. So I put my hand on his—my hieroglyphic veins and bony knuckles against his firm skin glowing with health—to soften my language. "Look," I say, a little sadly because he's becoming rather pathetic, trying to be the son others would admire. Why doesn't he wait until I'm too old or sick to fight back? He could be living his life with what's-her-name and the water spaniels, being a corporate lawyer almost as famous as his father, underwriting operas and benefit galas, getting his photo in the papers, and leaving me alone. But all that isn't enough for him; he needs to keep me under his wing. I suppose he's worried about the guilt he'll carry around if I drop dead tomorrow while he's in bed with what's-her . . . Oh, I know perfectly well her name is Diana; I'm just not thrilled with her. While he's in bed with her, or socializing with the stars of the Met, or touring Angkor Wat as he was last fall when he called me from Cambodia—*from Cambodia*—three times to make sure I was doing okay without him in the neighborhood.

Or maybe he's just trying to be better than his father, who dropped dead at sixty-nine–way too young these days, or, in fact, any day—leaving me to fend for myself. Or to depend on Matthew Bremer, He of the Broad Shoulders.

So I put my hand on his and say, a little sadly, "If you want to say I'm lying, go ahead and say it."

"I didn't accuse you of—"

"Look," I say again, still trying to be patient. "It isn't winter; I can't go skiing. I don't have much to do in the garden; the crew comes every week and does just about everything that's needed. I can't read more than a few hours at a time. I can't walk as much as I used to—I admit it," I snap when he opens his mouth to say something about my age. "I don't like television. Photo albums are depressing, and after awhile I begin to wonder why everybody's always grinning; surely the world had as many problems then as now. I browse the Internet, but that's tiring and so boring after awhile. Most of my friends are dead; it's a shame I never got around to finding people twenty or thirty years younger than me, but I didn't, so there you are. So I feel like I'm getting squeezed in a life that's narrower and narrower, and I need to get out of the house and there are only so many days I can visit the same museums I've been visiting for over eighty years, so I go to department stores. I like them: they're bright and colorful and crowded with people making themselves happy by buying things they probably don't need, and the salesgirls know me and make a fuss over me, which I like. I mean, you go to Antarctica and

Petra and Ephesus; for heaven's sake—you go to that place in Belgium *for dinner*—so I'd think my little adventures, pathetic as they are compared to yours, shouldn't surprise you. And I want to keep doing them! You might try to understand that. I don't want to be spied on; I want to be left alone to enjoy the little pleasures I find here and there. It's my life, and if I get absentminded sometimes and somebody thinks I've taken up stealing, I don't want anyone around to yell at me or tell me I'm too old to be left alone in a department store. I want to do what I want and if it looks odd to other people that's too damn bad. I can take care of myself, and I don't want my son or anyone else to interfere."

There was a long silence. "Jesus," says Matthew. "That's crazy."

I let a minute go by and then I sigh, a bit dramatically, I confess. "Did Philip and I do this to you? Raise you to be a prig? Wait, my vocabulary is better than that. Stuffy, stiff, straight-laced, prudish, anal. Did we do that to you? Or did social climbing do it?"

"You can't do this," says Matthew, and he's so angry his voice is tight. "You're an old woman and some excuses might apply, but being at the end of your life does not justify—"

"Wait," I say loudly, and heads turn. "The end of my life? What do you know about it? People live—"

"I'm sorry . . . Damn it, I'm sorry . . . I shouldn't have said—"

"—into their hundreds these days, and you have no right to talk to me about the end of my life when you haven't the faintest idea the stuff I'm made of. I don't feel old, can you understand that?"

"Yes. Good. That's great. But how you feel isn't the

top of my list right now; it's how you behave. If you'd think about anyone but yourself once in a while, you'd know you're jeopardizing others."

"Who? The chairman of Saks?"

"Your family. Me. Everything I've built up. I have a name in this town and all I need is a squib in the paper about my senile mother shoplifting . . . and then probably a video . . . I'll bet they follow you around the stores. YouTube, for God's sake."

I leap out of my chair. Well, it isn't quite a leap, but I slide across the banquette and hobble out. The problem is, I'm stiff when I've sat too long, and it takes a few minutes to loosen up, but I don't have a few minutes, I have to get out of there, so I go lurching between tables of high-powered executives who, when they see me coming, slide their chairs aside to make room. A few of them smile in greeting and since I've known them for years I smile back, although it may be mostly a grimace.

Matthew, I learn later, threw a fifty-dollar bill on the table and came after me, but with a lawyerly stride, his dignity intact, so I manage to be in a taxi by the time he emerges. We look at each other through the window and I give the driver my address and off we go.

Now let me explain that this conversation does not take place on one day over one quiche and salad and carafe of wine. In fact, it goes on all summer, in bits and pieces, and I do not leave in a huff every time, and Matthew does not call me senile and at the end of my life more than once, and most times, when we've finished our coffee, we have a friendly ride in the taxi and he waits until I'm well inside my house before telling the driver to go on.

As far as I know, no zealous reporter has written a story about the incident at Saks or any others that might occur now and then. It appears that Matthew's reputation is intact.

And so is the reputation of my other children, I'm sure, or I'd hear about it when we have lunch or when they invite me to dinner: my gorgeous Sarah, fifty-eight and looking better than ever since she shed husband number two, with a beautiful daughter and two grandchildren and a suitor whom I hope she marries because he seems the best yet; and Garrett, at fifty-six a teacher of eighth grade in a posh private school where his pay is low, his satisfaction high, his second marriage a solid success, his four children probably the brightest our family has yet turned out. And because Sarah and Garrett are offspring of Philip and me, they are delightful company: witty, informed, warm, a lot less stuffy than Matthew, who is also our offspring but increasingly seems to be an aberration. The problem is, all three of them have the same fixation when it comes to evicting me from my home and plopping me into a building dedicated to the doddering and the creaky waiting-for-the-end. Well, I know that's not completely true; I know that glitzy building has plenty of people as vigorous as I am, but I know a symbol when I see one, and that's all I need.

By the end of summer, when I'm taking walks in the park beneath trees burnished with copper and red and I'm thinking about the first snowfall and the first click of my boots locking into my skis, I'm tired of telling all three of them that I'm a capable, independent, clear-headed citizen, consumer, voter, homeowner and skier, and they should get the point and let me go my way without supervision. So finally I simply stop responding to their serious discussions. As soon as one of them launches a new foray, I nod at regular intervals, and when they fall silent, I launch into a sprightly review of the play I'd seen the night before, or a concert or opera. Sometimes

I give the plot of a book I'm reading; that can occupy an entire meal. Occasionally I rehash the news I'd read in the *Times* that morning. At that, Sarah or Garrett, whoever is that night's host, will laugh, and we'll have a fine conversation. Matthew, being Matthew, frowns, and I pet the water spaniels and soon it's time for me to go home.

But here's an annoying issue with life: just when we think it's settled into an agreeable and reliable pattern that we not only can trust but also predict, it changes, as if whoever is running things decides it's unacceptable for anyone to be able to nestle into comfort and stay there. And so, about the middle of October, a few weeks before my birthday, there is another lunch, the worst lunch, and of course it's with Matthew. It is a warm, beautiful day: what we used to call Indian Summer. I'm feeling chipper. We're in a new French restaurant that's had great reviews, and we order trout, both of us, with poached apples and a Sancerre. And Matthew says, "I have two Christmas gifts for you."

"Who's thinking about Christmas?" I say. "Time goes too fast already without you pushing it."

"I know it's early," says Matthew, "but sometimes early gifts are the best." He puts down his fork in a manner that says This Is Serious Business, and my back gets stiff so I'm sitting straight up, nowhere near the back of my chair. "I stopped by your house last week, around eight o'clock, on my way home from a meeting. You weren't there."

"When last week?" I ask, but it's just to stall, because I know what's coming.

"Wednesday. The night you were in the hospital after Maria took you to the emergency room."

"She shouldn't have said anything. She promised she

wouldn't."

"You shouldn't have asked her to promise."

"No," I say, and it's true. I wasn't thinking about Maria; I was only thinking about me.

"Anyway, you should have known I'd get it out of her. When she told me you weren't home, I asked her what had happened and she said she couldn't tell me, which was ridiculous, and she knew it. She was supposed to report to me every week, how you were, what was happening. So I told her I'd charge her with negligence if she didn't tell me."

"Report to you? Tell you what I did, what I wore, when I peed, when I—"

"Don't do that; she only tells me—"

"Since when? How long?"

"Three years. She never had much to report."

I'm still sitting straight, still holding my fork, but I'm not eating. "Poor Maria," I say, and I do feel sorry for her. She's the nicest person alive and she's been my housekeeper since Philip died, and I do believe she cares for me as much as I care for her, but I don't blame her for obeying Matthew; most people obey Matthew when he issues an order.

"So you fell," Matthew says after a minute.

"And didn't break anything," I say.

"They admitted you. Kept you overnight."

"For observation. You know that; you probably talked to every nurse and resident on that floor. My doctor, too, I'd guess."

He ignored that. "This wasn't the first time you've fallen."

"Everybody falls! You fell last winter."

"I fell?"

"When you were skiing in Aspen, some run—Silver

Queen?—one of your kids told me."

"Skiing, for God's sake. That is not walking across the bedroom. Now look. Please listen and don't shout at me." He puts down his fork. "I've paid your entrance fee at 55 East, and I have a buyer for your house."

I stare at him. I think my mouth is open, but my throat is stopped up and no words could come even if I could think of any.

Matthew looks away, then back at me. "Drink some water. Or—" He holds out my wine glass. I do not take it and he frowns, the famous Matthew frown we all try to avoid. "We've talked about this for months, all summer. It's time for you to be out of that house and in a place where you can get care any time you need it."

"Maria," I whisper.

"Six hours a day. You need someone available all the time. Listen to me. This isn't a dungeon you're moving to; it's one of the best buildings in the city. Your apartment is one of the biggest and they've done a terrific job: walnut floors—and your Kirman will fit in the living room; we measured it—walls painted your favorite colors, drapes the same as the ones you have now. Sarah took care of the decorating, you know how good she is, and the three of us checked it out and you'll be happy there."

The three of us. That's when my back slumps. It's as if a brigade comes over the hill and you realize how outnumbered you are, so you just shrivel up and wait for them.

"You can keep Maria if you want," Matthew is saying, "but they provide housekeeping and anything else you need. You'll love it there, you know, you'll meet people and in a couple of days it'll be home, a lot better than rattling around in fifteen empty rooms and no one you know close by. But other than that, your life won't change. You can walk and go to concerts and ski, whatever you like; you'll be on your own in your own home, the same as now, no one watching you, no one telling you what to do. But when you're home, you'll have a staff close by to call on if you need help. And a building full of people; you'll make new friends every day."

"My house." I'm still whispering; my throat is a knot and my head hurts.

"We got a good price. Considering the economy and how much work it needs, a damn good price. It went to a developer; we don't know what she wants to do with it, but she admires its lines and who knows? She may keep it as a house. Maybe an art gallery; that would be great, wouldn't it?"

Silence sits at our table. I am looking at the remains of my trout, half a poached apple, a broken piece of bread. "And," Matthew says, "if you find you don't need Maria once you're settled, I've opened a bank account for her that should last as long as she does, if she's careful. I know how much she means to you."

By the time the taxi gets to my house, I can walk just fine, but Matthew isn't sure, so he holds my arm and walks me to the front door. "Sarah will be here tomorrow to help you start sorting things before the movers come to pack. She said she'd come every day, so you can take it slowly; you don't have to be out of here for a couple months, plenty of time to go through every nook and cranny. We know it's a huge job—over sixty years in the same house—but we'll all help and you'll be amazed how fast it'll go. Six hands, you know, with you directing, and you're the best director around." He helps me turn the key in my front door—my hand seems to be trembling—and escorts me inside. In the foyer, he puts his arm around me and kisses my forehead, my cheek. His voice is deep. "We love you, you know; we want you to be safe and happy."

Sarah is efficient and fiercely focused; she empties drawers and sorts everything into neat piles for me to evaluate. I'm to decide what I absolutely must keep, what can be given to some charity or other, what gets tossed or given to a charity further down Sarah's list. We have sixty days and fifteen rooms plus attic and basement, and when Sarah gets home, she stays up late, drawing charts and making lists on her computer, sending them to Matthew and Garrett and me, so I'll be prepared when she arrives each morning. And on weekends, my two stalwart sons join her, lists in hand, and I sit in a chair and watch the three of them plunder my past.

I don't let them touch the rooms I've been living in these past years: the library and kitchen downstairs, my bedroom and dressing room upstairs. After four weeks, the rest of the house looks as if we're preparing for Armageddon: silver and china sorted for the packers; boxes of books filled but open, waiting for official tape; my clothes hung in tall boxes with built-in rods. Finally, at night when I'm alone, I make my dinner and eat it in the library: fireplace lit, television news briefing me on the planet's disasters, wine bottle and book at hand, draperies closed against the rest of the world. I look around, again and again, memorizing the room.

At midnight, this midnight, I make my way upstairs and prepare for bed, putting on a nightgown that was one of Philip's favorites, pale blue, with lace. When he gave it to me for some birthday or other, he said he liked the idea of seeing me in it before he saw me out of it, always with the light on, because it was good to share our bodies in full view, not let the dark smother them. In bed, I remember the two of us together, I can hear his voice, see his smile, almost feel him inside me. And perhaps I fall asleep, or more likely it is the kind of fitful doze that passes for sleep most nights now. Whichever it is, my eyes are open, the contours of my bedroom clearly visible in the light from the street, when the voices, men's voices, rise in a rumble from below.

Not my sons' voices; a different timbre, with a note of urgency. The word 'boxes' separates itself from the rumble, and I think they must have seen the deliveries of the moving company's boxes the last weeks, and guessed . . . what? That I'd died and someone was packing up so the house could be sold. That I'd moved to an old folks' home and my family was packing up so the house . . . etc. etc. That the house will soon be torn down. But how had they broken in so quietly? Two locks and they figured it out. What a shame they don't use such cleverness to do good.

"Fur coats" says a deep voice, and I can hear excitement in the words. Then the clatter of hangers sliding across the closet rod. And the back door opening and closing.

But of course they aren't really gone; most likely they're stashing the coats in their car or truck or whatever, and then they'll come back for more. They'll come back for the silver. And, of course, jewelry.

The house is so quiet: silent rooms, a silent street. As Matthew has said many times, there are no more houses here; everyone in the neighborhood is tucked away in cubicle apartments, soundproofed and isolated from each other . . . and from me. And the men will be back, any minute, and they'll come upstairs. And then what? That's for them to decide; I have nothing to say about it. I have no options.

Well, not so fast. I could talk to them, maybe tell them something that would interest them. Or I could explain that they're ruining their life, though probably they'd heard that before, from a parent or a friend or a judge. I could sweet talk—old ladies do that, sometimes to good effect—so they'd be content with the fur coats and leave.

But why? Why would I put up a fight for my possessions? I don't care about them and my children never did. Let them take everything; the absence will change nothing. I can even tell them the combination of the safe; what difference does it make?

Well, but it does. Once I see their faces, I'm the witness they have to get rid of. Even if I promise I won't say they were here, that I'll tell everyone I slept through the whole thing, never saw anyone, they won't trust me. And probably they'd be right. Once Matthew got going on me, or Sarah or Garrett, I couldn't keep lying; I've never been good at it. And if I saw the men again, in a lineup or photographs, I probably could identify them, especially if I'd watched them go through my bureaus, if I'd given them the combination to the safe, if I'd had a conversation with them.

I really don't want them to kill me. What an awful way to end a life: bludgeoned to death, stabbed, shot, strangled... a stupid way to go. I know how I want to go; I've known since Philip died. On my own terms. Not clutched by an illness that strips the body to a ghastly caricature, not with a heart attack, or under the wheels of a car, or on a flight of stairs after missing the top one, or skidding on an icy sidewalk into a lamp post.

Of course I've thought of those, and a few dozen more, and try to avoid all of them. Which is why I walk like an old woman. Because I will choose my ending, not have it forced on me. And I am prepared to choose, though my preference would be to put it off well beyond where I am now.

Of course I've never discussed this with my children; the scenario is too predictable: "You're being overly dramatic," they'd say, a little too vigorously, to drown out the thought that maybe I'm right, maybe it's time for me to go. "It's too early to be thinking of such things; you have a full life—why not enjoy it instead of indulging in maunderings that could lead to tragedy?"

Oh well, talk about being dramatic. My offspring, indeed.

But now there's something new. I'm losing my home. I'm being shifted to foreign territory that, however elegant, is not mine and never will be. Being shifted. The most terrible thing: the passive voice. Somehow, overnight it seems, I am not in control of my life. I don't have any say in what comes next. Something like being abducted, which is far worse than anything I imagined for my advanced years. How could I have contemplated this? So much praise from my children in the past decade or so—"What a remarkable woman you are!"—who would have guessed?

So, on all counts, this is the time: certainly not the one I would have chosen, but still, the right time.

On the table beside my bed, as every night for many years now, sits a glass of water and a small box with three pills. For all those years, with the help of a good friend, I have replaced them at regular intervals, to keep them within their expiration date. As Matthew has said, I am a good director: I keep track of details.

My family will think I died quietly in my sleep; it's clear they've been expecting it since whatever birthday suddenly seemed to them ancient. My family will believe it, and so will anyone else who is interested, except the friend who has helped me, and she is discreet and completely trustworthy, besides having the same three pills and water glass beside her bed, and a friend who will help her when the time comes.

As for the intruders, won't they be surprised to come looking for jewels and find me dead in my bed. Probably scare them out of their wits. Serve them right. Maybe make them give up a life of crime.

I hear the voices downstairs, but it is no longer important what they are saying. I put the three pills on my tongue and swallow them quickly, before the first steps upon the stairs.

And that is that, I think, lying back on my pillow and pulling the quilt over me, neatly, up to my chin. It's time.

So, in the end, the old lady wins. Let them put that in their pipe and smoke it.

Eleanor's Room

WHEN ELEANOR TOOK WALKS through the city or shopped or rode the train to and from work, she was an ardent observer of lighted rooms visible through uncurtained windows. She did not focus on the people in the rooms, though she made swift judgments on what women wore and how they carried themselves. What attracted her were the trappings: the choices people made as settings for eating, sleeping, entertaining friends, curling up with a book; the art and fabrics they selected to decorate walls and windows; the purchases they made to provide their entertainment, music, and news of the world. Each room she studied, she measured against her own space. It was not that she found her surroundings wanting; rather, she was animated by choices: how her own selections stood the test of comparison; how, seeking novelty, she might rearrange furniture and works of art, or add or eliminate certain colors to more dramatically greet and buoy her each time she stepped inside and locked her door behind her.

She had the same general thoughts about Martin, who visited her. Other men were handsomer, their bodies leaner, the planes of their faces sharper, their eyes warmer. Often she would focus on one man or another as she scanned faces across the aisle of her commuter train or met a glance in the supermarket or department store and picture one of them in her room, searching her bookshelves for clues to who she was, holding her chair at the small table where she would serve dinner, lowering his weight on her in the bed he helped her open from the couch that took up one wall of her room.

Sometimes, briefly, she thought up names for those men,

professions and hobbies, but she abandoned them quickly, knowing too well the seduction of fantasies. Living alone, she recognized her vulnerability; the first time it happened, she grew frightened by the ease of skidding past an unmoored daydream to an image that threatened discontent. She would not even allow herself fleeting, playful images of an unnamed man comfortable in her room or raising a glass at dinner; she knew how little was required for her to fabricate an entire scenario that, in the end, would not satisfy or even please, in fact, could destroy.

She did not have to fabricate with Martin; he was familiar in her room. The reality of Martin—stocky, with features running to fleshiness and a minimal chin—was solid and present, and even though, now and then, she questioned her easy willingness to let him dominate her room, she could suppress that beneath the pleasures of companionship and the gratifying, if tenuous, fact that he continued to visit.

Eleanor's room was large: a spacious rectangle artfully arranged into living and dining areas, reading, and media space. The galley kitchen was in one corner opposite a small bathroom closed off by a pocket door. The wall between them was taken almost entirely by a window looking upon a busy street two floors below, with, beneath it, an expandable table for dining and two chairs tucked against it. A modern black walnut cabinet opposite the couch held equipment for music, films, radio and television.

Eleanor had made the space bright, almost riotous: stripes in bold colors for the couch, plaids for two deep armchairs, the floor covered by overlapping Turkish rugs from the days when she had been a traveler. Prints crowded her walls, the collection expanding as her preferences shifted:

Kandinsky and Malevich followed somewhat later by Miró, Gris, and Picasso, rearranged to make room for Jacob Martin and Munch. Most recently, feeling it obligatory to include women artists, she had added Marie Laurencin and Paula Modersohn-Becker. Small Inuit sculptures stood on tables and shelves, alone or in clusters, appealing to Eleanor with their cool surfaces hiding intense emotions. The room was cheerful and embracing, almost relentlessly so. Martin liked it. He often told her how good and pleasant it was to be there.

They had met when he came to help a small, well-known orchestra in which Eleanor was principal flute. "Extremely fine. Extraordinary," the conductor had declared at her audition and assigned her the first chair. The orchestra rehearsed three nights a week and on weekends before concerts, and performed twelve times a year in a neighborhood church famous for its fine acoustics. Martin was an accountant and had been asked to assist the executive director of the orchestra by straightening out the books and helping to plan a fundraising event. He was given one of the church offices and, on his first night, when he opened the office door to go home, he heard the cadenza in the opening movement of Mozart's Flute Concerto No.1 in G. He slid into a pew for the remainder of the rehearsal, and when it was over, he introduced himself to the conductor and asked if he could come back often, since, he added with a look at Eleanor, he thought his work would keep him there for quite a while.

He became a regular, so quiet in a shadowed corner they usually forgot he was there. But he was in the first row when the orchestra performed the program they had been rehearsing, ending in an unexpected burst of seasonal jubilance with Sousa's "Stars and Stripes Forever."

"You know, I usually ignore the fourth," Martin said to Eleanor, joining her for the first time as she left the church, "but how can one, with Sousa? Thank you for that lively reminder." He stopped, which forced her to stop beside him. "Wonderful concert; thank you for that, too. I've been wanting to ask you—of course I didn't want to bother you before the concert—ask you if we could, that is, if you would care to have dinner with me. I thought, a traditional fourth, you know, fireworks and so on. There's a restaurant with a good view of Navy Pier, and I made a reservation, that is... I thought, on the chance that you weren't otherwise... They're hard to get, you know, especially for tonight. Eight o'clock? The fireworks begin at nine. That is ... of course ... if you're not already —?"

He seemed so ingenuous that Eleanor felt defenseless. She knew nothing about him, nor he of her. She had no idea how he had come to this point.

"May I pick you up?" he asked.

He was earnest, a supplicant. Eleanor could think of no good reason to refuse. She told him her address, and he wrote it in a small book he carried in his inside pocket. "Seven forty-five," he said.

And at the restaurant, small, chandeliered, known only to members, with red wine poured and menus still unopened, he said, "I've been watching you. So beautiful. And when you play: glowing."

Eleanor was struck, as she would be many times to come, by how easily, if incongruously, his courtliness sat on his rounded accountant's shoulders. It was, at the very least, disarming. At best, she found it seductive.

Most of the time they were in her room, where Martin visited twice a week and Eleanor served the excellent meals he always acknowledged with praise and a familiarity with ingredients and technique unexpectedly as vast as his lore of wine. From time to time, so rarely Eleanor still kept count, they ventured out, to offbeat art theaters and small, unadvertised restaurants that catered only to members and their friends. Occasionally, Martin spent the night in Eleanor's bed, which he helped open from her ample couch; most often he left at midnight or a little later, having announced, on arriving, that he had a particularly early appointment the next morning or a plane to catch practically at dawn for a business meeting.

Their first trip together, to San Francisco where Martin was speaking at a CPA conference, was, for Eleanor, a honeymoon: they strolled the Embarcadero and the Marina and North Beach, went to a concert with dinner afterward at a popular new restaurant, and climbed to the top of Nob Hill where they were disappointed to discover there was not the view they had anticipated, but where Eleanor, her bulk quivering, was triumphant for having stayed the course.

"Rose would not have done that," Martin said of his wife, admiring Eleanor for her achievement as they stood, catching their breath. "She never tries anything she's not already sure of. Like a lawyer who never asks a question unless he knows the answer in advance. Rose would have made a good lawyer. Sharp." He shrugged. "And needling." He smiled at his pun.

But Eleanor thought of Rose as her namesake flower—slender, graceful, perfumed, strongly defended—and was as envious as she was jealous.

"She was impressive and I was young, so immature," said Martin seriously, when she asked him. "And enthralled. Possibly her perfume, wafting visions of minarets and royal gardens. Or . . . perhaps not. Because there was something homey about her too, as if she was always ready to put on an apron. But then, she was glossy, well put together. Her hair was always perfect, even when she woke up in the morning. And the way she walked . . . in a way like royalty. That combination, you know . . . hominess and . . ." He would gesture, as if helpless to explain such mysteries.

There were four children. There was a house in the suburbs, forty minutes north of Eleanor's room by expressway, with lush grass and spreading maples and rose and peony beds. There was a dog. There were school plays and recitals, parent-teacher conferences, clubs and swimming meets. There were evenings with the neighbors around barbecue grills and trips to Wisconsin to see the fall colors and pick apples.

Eleanor collected the information that came sparsely but with sufficient detail to explain visits only twice weekly, and often not even that. "Because Rose doesn't always have rehearsals on a regular schedule."

Rose starred, and sometimes directed, in a Gilbert and Sullivan community theater in their suburb. "They're very good," Martin said. "Strikingly professional on occasion. Of course they're totally dedicated; they spend a good part of their waking hours in rehearsal."

Eleanor asked how many were in the group, and when Martin told her, she exclaimed in surprise. "What surprises you?" he asked.

"The number of bad marriages," she said with an artlessness that, in retrospect, embarrassed her.

To that, Martin made no reply.

In her workday, Eleanor was busy; her days passed pleasantly. Receptionist for a group of six physicians and their nurses, she greeted patients, provided forms for them to complete, and used the computer skillfully for a multitude of tasks. She kept the coffee urn full and spent much of her time on the telephone, routing calls, phoning in drug prescriptions, making and reminding patients of appointments in her warm, inviting voice. Her place there, in a high-backed swivel chair within the curve of a gleaming desk piled with secretive folders and printed forms beneath paperweights embedded with a caduceus, was as much her own as the room in which she lived. She was at the heart of it, well-liked and admired for efficiency, not as the ruler of a realm but as one who served: an acolyte, she liked to think, serving health in the office as, at home, she served beauty in the furnishings and art of her surroundings.

Eleanor bought prints for the doctors' offices and corridors, and flowers for the examining rooms, until told fresh flowers were not allowed there, at which she moved the small vases, with arrangements matching the seasons, onto tables in the waiting room and clustered on her desk.

She thought there should be an abundance of beauty in the world, to counteract misery. She was sure beauty existed in a multitude of settings; it was just a question of ferreting it out from the muck of errors, missteps, and cruelty, and bringing it home intact. And if it turned out there never could be enough beauty to lift the weight of sadness and ugliness forcing everyone, at one time or another, to bend, to crumple, all the more reason to clasp what one could find, and treasure it.

But then, there was Rose. Rose who, in numerous photographs on the Gilbert and Sullivan website Eleanor checked with compulsive frequency, had a small nose, a wide mouth, and glinting hair. Not beautiful, she drew attention with lively eyes, a mobile face, and a slender dancer's body.

Eleanor thought of Rose often, and she thought of the two of them, Eleanor and Rose, as artists bringing music and drama to the world, enriching lives, while Martin, the plodding accountant, brought numbers into careful balance, enriching corporations. Yet, she thought, arranging heather in an amethyst vase on one of her shelves, he spoke authoritatively of food and wine, and appreciated music and literature, though not, she added critically, with the insights of an artist. He was ignorant of art and philosophy and did not think of that as a character flaw.

Rose and I, thought Eleanor, and Martin.

But neither character nor Rose was discussed in Eleanor's room when Martin was there. When he shared dinner at the small table beside the window, when he used Eleanor's desk to find information on her computer, when he sat on her couch with stockinged feet on the coffee table and his arm around her shoulders, "There is no them," he said. "Anywhere. Only us."

He sang to Eleanor and told her she was beautiful. He traced with fingers made supple by calculators the deep folds in her flesh, the wide mound of her stomach, the smooth pillows of her wrists. He sang Cole Porter and Rodgers and Hart and George Gershwin; he had a light tenor, pleasant and unassuming. To her flute accompaniment he sang Andrew Lloyd Webber and Hoagy Carmichael and more Cole Porter: "Let's Fall in Love." "I Get a Kick Out of You." "In the Still of the Night." He sang as he arrived at her front door, flowers or wine or candy in hand; he sang as he flung back the bedcovers at midnight or one o'clock and dressed to go home; he sang snatches of "I've Got You Under My Skin" on the telephone when he called to say he could not, after all, come to her that night, because Rose had invited friends for dinner.

"There is no them," he told her the next time, in bed with the drapes closed. "Only us."

Eleanor, wild with love within ardent rolls of flesh, transfixed by the memory of computing fingers on her yielding depths, played the flute with such ardor in her next concert that music critics for the city's newspapers singled out her performance as inspired and magical. That night, Martin brought champagne, celebrating her triumph. "My superstar. You are a wonder, wondrous." He took her hand, and they opened out the couch to reveal their bed. He sang, "I cain't say no," and laughed as he mimicked Ado Annie's twang. "My treasure. My pleasure." He laughed again. "My measure. Of delight."

And it was not until he dressed to leave, a little before midnight, that he announced that this was also a farewell: he and Rose were flying to London with her theater group, then, with a few friends, to Portugal and Morocco, an extended vacation with no set date of return.

When Eleanor walked through the city or shopped or took the train to and from her job in the doctors' office, she studied rooms through uncurtained windows to see signs of distress or hints of trouble. Moving beyond her previous habit, she concentrated on the people within the rooms, and when there were no obvious clues, she created scenarios: a woman writing a letter hinted at planned trysts, furtive glances of longing, snatched moments. A man buttoning a tuxedo foretold glittering galas with unmarried couples dining by candlelight, dancing to small orchestras, counting the minutes until they could get away, to close a door behind them. A man and child sitting in silence on a sofa meant loss: a wife and mother having fled with a lover, abandoning everything familiar for a flare of desire. A crying infant was prelude to a nurse rushing in, late because of an assignation that miscarried when her lover failed to appear. Eleanor had never been a storyteller, but, with Martin away, his emails infrequent and cool, her room empty even of echoes, she found deep within her a cornucopia of narratives that came to her complete but amorphous, drifting away even as she contemplated them, to be replaced with new ones at the next set of windows.

In a coffee shop in a neighborhood of boutiques and ethnic restaurants, she met Sophie, who was reading and sipping a latte. There were no empty seats in the crowded room, and Sophie, glancing up from her book, met Eleanor's searching look and gestured to the other side of her booth. When Eleanor had ordered an éclair and coffee, she read the title of Sophie's book and said, "I haven't read Berlioz's *Memoirs*. Is it good?"

Sophie's mouth tightened with the exasperation of someone who had known a good deed would have bad consequences, and she nodded without looking up. But Eleanor had not talked to anyone all weekend. "I've played his Trio for Two Flutes and Harp; it's very fine, even though he didn't like writing for solo flute."

At that Sophie did look up. "You play?" then so quickly that it emphasized rather than hid the insult, "I didn't know he wrote one."

"Four or five I think. This one is part of *L'Enfance du Christ*, very lovely, and short, about six minutes."

"I've sung Beatrice in his *Beatrice and Benedict*," said Sophie.

Eleanor was astonished: in that entire city, to have found another musician, and a singer at that. She was not one to expect good fortune. "You're a mezzo, my favorite voice," she said, and they beamed at each other as they shook hands across the table and exchanged names.

"Seventeen and a half," said Sophie in response to Eleanor's question.

She was a sophomore at Northwestern University, having leaped ahead in her classes. "I'm actually brilliant, and I couldn't, like, wait to get to music. If you're smart enough you can, you know, do whatever you want; I mean, high school teachers, like, focus on the dumb ones, anybody who makes them, you know, feel smart, so they'll do anything for the smart ones, just to keep them from, you know, showing up the big guru supposedly in charge."

"If you're going to be a singer," Eleanor said seriously, "in the public eye, you should watch the way you speak."

"My mother says that. But you should lose weight. I'll bet your mother tells you that."

Eleanor glanced at her éclair. "She did."

"So now she doesn't? She gave up?"

"I guess so. We don't talk much."

"Oh, I wish. My mother never gives up."

In a moment, Sophie returned to her book. Eleanor ate her éclair one slow bite at a time and drank her coffee even though it was cold. "I live not far from here," she said to the top of Sophie's head. "Would you like to go there and sing some duets with the flute?"

Sophie shook her head. "Sunday dinner with my parents. But I could call sometime."

She did, to Eleanor's amazement, two days later. And after that she came often. In place of Martin's light tenor, Sophie's warm mezzo filled the room, and Eleanor and Sophie smiled at each other, pleased with the music they made and with each other. Eleanor, blissful with another presence in her room, always asked Sophie to stay for dinner, and occasionally she did, and they talked at the small table where, until then, there had been only Martin. Sophie drank a large amount of Eleanor's wine, especially Malbecs—"my favorite"—and Eleanor did not mention her age; she was not familiar with the state's drinking laws, but she had no interest in researching them. Given the choice of adhering to whatever was legal or risking the loss of Sophie, there was no contest. No one knew or cared what was done within Eleanor's snug enclosure, so Eleanor was content. The wine flowed, accompanied by coffee and truffles, and Sophie talked about music, about college, boys, dates, the suburbs, families.

"I'm talking too much," she said comfortably one night. "I love to talk about me. At home nobody, like, gives a shit. My brothers are, you know, morons, and my parents are into bridge and lawn mowers and barbecues. Totally suburban, totally, you know, stifling."

"That sounds like every teenager's description of parents," Eleanor said.

Sophie scowled. "They're worse. You wouldn't understand."

"Tell me," said Eleanor, making amends, and Sophie talked some more. "They wind each other up every morning so they can, you know, go through the motions until bedtime; all habit, no surprises, no upsets." Her father owned a real estate company—"He's got a sharp partner; otherwise he'd be, like, toast."—and her mother cooked the solid Midwestern meals she had learned at home: "She wears a blindfold when she gets to the spice section in the grocery store." She dismissed her two brothers in college. "Nerds, like all they know is sports and, you know, video games; I mean, God help any girls stupid enough to go out with them." And her parents' friends drew a snort. "Totally the worst: if you put them all together, you wouldn't find one original idea. I mean, they get all, like, chirpy when they see me—'Oh, Sophie, we heard about your concert, you're a singer, that's so wonderful; isn't it wonderful, Kurt?'—that's my father—and he'll say it sure is, they're all so proud of their little girl and all that, but it doesn't mean anything; I mean, I'm an artist, and they haven't a clue; my father's best friend is an accountant, for God's sake, and it's like we don't even come from, like, the same planet. You know what they get emotional about? Business and golf and bridge. Oh, and if the trash gets picked up on time. That really turns them on. God, what a crock. One of these days I'll throw water on them so they melt into a puddle, like the wicked witch of the west."

Eleanor, unnerved by youthful cruelty and impaled on "an accountant, for God's sake," moved on. "You must have boyfriends."

"Oh, tons, but they're mostly losers, you know, okay for a night or two, but that's it. I mean, the music guys spend all their time in music, and the others are into, you know, rock or whatever, but not *music,* and that's it, that's all they know. They're still kids, like my brothers, and who needs that? Or they're too old, and who needs that?"

"Too old?" Eleanor pictured faculty preying on young girls.

"Guys in graduate school, a couple of assistant professors, whether they're married or not. Most of them, all they want is to, like, fuck and drink. You know."

Eleanor nodded, knowing nothing. "Is there anything or

anyone you like? Or approve of?"

Sophie, too absorbed to notice irony, said, "Well, yeah, there is this guy, he's famous, you'd know his name. Concert pianist, travels to play with, you know, different orchestras, tall and handsome, sort of brooding—like Heathcliff? God, I love that book. And he's cool, I mean he's into music, real music, and books and movies and even, you know, politics, not that I am, but anyway we don't talk much, not in bed, and that's mostly where we are. He's a lot older, but with him that isn't important. The big thing is, he's married, I mean they all are, all the good ones, but she's this big socialite in New York, like bow down and grovel my husband's so famous and we're so rich, and she's probably got some guy in her bed, so I don't, you know, think about it. Except that's he's, you know, taken, and that is so totally boring."

Sophie was in and out of her chair as she talked, gesturing broadly, drinking wine, scanning Eleanor's bookshelves, eating a truffle, picking up a paperweight or small sculpture, combing her long hair with her fingers. She was like a flame, Eleanor thought, envying her vitality, the fluidity of her body: tall, bright, leaping, swooping, pure energy rippling the still air of her room.

"So, what about your boyfriends?" Sophie asked. "You never talk about any. You don't talk about yourself much."

Eleanor did not mention the lack of space in Sophie's lexicon for someone else's confidences. "I have friends," she said. There seemed no way she could string together enough sentences to match Sophie's monologues.

Sophie's chin came up, toward a photograph of Martin. "That guy one of them?"

Eleanor nodded. She had not thought Sophie was

observant, though at her first visit, she had repeatedly exclaimed in amazement, "What a fantastic place—the colors, everything so bright and like gorgeous. You look so straight," she had said, almost accusingly. "Straight, straight, straight. Except you're so fat. God, you're really huge. Why don't you lose weight?"

"I know," Eleanor had said and took out her flute.

Now Sophie was looking at the photograph of Martin seated on Eleanor's couch, his tie loosened, thinning hair smoothed back, his smile easy and faintly pleading. "He looks straight, too. Is he in your orchestra?"

"No," Eleanor said. "But he helps out."

"Like how?"

"Organizing benefits, things like that."

"So why isn't he around?"

"He's out of town." Sophie's eyebrows were up. "And he's married."

"Oh, shit, another one. Crawling all over the place, bastards, scooping up whoever's loose in their playground, not giving a damn about anybody's feelings."

Eleanor was gratified by Sophie's harshness.

"But you're nuts about him, right?" Sophie asked.

"I like him. He's—"

"All you've got. Right." And then, "He can't be the first, not at your age. Don't tell me. He is? Really?"

Sophie's eyes were dagger points of curiosity, but Eleanor found them oddly comforting. It was not because of any special bond between them—she knew they would never be able to bridge the gaps in their worlds except in ad hoc and shallow ways—but because Sophie's eyes were, beyond eagerness and curiosity, neutral: within their pale blue depths lay neither pity nor censure, nor the derisiveness of a freak show barker.

And so, to Sophie's question, Eleanor nodded.

"Right," said Sophie. "So, if he's the first, how do you know he's any good?"

Eleanor was silent.

"Most of them aren't, you know. Like all they care about is proving their dick is more potent than it looks, a weapon of, you know, mass conquest, when what it really is, is like something you planted, a bean or flower or whatever, and this little shoot comes up and sort of looks around and waves at you, you know, bravely every time you walk past."

Eleanor cringed, and then she laughed. There was something delicious about Sophie's nastiness, and about her own laughter, as gratifying in its skewed way as looking out from the sharp-edged landscape of Sophie's world.

"I don't know," she said. "I don't know if he's any good."

"Right. So, what's his name?"

Eleanor told her; by then, everything was open, everything was fair game.

Martin called a week later. "We're back, but I'm tied up in meetings. I'll call you as soon as I can draw a breath. I miss you."

Eleanor thought, I didn't tell Sophie you're an accountant; the least you could do is spend some time here and show me you're more than that. More than a little shoot waving at me when I walk past.

But she lacked Sophie's ruthless certainty, and since she knew her thoughts and comments about Martin these days were protecting herself, not him, she replied that she missed him, too.

Weeks followed, and he did not call. Eleanor's flute playing grew melancholy; her conductor asked her to stay after rehearsal to discuss it.

"We've had so much rain," said Eleanor. "Everything is so gray. You know," she added, sounding like Sophie.

"No . . . other problems?" asked the conductor . "Money, your health, maybe . . . social?"

Meaning romantic, thought Eleanor. Meaning, how could romance possibly be part of my life? She kept her eyes on her flute, lying across her lap, not knowing whether the conductor was looking at her or out the window. She was accustomed to people looking past her, and she had come up with ways of interpreting that: her bulk made others so uncomfortable their glances skittered over her and away, like a bead of mercury on a cold surface, or they liked her so much they willed themselves to avoid eye contact that might lead, in spite of their affection, to a blurted gaffe: *God you're really huge; why don't you lose weight?*

"No," she said to the conductor. "No problems. I'll try to do better."

Sophie came dancing in on her next visit, brandishing a photograph. "His house," she said. "Martin's. And what's-her-name."

"Rose," said Eleanor automatically. "How did you get that?"

"Took it. Drove past on the way to my parents' last Sunday. Would you believe it, they're only about a mile away. And totally, you know, suburban, same kind of street, same kind of boring house. Straight, like him. Or is he kinky? I never asked you that."

"You drove past his house? But he could have seen you."

"So what? He doesn't know me. Her name is Rose? Lots of roses in front. You know, bushes."

"What else?" Eleanor asked.

"Oh, you know, the usual stuff, it's all in the picture. Basketball net over the garage, chimney, big picture window, brick—"

"What color?"

"Red. Light red. Sort of rose." Sophie laughed. "Rose drapes in the window, too. I'll bet the whole house is rose, you know, furniture, carpets, walls. God, like living in a brothel."

"You noticed the drapes?"

"I notice things. And I was paying attention, for you."

Eleanor looked at the photograph. "It's a nice house."

"But boring. Let's make some music."

The next week Martin called. "Still tied up. Shit, Congress is going crazy; new regulations, new forms, new requirements. I miss you."

He no longer came to rehearsals. He had finished his work for the church.

Sophie came with news. "Rose buys at Whole Foods. And Saks and Martha Turner and Escada and Ferragamo. He must be cleaning up."

Eleanor said, "Are you sitting in front of the house, waiting for her? Watching?"

Sophie shrugged. "It's not a big deal, I only go when I'm going to be in the neighborhood. I mean, it's like fun; I park somewhere and do homework, and when she comes I take a quick look and then leave. Just long enough to get, you know, information."

Eleanor, greedy and ashamed, asked, "What else did you get?"

"I never see kids. They don't live at home?"

"I think some are. And some in college. Two, I think."

"You're not sure? He doesn't talk about his family? How

old is he?"

"Forty-five? Fifty?"

They were talking in questions. Like clumsy amateurs, Eleanor thought, and with the thought an oppressiveness settled over her, a stale shroud of conspiracy that made her room seem smaller, heavier, less welcoming.

"I'll know at Christmas," Sophie said. "If there are any, they'll be around."

A few days before Christmas, she brought a photograph. "Two boys like college age. Plus a girl and boy, lots younger. Like, second thoughts? They're all totally awesome. They don't look like Dad, though. Is Rose gorgeous?"

"I guess you'd say striking."

"So you've done it too . . . gone for a look."

"No, of course not . . . I wouldn't." Eleanor told Sophie about Gilbert and Sullivan and photographs on the theater website. "So are they any good?" Sophie asked.

"I don't know. I've never been."

"Oh, come on; you must be curious. I mean, at least see her do her song and dance. So you go to one of her plays. Why not?"

Eleanor shook her head.

"Oh, you're worried he'd be there, but he wouldn't. Listen, I know about performances. I mean, opening night for sure, but after that, God, a guy with all those, you know, free nights, why'd he want to sit in a theater when he could be in bed with his girlfriend? I know what. I'll go. What're they doing now?"

"*Patience.*"

Sophie laughed. "You ought to go; that's your specialty." There was coarseness in Sophie's voice, but Eleanor did not dwell on it. They made their music and Sophie left early. "Lots of homework."

Eleanor held the door for her, trying not to ask, and then did. "Are you going back there? I mean, besides seeing *Patience*?"

"You want me to? Really, really? Well, I might. I'll let you know."

The next day Sophie called. "They're going away. Christmas holiday, I guess. Lots of suitcases. Skis. Did you know he skis?"

"No," said Eleanor and went out for dinner, to a new Thai restaurant that was quiet and inexpensive, with heaping plates of food.

Sophie, too, was gone at Christmas, so both she and Martin missed the holiday concert featuring Eleanor's playing of the Telemann *Fantasia for Solo Flute* and the flute solo in Tchaikovsky's *Dance of the Sugar Plum Fairy*. The newspaper critic called her playing soulful, not as ardent as before, but deeper.

In January, Martin did not call; Sophie did not call. Eleanor called Sophie and invited her to dinner. "No, sorry, I've got finals. Such a crock, finals after vacation. I'll call when I'm, you know, done."

Eleanor had not seen Martin since his trip to London in October. But he called, three weeks into January. "New tax laws, everything's screwed up. I miss you."

"Did you have a nice Christmas?"

"Oh, dull, the usual thing. I'll call soon."

When Eleanor walked through the city or shopped or took the train to and from work, she saw, framed in uncurtained windows, tragic lives. A sobbing couple slumped together while men in overalls piled furniture on the sidewalk below their window. A woman slouched at a computer, reading job descriptions and drinking from a nearly empty bottle of amber liquid, a fresh bottle nearby. Black-clad, sobbing mourners sitting in a circle of straight-backed chairs, an elderly man holding close the tearful woman beside him, a soldier's photo on a mantelpiece draped with a black ribbon and an American flag.

Brutality is everywhere, Eleanor thought. Happiness is a brief lull between catastrophes.

On Sophie's next visit, after they made music, Eleanor opened a new bottle of wine and Sophie talked of skiing in Sun Valley and her lover, who was on tour in Europe, playing the complete Beethoven piano sonatas. "And where's your great lover?" she asked Eleanor.

"Working on tax laws. He's an accountant."

"Oh," said Sophie. "Oh."

"It's a busy time of year."

"Right. Well, that's kind of funny. When you think about it."

They laughed, and Eleanor thought, We're two artists laughing at an accountant. Because he is by definition beneath us?

"I saw *Patience*," Sophie said. "I bet you were trying not to ask." Eleanor, needing to hear more, was silent. "It was terrific. I couldn't believe it, you know, community theater, housewives and whatever. But they're really good. Voices, sets, costumes, the works. Big audience. Rose got cheers. She isn't, like, gorgeous, but she's got something. Sort of a spark, striking, like you said. Wakes up the stage. You know. Anyway, I'll see what else I can find. I'll call."

She did not call, and neither did Martin. Everyone is so busy, Eleanor thought. Such busy lives self-centered people lead.

In the evenings she spread on her desk the photographs

Sophie had brought, and studied them. How ordinary it all was: a respectable suburban couple—successful husband becoming a little heavy in satisfied middle age, talented, lively wife magically staying rail-thin—with two handsome sons in college learning how to make money and two younger children growing up in privileged lives. And the successful husband, for ego or simple diversion, has an affair in the city while his wife is cheered by audiences for her ego and diversion. Upstanding citizens of their town, keeping their meticulous lives intact: neighbors, barbecues, evenings at the movies, bridge nights, ski vacations. They keep a lid on, they don't let things get out of control.

Whatever else they do, went Eleanor's thoughts, they live together, travel together, sleep in a king-size bed with snuggling duvet and pure white sheets blemished only by the night's eruptions; waken to the rosy rooms of their neat brick house with broad, dense trees and basketball net and a chimney that sends smoke into the night when they sit in front of their fire, having a late night drink. And where does a single room filled by lonely obesity enter into this happy picture? Oh, how could it? It does not fit. It is an insignificant square peg off to the side of the roundness of their life, briefly tantalizing for a difference in configuration, but not the fit with which one could contemplate a future.

And not surprisingly, Eleanor thought further, tantalizing no longer cuts it. Ephemeral to begin with, it soon fades—a change in the weather, a curve in the road leaving behind a configuration once new, now mundane—while home, a warm familiarity requiring no logistics, moves center stage again, attractive and even necessary. Until, of course, the next time, but by then Eleanor and her colorful, complaisant room would have been forgotten, replaced by a new, newly tantalizing pursuit. How incredibly ordinary it all is, she thought. And, of course, brutal.

In February, during a heavy snowfall, when Eleanor had eaten dinner at home instead of going out, Martin called. "Have you hired someone to spy on me?"

"Have I—? What are you talking about?" She was trying to adjust to hearing his voice again, and then to its abrasiveness. "What does that mean?"

"My wife says some woman has been sitting in front of our house off and on for weeks, taking photos. We called the police, and she told them she's a realtor photographing neighborhoods. Of course that's a lie."

Eleanor nodded.

"Call her off," Martin said. "I'm warning you."

"I didn't hire—"

He hung up.

Eleanor paced her room. She called Sophie's cell phone but received only her recorded mezzo singing "Let's Do It Again." She paced, wall to wall, window to door. Her hands were clenched. "He should not talk to me that way," she said aloud. "Warning me."

She stopped again beside her desk and picked up her telephone. Then she stopped. "I don't know his number," she said. "That is ridiculous." He was listed in an Internet directory and, before debating it, she dialed the number.

"How dare you call here?" he demanded, and Eleanor realized her number had appeared on his telephone display.

"You threatened me," she said rapidly, breathlessly, to get it all in before he hung up again. "With what? You said I'm warning you. With what? What will you do? What are your weapons?"

He was silent, and in that silence Eleanor felt a sudden burst of exhilaration.

"Show me your weapons. Your plan of action. You're always adding things up. What does warning add up to?"

She heard herself babbling and took a breath. "What can you do?" she asked, still wildly excited. "I am intensely interested in what you think you can do."

Still he was silent. Eleanor pictured him, stunned, scowling, holding the receiver away from his ear, denying an Eleanor he did not recognize. She felt giddy. Sophie would be so proud. She could see Martin, a Martin she did not know any more than he knew her, thinning his lips in anger, blaming her for deluding him all these months, hiding aberrant tendencies. Beautiful, he had called her. Glowing.

"Bitch," he said. "Leave me the fuck alone." And hung up.

But in less than a minute he called. "Sorry," he said. "Didn't mean that."

Eleanor said nothing. Her giddiness was gone; she was drained and cold and sat on her couch.

"Didn't mean it," he said. "I care deeply for you. We had good times, wonderful times; I was sorry it had to end. Truly sorry. You're an amazing woman, a fantastic musician; I'll miss you. But these things end. You know that; you're not a child, you're—"

"Amazing. Yes, I know."

"And of course I wish you well. All the best."

She hung up gently, soundlessly, and sat beside the telephone. She picked up her flute and ran her fingers over the keys. When the phone rang a few minutes later, she gazed at it until it fell silent. How boring this all is, she thought. He could have come up with something interesting to say, something creative. He could have done me that courtesy. But why would he? He was finished. These things end. I'm not a child. I'm supposed to know that.

At Eleanor's next concert, critics found her flute resonant and melancholy, communicating, they wrote, depths of universal sorrow achieved by few musicians. The conductor began choosing selections with prominent parts for the mellifluous darkness of her playing. Sophie, preferring liveliness, came less often.

A short time later, when Eleanor asked, Sophie drove her to Martin's suburb and pulled up across the street from his house, but a police car appeared in the rearview mirror, and Sophie accelerated and drove off. "Thank you," Eleanor said. "That was quite enough. Coda."

"You'll find someone else," Sophie said brightly. "There's not a ton of good ones out there, but you'll find one. Better than Martin. At least, single."

When Eleanor took the train to and from her job in the doctors' office, she no longer focused on the lives framed by the uncurtained windows they passed; now she directed her attention to her fellow passengers. She was not in a great hurry; she let the days pass in patient scrutiny until she found one in particular who drew her interest.

He always took the same seat, beside a window in the middle of the car, and was reading a hardback copy of Albert Camus' *The Fall*. Eleanor walked down the aisle to sit beside him and took from her handbag her own paperback copy. As all readers do, he glanced at the book as she opened it to a marker halfway through. She met his eyes and looked down at his book. "Oh," she said, a thread of wonder in her voice. "You're rediscovering it, too. Quite remarkable, isn't it?" And whether she was referring to Camus' tale or the coincidence of two people on a train reading the same book, she knew, from the interest in his eyes, they would begin a conversation.

The Specialty of the House

FROM THE WINDOW SEAT in her bedroom, Dorothy could see the long driveway leading to the front of her house and watch everyone who came and went, even at night when the lights flanking the front door illuminated a wide swath that prevented anyone from sneaking in. She was sitting there, hidden by heavy drapes, the day Lawrence arrived. She watched the car come to a stop in the circular drive, saw him step out and take a long look at the front door before turning slowly in place. "Surveying," Dorothy said aloud. "Taking a survey of our house." She leaned forward to count the times he turned, once, twice, three slow revolutions before making a half turn to take two suitcases from the car—big ones, for a long stay—and set them in the driveway. She knew his name was Lawrence, but she would never call him that. He was only 'he' and 'him.' The stranger. The intruder. The thief. He straightened up and studied the house, the late afternoon sun picking out the gray in his dark hair and beard and glinting off his glasses. He's old, Dorothy thought. And not even handsome.

Still standing beside his suitcases, he scanned the wide sloping lawn and beds of chrysanthemums and asters the gardeners planted every September. He contemplated the pond with flashing koi, the towering trees shading flagstone terraces, the stone steps at the far end of the lawn leading down to the beach and the lake. And then, abruptly, he looked up, to the second floor of the house.

Dorothy leaped back, but she was sure he had seen her, and she knew why he had looked up: her mother had told him to. Her mother knew she liked to sit there, knew she would be watching for him, and she probably said, "Look at the window above the front door and you'll see Dorothy; she peers at the world from there." And she would have laughed, because she always teased Dorothy about being more of an onlooker than a participant. "Make new friends," her mother would urge. "Go to parties. Nobody cares that you don't have a father or how he died. I'll bet lots of others in your school don't have fathers."

To which Dorothy always shook her head. "They have fathers. Even if their parents are divorced, there's a father, and even if some of them died, they weren't *murdered*."

Her mother would have forgotten they'd talked about that. She would have laughed about Dorothy sitting in her window seat watching their driveway and the cars and cyclists on the road some distance away, and the houses on the other side, more visible in winter when the trees were bare. Laughing with a stranger, betraying her only daughter.

She heard voices at the front door and leaned forward again; no one would pay attention now, because her mother had come out and the two of them were looking at each other, not touching, not even close, talking inanities.

"You made good time."

"Your directions were perfect. And the traffic was light."

"That was lucky. Afternoon traffic can be so bad. The rush hour..."

"No, it was an easy trip. Though I kept wishing it was shorter."

They drifted inside; the houseman picked up the two suitcases, and the front door closed behind him. Dorothy sat in the silence of her room, in the silence of the house beyond her closed and locked door, and thought about her mother, and then she went to her closet and took out her charms.

They were in an old dress box of her mother's she had found in the trash, still bright and shiny, still filled with red tissue paper, large enough to hold neat rows of charms and hexes. Dorothy had many ways of arranging them on the round table in the center of her room and she debated, finally settling on concentric circles covering the leather top. Her father had brought her the first one from Egypt. It was just a few months before he died, and she remembered how mysterious he'd been, handing her the charm tightly wrapped in its embroidered cloth. Maybe Egyptian charms lose their potency in a Chicago suburb, he had said seriously, but you couldn't be sure. Dorothy would know how potent it was the first time she used it, and she could tell him about it and whom she'd zapped; he was curious to know whom his eleven-year-old daughter would choose as her victim.

All the others in her collection she had found on the Internet, following links on sites selling preteen bras and T-shirts and low-slung jeans, and as soon as she'd saved enough of her allowance to pay for a new one, her brother would buy it with his credit card. He was nine years older than Dorothy, not at all interested in what she was buying, or why, so she could trust him. He liked being necessary, but beyond that he barely noticed her; all he saw clearly were girls and his favorite hockey team.

The links on the Internet led to riotous pages of charms and hexes scattered about like confetti, little balloons floating above them as if they were talking. "Control your destiny!" "Your fate in your hands!" "Change your life!" "Make friends bend to your will!" "Add to shopping cart!"

Her brother had left for college two years earlier, when

she was nine, but each time he came home for vacations, Dorothy had two or three new charms for him to order, and now she had ten charms and nine hexes. Every few days she took them out and arranged them in rows or circles on their embroidered cloth, memorizing details of each so she could imagine them clearly when they were tucked away in her closet. They were all colors and sizes, no two the same, but all of them dazzling: wildly decorated with bright gauze and silk, feathers and sequins, velvet ribbons, lace, tiny beads, diminutive sinister spikes, all in intriguing combinations that made Dorothy think of her books on India and Kazakhstan: whirling dervishes, dark-skinned snake charmers, red-caped magicians, golden-haired princesses in locked towers threatened by menacing figures in the shadows. The hexes were weighty with the mystery of their latent power, the charms more fragile. Some were flexible, some rigid, but each one had a story to tell, written calligraphically inside its own scroll tied with a red silk ribbon.

Dorothy knew there would be a time to use them, a crisis that cried out for powerful hexes and charms, maybe all she had, to make life orderly again. It would not do to waste them on everyday problems or aggravations: she had chosen only the most expensive and unusual of those she'd seen, so she could be secure in the knowledge that she had the perfect antidote to whatever traumatizing events arose.

A bell rang, a musical phrase trilling from a box near the ceiling. Her mother wanted her. Long ago, when the house was built, the bell rang from the bedrooms to the servants' quarters, and was louder and more peremptory: ladies in flowing negligees summoning their maids to help them dress for the day; men tottering home in the early dawn after too much to drink, demanding a butler remove their tuxedos before they collapsed on their beds; someone sick calling for the butler to summon a doctor. When Dorothy's parents had had the house renovated, they had not eliminated the bells in her bedroom and her brother's but had rewired them melodically to call them to breakfast or dinner or a sail on the lake, or perhaps to make sure they were in their rooms at bedtime.

She's probably tired of kissing him, Dorothy thought; that's why she's calling me.

But how did they kiss anyway? His beard would scratch, and his glasses would knock against her mother's glasses. Unless they took their glasses off, the way they took everything off when they went to bed. How could her mother stand looking at him when he was naked? With nothing on he'd be ridiculous, like a skinned stork, tall and bony and white except for his dark beard and his thing flopping that somebody in school said was always red. It was boring to think about.

The bell rang again. They'll show off, she thought; that's why they want me there. And he'll call me Dot. She replaced the charms and hexes, laying them in neat rows on their cloth and covering them with the long overlapping ends. I hate that name. He should know that. She slid the box into the closet and covered it with a pile of shoes.

And she'll smile all the time, the way she does when she says his name, when she reads his emails. Like she's got a secret.

"This is Lawrence," her mother said, standing beside him in the living room and smiling. "I've told you about him."

He was holding out his hand. Dorothy's hand came up to meet his, and she shook it once, hard, then stepped back so she would not have to look straight up at him. He was taller than he'd looked from above, but she'd been right about his being old and not handsome.

"It's a pleasure to meet you," he said formally. "I was thinking about you, driving here today. I hope we'll spend lots of time together and get acquainted."

She squinted at him. "Why?"

"Because I'd like to get to know you."

"You came to see Mother."

"And I will," he said. "But you and I should be friends."

"Why?"

Dorothy's mother frowned. But he was smiling, as if Dorothy had said something amusing. "Families are happier when they're all friends."

"Mother and I are our family. Our whole family. And we're friends."

"Dorothy," her mother said, "I asked you to be polite."

"I shook hands with him."

"Lawrence is offering you friendship."

"Why?"

"Because he is; that should be enough. Do you think there's so much friendship in the world you can afford to reject it when it's offered to you?"

"I didn't!"

"I'm ashamed of you. To turn your back on—"

"I didn't!"

Their voices crossed each other, and Lawrence said, "She didn't exactly reject it, Carol." He put his arm around her mother and smiled again. "We don't have to examine the subtext."

"She's being unpleasant. And I specifically asked her—"

"I'm not unpleasant!" Dorothy glared at them, close together, touching all along their sides. "And I don't even know what subtext is. I just asked why. Can't I even ask why?"

"What do you want to know?"

"Why you let him butt into our family! He's a foreigner. He doesn't belong with us."

Her mother's chin came up. Dorothy knew that look: mostly it had been aimed at her father, but now and then at her, whenever she said something her mother called inappropriate. Her mother tried to avoid controversy—she said she'd had enough of it in her life, and each time people got swept up in it culture took a step backward—and anytime Dorothy made caustic comments about a student at school or joked about how someone looked or mimicked a teacher she didn't like, her mother drew back into that uplifted chin and Dorothy knew she had Undermined Culture.

It was odd, Dorothy thought, that her mother had worn that look for days and weeks after her father died. Dorothy had been prepared to comfort her; she was six years old and struggling with her own terrors, but she was prepared to be a source of strength to her mother. She would follow her from room to room, waiting for tears and heaving shoulders to match her own, waiting for a fainting spell or collapse, but there was nothing. Her mother had turned to stone, pale, tightly wound, her lips a thin line, her chin high. That was the worst time, Dorothy thought, everything was the worst then, except for now, with Lawrence standing there like he never would leave.

Her mother stepped sideways, out of Lawrence's enclosing arm. "This isn't like you," she said to Dorothy. "You're usually so grown up. I've been so proud of my grown-up daughter, someone I could count on. What's wrong with you? All I asked was that you meet my friend and begin to get to know him. But you're not even giving him a chance. You've never met him before, but you decided in advance you wouldn't be friendly."

"He wants to own us!" Dorothy cried. "He looked at our house like it was something in a store he was going to buy. He kept turning around and around, looking at everything, studying everything. Like he wanted to see what we had and make sure we were rich enough for him."

"Shame on you," her mother snapped. Her voice was like a knife.

Dorothy had never heard that voice, but she felt it cut and she began to cry. She had to go to the bathroom and she squeezed herself, trying to hold it in, trying to hold back her tears, trying to catch her breath. "It's true, though," she said. "I know it. He doesn't love us; he just wants to own what we've got; I saw him, I know it."

"Well, now," Lawrence said with a small smile. "I think this is something we should talk about." He held out his hand to Dorothy, palm up, as if offering something, but Dorothy was staring at her mother through her tears.

"I watched him, he knew I was watching but he didn't care, he just kept checking us out, our house and the gardens, looking and looking. Surveying." Her mother was looking across the room, and Dorothy turned to see what she was looking at, but there was nothing special, just their usual furniture, in all the usual places. "It's true, it's true, it's true!" she cried, and turned and ran.

"Dorothy!" her mother called. "Come back here! This minute!"

Like a dog, Dorothy thought; she shouldn't yell at me like

that. In the foyer, out of sight, she stopped and listened.

"She's unhappy," Lawrence said.

"Really? How clever of you to notice. Oh, God, I'm sorry, Lawrence. I didn't mean that. Please forgive me."

"You're upset," he said, and even though her mother was silent, Dorothy knew she was thinking he'd done it again: said what was obvious. He didn't sound very smart.

"Let's take it slow and easy," he said. "Too many high emotions boiling away all at once."

"I know what to do," her mother said, sounding annoyed. "I can handle Dorothy." She walked into the foyer and Dorothy fled, running up the broad, curving staircase. "Okay," her mother said, looking up at her. "You made your point. You don't like Lawrence being here, you don't like it that I'm happy he's here. You want things to go back to the way they were. But that isn't going to happen, you know; things change, people change, and we have to get used to it and find what's good about the way things are now. You can do that, Dorothy, you're smart and I know you love me and want me to be happy. I trust you, you know, I trust you to help me when I need it. And right now I need you to be pleasant and help us adjust to something new."

"It's only five years!" Dorothy shouted. "You were mad or sad when Daddy died, I don't know, you never cried, even when I did, all the time, but you said we were together, you and me, and that was what counted; you said we'd take care of each other, that we were our family. I remember you saying that!"

Her mother was looking up at her, and Dorothy was sure there were tears in her eyes. "And I meant what I said. But your father was the one who died, sweetheart; I'm still alive. You are my family, you're my dear, beautiful daughter, and I love you, but I have other needs that you can't understand yet. I want you to sit with us so we can talk about it."

"I'll talk to you, not him." Dorothy stomped the rest of the way upstairs, as noisily as she could on the thick carpet. "You keep telling me how smart I am," she shouted down to her mother. "So how come there's all these things I don't understand?" She slammed her bedroom door behind her and rushed to the bathroom. She was crying and thinking she'd almost wet her pants, like a baby, and maybe her mother thought she was a baby, acting like a baby, and that was why she'd talked to her that way, hurting her.

She knew she'd messed up; she should have been nicer. She didn't have to be really nice, just enough to keep things from blowing up. But as soon as she'd seen them together, with her mother inside his arm, she couldn't help it, she said what she thought, let them see what she felt. So now everything was worse than before, and when she sank into the pillows on her window seat, she decided she'd stay there forever; even if the bell rang a million times, she wouldn't answer, and then her mother would feel sad and tell what's-his-name to go home. Or he'd make her let him stay and they'd wander around downstairs and get old, they'd have gray hair and hobble around on canes and they'd need help getting up the stairs, but she wouldn't come out. She couldn't. They didn't want her. They'd stood there like they knew something nobody else knew, his arm around her so tight there was no room between them, not even for a daughter. A dear, beautiful daughter.

She flung a stuffed owl across the room, and a fuzzy dachshund, and kicked her American Girl doll that had fallen off the dresser, and that she was too old for but couldn't bear to give away, then held her Raggedy Ann in a tight hug. She'd outgrown Raggedy Ann, too, but she knew there would always be times when she'd need it, and maybe the stuffed animals, too. Like now, when her mother had abandoned her.

There was one thing that was good. Her mother had heard what she said. She could stand close to him and they could talk and talk, they could go to bed if that's what they wanted, it didn't matter, because when Dorothy said he'd studied their house to see what he was getting, her mother's eyes had closed for a minute, half a minute maybe, and that always meant she had something new to think about. For the first time—or maybe not the first—her mother wondered.

* * * * * * *

Dorothy's father had teased her. He was a big tease; everyone called him that. He had a memory for things others forgot, and he registered little traits nobody else noticed, and he used them to tease. People laughed when he was really on, soaring on a current of cleverness, flicking little stilettos into his target and twisting until he heard a yelp of pain, sometimes outrage, at which he would let others direct the conversation, until something gave him an opening to turn on someone else. People laughed, until they became the victim; then they would scowl or flare up—*Fuck off, Brian, you're such a shit*—and sometimes walk out, even if that left an awful gap, louder than words, in the small dinner party in the silk-hung dining room with an attentive waiter looking at the ceiling but taking it all in.

Eventually there were fewer dinner parties, fewer invitations, fewer friends, and Dorothy's parents fought at night. They quarreled about his behavior, about his company, which he hated and kept threatening to leave, and Dorothy's mother would say there was no way she would tolerate that, they didn't have the money they used to have, and he would shoot back well then, she could sell her fur coat and learn to cook hamburger meat. They quarreled about the times he hardly noticed his wife, shutting her out "as if you don't see me," and about the way he treated Dorothy and her brother. Until one Saturday, after a dinner party the night before with people they'd met only once, when two of the guests had left before dessert, Dorothy's mother said, "You are, Brian. You are a shit."

The four of them, Dorothy and her parents and brother were at lunch in the alcove off the kitchen, and Dorothy, shocked at what her mother had said, picked up a green bean and began nibbling it with tiny, nervous bites, from the tip to the end. Her father held his water glass to his mouth, like a microphone. "Gaze at those table manners, audience. Ever seen such elegance? Such grace? Would you not suspect noble genes if you didn't know better? Much better?"

Dorothy burst into tears. "Lay off, Dad," said her brother.

"You are a shit," her mother said. "Even with your children."

"Wait a minute, hold on just a minute, is that any way to talk to the loving father of these wonderful children? I love this little angel and she knows it. I tease with love and she knows it. I wouldn't tease her if I didn't love her, and she knows that, too."

"Don't do it again," her mother said. "I can't stand it. I hate it."

"Hate?" He stood and looked at them one by one. "Hate? A strange word to use at a loving family lunch. Almost as bad as shit. Words used by people of small vocabularies and even smaller minds. Once you found me amusing. I made you laugh."

"Once you were amusing. Now you're monstrous.

Solipsistic and sadistic."

"But sexy. You liked that. Remember? All you wanted was to be in my bed. You tried to get my attention with a new hairdo, some kind of weird beehive that was, I believe, the fashion for desperate misfits, and I noticed it with amusement, recalling that a fashionable Carol was, at best, an oxymoron."

"Stop it! You're doing it again."

"Those days, when I made fun of someone, you said it was good to take arrogant people down a peg or two."

"Meaning your daughter? Meaning your wife?"

"It's the way I am. You knew it from the day you met me and decided you wanted me. For sexiness and all else, of course, but also because you were afraid no one else would take you seriously: there was, we all knew, so little there. You know, my dear, you are a nice, simple woman. I thought when I married you I could bend you toward eccentric or whimsical—perhaps, God willing, even fey—but you are resolutely common. Such a disappointment to those of us who enjoy the intellectual side of life. To be solemnly wedded to a limited, middle-aged woman with no sense of humor. Vanilla, as they say. Our friends have been driven away not by my wit, but by your deadly dullness. And now you have learned some new words. I do not like them. Who hates my speech hates me. I shall therefore take my leave." He bowed and left the room, left the house, and did not come back.

The house was empty and echoing. The last quarrel reverberated through the rooms. Dorothy's brother swore furiously. "They could have waited, had their dogfight when you weren't around; you're six years old, for Christ's sake; they don't give a damn what they're doing to you." But then her brother went back to college and she was left to walk around the house and remember all the words, and the anger. Even with time, nothing faded: the memories tangled with her thoughts: every word, every grimace, the cutting voices, her mother's clenched fists, her father's mocking smile as he bowed.

She and her mother did not talk about it. Once Dorothy tried, but her mother waved her words away as if they were annoying insects and shook her head with a finality Dorothy recoiled from. She never asked the questions roiling inside her about love and marriage vows and the long-ago dreams each of her parents might have had, and shared. She never knew what her mother thought or felt after that awful day, and could not ask about the words they'd spoken, what they really meant, afraid of her mother's chin going up and her lips tightening, and all the anger coming back. Instead, the two of them spoke quietly. At first her mother said, "He'll be back; he's done something like this before; it's a joke." Later she said, "Of course he'll be back, this is the only life he knows; he's trying to force me to beg him," and when Dorothy asked, "How? You don't know where he is," her mother said, with a narrow smile, "He has an office. And he has email; he knows I can reach him anytime; he's testing me." When he had been gone a month, she said, "You'll hear from him. He'll have to prove what a good father he is; what else could he use in a courtroom? Of course it won't come to that, but if it ever did . . ."

But Dorothy did not hear from him, and he did not come back. Finally, Dorothy's mother said, "The bank says he's been withdrawing funds. So he's having a midlife crisis. Hardly unusual; men have them all the time. They get over them. Eventually he'll show up. What else can he do? No one else will have him."

They settled into a routine that seemed to please her

mother, but Dorothy could not sleep and her schoolwork suffered. She begged her mother to find him and bring him home. "A detective! You can hire one; they always find people."

"Maybe later," her mother said. "Give him time; believe me, he doesn't have the guts to make a life alone."

At school, Dorothy overheard two girls in the locker room. "My father says he's shacked up with somebody new. What does shacked up mean?"

"What is shacked up?" she asked her mother at dinner. "Somebody said that's where Daddy is. Like, living in a shack?"

"They're talking about us?" Dorothy's mother asked. "How do they know? I've only told a few people."

"But what does it mean?"

"I suppose it means in a shack."

Her mother called his office. He had called in sick and had not been seen for a month. She sent him an email. It was returned as undeliverable. "Fuck," she muttered, and Dorothy pretended not to hear.

Six weeks after he left, a lawyer called, talking of division of assets and settlements and visitation.

"It won't happen," Dorothy's mother said. "He's trying to frighten me. He really is a shit."

"I love him," Dorothy said.

"He was mean to you."

"I don't care. I love him and I miss him and I want him to come home."

The lawyer returned twice. "I won't sign anything," Dorothy's mother said, "until he talks to me himself."

He called the next morning. "We have to talk about this," she said. "You have obligations. We have two children."

"Children survive divorce just fine," he said. "We'll find

you a place to live that's in the same school district and they'll hardly notice any difference. They'll see me two or three times a week; they won't lose a father, they'll just discover what a dull mother they have on the days they have to spend with her."

The next day, Dorothy's mother went to his office. He had left, they told her; he said he had a greater opportunity elsewhere.

And then, before divorce got any closer, before any papers could be drawn up, much less signed, the police came, just after midnight on a Saturday night, to say that Dorothy's father had been robbed and shot dead outside a bar in the city. They wanted her to come to the morgue to identify the body.

To Dorothy's tears, her mother said, "He would have come back; he just wanted to see how far he could push me."

Dorothy hurt inside. "He only left because you made him."

"Stop it; don't talk about things you don't understand. Six years old: how can you know anything about it? We'll talk when you're older. Right now, just leave it alone."

But Dorothy could not leave it alone. She brooded about it in her room, at school, walking on the beach below their wide lawns and gardens. She made up stories about her father: he was not dead, just faking, to get away from her mother; or he was in a hospital somewhere, being treated for gunshot wounds that had made him lose his memory; or he did die, and left behind a long letter to help Dorothy get through the years without him, but her mother had hidden it so Dorothy would forget him and now she had to figure out where it was.

Still, she clung to her mother. They stayed close together in the big, empty house; she helped her mother in the kitchen, or they chose restaurants together for dinner; they shopped for clothes together, and at night Dorothy would do her homework in the den while her mother read nearby. At the same time, her mother was redecorating the living and dining rooms and her bedroom, hers alone now, supervising the crews who came each day and took apart the rooms and put them together again with new paint and new furniture and bright paintings on the walls. There were no more dinner parties, and even when Dorothy's brother was home from college, the three of them ate in the breakfast room, newly decorated to look like summer, with pale blue patterned wallpaper and old-fashioned yellow-painted round table and chairs. Even in winter, a bouquet of white and yellow narcissus was always in the center of the table. And Dorothy's father was less and less a presence in her daily life: only, at night, the dominant force in tentacles that still wound through her dreams.

And when she arrayed her charms and hexes on the table in her bedroom, he seemed to be standing beside her, kind and humorous as he had been the day he brought her the first one, saying he'd missed her when he was in Egypt and next time he'd be sure to take her along.

Now her mother was with a stranger and they were downstairs, plotting things or kissing or whatever. Dorothy sat at her window, looking at the cars on the road at the far end of their driveway. Once she thought her father might be in one of them and the car would turn into their driveway and she would run downstairs to greet him. But now she knew her father truly was gone, seemingly as forgotten as if he had never walked through their house laughing and saying funny things about the day, the city, the people he worked with, funny things she and her mother would laugh at and quote to their friends. "So clever," her mother would say to friends. But that was a long time ago, before he made people angry with his quips, and now he'd gotten killed. That wasn't very clever, Dorothy thought.

The gardeners had cleared a sinuous path along the driveway and were planting tulip and hyacinth bulbs for next spring, smoothing dark soil over them, using blowers to clear the walks. They dragged skinny shadows of themselves, like long tails, as they moved slowly in the late afternoon sun.

"Dorothy." Her mother was on the other side of her door. "Sweetheart, you've been up here long enough. We'd like you to come to dinner."

"I'm not hungry."

"You're always hungry for dinner. Even that time the bee stung you and you came screaming into the house and I held you on my lap and sang—"

"I don't care!" Her face was wet and hot and she did not even wipe away her tears. That had been the most wonderful day; she remembered all of it. She had curled into a tight ball in her mother's lap, crying from pain and fear of the bee that seemed larger and deadlier the more she thought about it, and her mother had held her close, warm and soft, and she was safe and everything was good. At that moment it was not so devastating that her father was dead and her brother at college; everything was all right because she and her mother were together, and her mother was protecting her.

"But that night you were hungry, too," her mother said through the closed door. "After we'd put cream on your arm and you felt better, we sat for a while and I sang some of your favorite songs, and then, all of a sudden, you said, 'What are we having for dinner?' And we laughed. So I know you're hungry now."

"Leave me alone!" Dorothy's stomach growled and she tightened her muscles to clamp it down. "You don't know anything about me. You don't care about me."

"Dorothy."

"You used to," she said stubbornly, "but you don't anymore."

"You know that's not true."

"It is too. You don't listen to me or ask me what I think about anything. Like who you let in the house. You think grown-ups don't have to ask kids about things like that, but I thought we were different. You should have asked me!"

No sound came from the other side of the door. Dorothy waited. She stood up to open her door to see if her mother was still there, but then she sat down. Just because her mother had come upstairs to talk to her, nothing had changed. What's-his-name was still downstairs, probably counting the silver. Her stomach grumbled again and she pounded it with her fist to subdue it and to squelch her rising panic. The silence pressed down, making her room heavy.

"Maybe I'll eat later," she said at last.

"I don't think that's a great idea," said her mother.

Still there, Dorothy thought. So everything was okay. "Just leave it, then. In the hall."

"Did I ever do that before?"

"No, but you never talked mean to me either. You never asked somebody to bring suitcases and move in. You never did lots of things."

"Well, you're right; lots of things have changed. Why don't we talk about it at dinner?"

Dorothy was pacing. The Prowler, her father had called her, and it had seemed only a little bit funny, but then he brought home her first charm and was nice and she'd kissed him.

"Dorothy." Her mother sounded very serious. "We can

talk about anything you like at dinner, or we can be quiet, whatever you want, but you have to come downstairs. It's getting late."

"It's eight o'clock."

"I know what time it is. It's dinnertime, and I expect you downstairs in . . . two and seven eighth minutes."

Dorothy laughed. She tried not to, but the laugh trickled out. This was their game, hers and her mother's, no one else's. They had a few games that were just theirs, and whenever they played them, Dorothy's world seemed ordered and manageable.

"Three," she said.

"Two and three-quarters," her mother said quickly.

"Two and five-eighths."

"Two and a quarter, my final offer."

Dorothy opened the door. "Two and three eighths?"

Her mother pulled her close. "I love you." She wiped a remaining tear from Dorothy's cheek. "Dinner?"

"Okay."

They were eating in the dining room. Dorothy preferred the breakfast room, small, octagonal, cozy, with the dinner dishes spread out on the kitchen counter so they could fill their plates as many times as they liked. Tonight, even though her mother had cooked dinner, the maid served it. After deciding she would not eat, Dorothy could not stop; she heaped her plate from the platter of roast chicken and fingerling potatoes in browned butter the maid held for her.

"You remembered," Lawrence said, smiling at her mother. "Our first dinner together, at that little place on 58th Street. The specialty of the house."

"She made it for me," Dorothy said. "It's my favorite."

"Then it seems she made it for both of us."

"No, she's made it for me lots of times. She knows—"

"Well, it has happy memories for both of us."

"I made it for myself," her mother said.

"Good Lord, I am sorry," said Lawrence. He shook his head. "Why I let myself . . ."

It was too late to leave her food untouched, to show them what she thought of them, so Dorothy kept eating.

After a minute, Lawrence said, "I still want to talk to Dorothy. First, do you like to be called Dot? I really don't like that name and I'll bet you don't either. Is that right? I'd rather call you Dorothy, if that's okay with you."

"You told him," Dorothy said to her mother.

"I did not," her mother said, but Dorothy knew she was lying. Her mother lied a lot these days.

"Well? Is it Dorothy?" Lawrence asked.

Dorothy shrugged. "Fine. It's fine."

"Well, then, Dorothy, tell me about school. Which part do you hate the most?"

"I don't. Why would I? I don't hate any of it."

"Lucky you. I hated a lot about school."

"Where was that?" her mother asked.

"Hell's Kitchen."

"Hell's Kitchen?"

"A neighborhood in Manhattan. We lived at 35th and 9th. A reporter called it Hell's Kitchen a long time ago. Eighteen eighties, I think. He said it was the lowest, filthiest part of New York City."

"Was it really filthy?"

"You know, I suppose it was. Tenements crammed with railroad workers, stockyard workers, peddlers, all of them new immigrants. But kids don't see that, and even if they do, they don't care. It was home. It was ours."

Dorothy's mother asked another question and then another, and Lawrence talked about Hell's Kitchen, the neighborhood, the people, his friends, the school. He talked easily, amusingly, and Dorothy's mother smiled and laughed, but Dorothy knew it was all play-acting, because wouldn't he have told her about himself when they were getting acquainted, like she and her friends did? Her mother must have heard all this stuff before, but she wanted to make it seem they were a real family having a fun evening together, telling stories about being young, even in an awful place, acting interested and curious and laughing. But Dorothy didn't laugh, except once, when he told a story about a pet lizard scrabbling around the mashed potatoes on the dinner plate of a boring uncle.

Which probably never happened; he was making it up; but it was funny anyway and she laughed.

"... six to a room," he was saying, "which actually helped keep us warm at night."

"He was poor," Dorothy said to her mother.

Lawrence tilted his head as he looked at her. "I sure was. Is that a problem?"

"They lived in a tenement. A slum. Rats and ... whatever."

"Well, we don't know about the rats, do we?" her mother asked.

"And they probably talked about how they'd all find a way to get rich someday."

"Oh, for heaven's sake." Her mother sighed. "We were poor, you know."

Dorothy looked up, at the shimmering prism of the chandelier. "We're rich."

"We are. But that's because of your grandfather. And he was poor; he came from Europe with nothing: he didn't even know English, and he worked—"

"Did he marry somebody rich?" Dorothy asked.

"He married a girl as poor as he was." Her mother's voice was even, and Dorothy knew she was angry. "She was sixteen, he was twenty three, and they both worked and saved everything they could and finally bought the building they lived in and then more buildings, but they never stopped working. They worked hard all their lives and they were fortunate: they made a great deal of money that we're still enjoying."

Dorothy looked at Lawrence.

"Not me," he said lightly. "Not everyone figures out how to get rich; it's an art. And some luck in there, too. Now how about telling me about school? Unless there's something else you'd rather talk about."

"Your job. If you have one."

"Sure I do. Lots of them. Lots of clients, that is, and I solve problems for them."

"Problems."

"Computer problems. I take over their computers from my office and get rid of bugs or whatever else might be wrong with them."

Dorothy wanted to act bored. Instead, she said, "What does that mean? Taking them over."

"I take control of them. If I took over your computer, you could sit at your desk and watch the cursor move around and the screen change and words appear and disappear because I'm doing all that at my desk."

"You're a hacker."

"Nope. It's legal and I get paid for it. People give me

permission to take over their computers because they'd rather not haul them down to my office to get them fixed. This way they can do what they want—read a book, go out for lunch, whatever—while I do the work, and when they come back to their desks everything's in fine shape and they're in control again."

"Compufixers," Dorothy said to her mother. "This group of kids in the high school. They come to your house and fix your computer and they get credit for it, it's part of their computer course. It's not a big deal; any high school kid can do it."

"Dorothy." Her mother clicked her tongue. "You're trying so hard to ruin things. I wish you'd try that hard to be pleasant and give Lawrence a chance. You might like him. You might even have a good time."

"But I'm not having a good time! You want me to pretend!"

Her best times were at school, where she was good at what she did, and each day was like every other day, without big changes. She had friends, not as many as the popular girls, but two special girlfriends who liked the same things she did, and the three of them were a group. They weren't friends she could talk to when bad things happened, like her mother all of a sudden talking about somebody, it seemed like overnight: like one day there was nothing, and the next day his name started popping up, like a gopher poking its head out, then vanishing, then popping up somewhere else. If she told one person about that, it wouldn't be five minutes before whoever she told, even sworn to secrecy, would tell a friend and swear them to secrecy, and then the story would travel, changing shape each time it was passed on. And then everyone would ask when her mother was getting married, and would Dorothy be bridesmaid and her brother best man, and where would she live while they were on their honeymoon, and were they going to keep living in the same house because lots of times new husbands didn't want to stay where old husbands had lived, and how did Dorothy like having a new father?

"He won't be my father," she said to her mother. It was early afternoon four weeks after Lawrence's arrival, and she and her mother were in the kitchen, chopping vegetables for dinner while he was in the city, Christmas shopping, he said.

"Whatever you want," her mother said, thinking about something else.

"Why doesn't he ever take us places?" Dorothy demanded loudly. "We go on picnics that you make, or walks, or we drive someplace and then we come back. He could take us to dinner or a movie or something."

In an email to her brother, Dorothy had said Lawrence was a fortune hunter. Her brother had written back that she should keep her mouth shut until he could get there and check things out.

"I thought you liked picnics and long drives," her mother said. "You always used to."

"I don't anymore."

"Well, we can go out if you like. I'd rather eat at home myself."

"You like restaurants. You and Daddy always went to restaurants. It's because of him. Because he won't pay for anything."

Dorothy's brother was not coming home for Thanksgiving. "Come home," she wrote to him in an email. "You have to come home."

"I'm going to New York," he wrote back. "You'll be fine without me. Mother always invites a horde for dinner anyway."

"You're going to your girlfriend's house," she wrote

accusingly.

He called her up. "You never cared before this whether I came home or not."

"I care now. You care more about what's-her-name than you do me."

"She doesn't complain the way you do. I may want to marry what's-her-name. Which is Natalie, as you well know."

"I don't want you to get married. I want you to come home and kick him out."

"Oh, come on. Our mother is a grown-up lady who'll make up her own mind. What's wrong with him?"

"You said you'd come and check him out. Then you'd know what's wrong."

"Well, I'm not there. So what's wrong with him?"

"I told you: he just wants our money. He's a liar. He's not honest."

"You know that for a fact? How about your imagination's in overdrive? Mom's pretty smart, you know. I don't think she'd be fooled. Listen, sweetheart, eat a lot of Thanksgiving turkey and relax. Maybe he just likes Mom; she's pretty likeable, you know. Good looking, too."

Everybody was satisfied. Everybody was blind. She was the only one who saw what was happening. "Isn't he ever going home?" she asked her mother.

"I hope not. Honey..." Her mother brushed the vegetables into a colander and sat at the kitchen table, holding out her arms. Dorothy perched on her lap. "I am asking you to give him a chance. Let yourself love him."

"I won't love him."

"Well, you don't have to, but you might like him. You might let yourselves be friends. It would make things a lot easier, a lot happier." She slid her hand over Dorothy's hair, smoothing it. "Honey, we're going to get married—we were going to tell you tonight, at dinner—and after we're a real family—"

"You can't! He's a bad man! He's only pretending until you get married and then he won't have to be nice anymore. All he wants is our things. He's always picking them up and looking at them like you look at something in the store before you buy it. He walks all over the house picking things up."

"How do you know that?"

"I see him do it."

"You follow him? You spy on him?"

"I just see him."

"You peer around corners and hide behind chairs and scuttle after him? Shame on you. What a nasty child you can be."

"He doesn't love you!"

Her mother stood up, and Dorothy slid off her lap, off balance until she caught herself. "He says he does," her mother said very quietly.

"He's lying! He wouldn't even be here if we weren't rich. Tell him he can't have any of our money. Tell him he can stay here but he can't have any of our money, and then you'll see, he'll go away and we'll never see him again and it will just be us, the way it used to be. The way it's best."

Her mother laughed, a soft, sad laugh. "I won't tell him that, sweetheart. You and I will always have each other, but it will be with Lawrence, too."

"But he doesn't love you! Or me. Just our money."

"That's not what matters." Her mother walked to the window and put her hands on the sill, hunching her shoulders, looking up at the sky and the trees. There was nothing interesting out there, but she kept looking, leaving Dorothy to pay attention or not. "He might really love me. I don't ask. But it doesn't matter. What matters is that he wants to live the way we live, in this house, with all these things. And they're mine, and always will be, so he'll be good to me. I'm pretty sure he likes me, I don't think I'm imagining that, and if he's good to me and treats me as if he loves me, and you, too, what difference does it make whether he really does or not? It's like the doll's house I grew up with; I gave it to you, but you never cared for it the way I did. It was so beautiful, green shutters and a cedar roof with three chimneys and all those sparkling paned windows . . . but when you walked around it, you'd see there was no back and it was just a hollow box with plain cubicles for rooms, and even though I filled them with furniture and little rugs, the fireplaces could never have a fire, the windows would never open, there wasn't even a stairway to the second floor. Nothing about it was real. But as long as you only looked at the front you could believe in it, believe that it could be real and that wonderful things could happen there."

"You're being awful," Dorothy said.

"Well." Her mother turned back from the window and turned her hand up as if she was letting something fly away. "The world is filled with things beyond our control, sweetheart; we do what we can with what we've got, or with whatever we can latch onto. That's the way it is. I can't live without it. You'll understand that someday." She waited, for herself to find something more to say, for Dorothy to ask a question or make some sign of acceptance. Finally, in the stretching silence, she returned to the counter, hefting the knife, making slow, careful slices of zucchini and leeks. "This is between us. I do not expect to hear from Lawrence that you have said a word about it. To him or anyone. I want your promise."

"I promise. Can I go now?"

"Say it again. As if you mean it."

"I promise. Can I go now?"

"Of course. Dorothy."

"What?"

"I love you."

"You're ruining my life," Dorothy said.

Upstairs, she arranged her hexes and charms on their white cloth on the table. It had to be something powerful: getting mugged and shot, with blood running all over him, like it had been with her father; or getting squashed like a bug by a drunk driver while he was crossing the street; or falling asleep while driving and veering into the path of a truck that crumpled his car like a paper cup and didn't leave anything of him but little pieces. It had to be something powerful and sure, something she could conjure up as if she were painting a scene. Then, a little while later, she'd hear the phone ring. Her mother would answer it, there would be a pause . . . and a loud shriek, cries and sobs, and she'd scream out Dorothy's name because she needed her.

And Dorothy would run downstairs and throw her arms around her mother, cradling her, pouring a glass of water . . . no, wine . . . no, bourbon or scotch or whatever people drink when they're devastated and need to be taken care of. She'd hold her mother's head to her chest, the way her mother did when bad things happened to her, and tell her things would be all right: they were together and she would watch over her and take care of her forever, and they didn't need anybody else. They'd be fine because they had each other in their own sheltering house.

She read the instructions on each little piece of paper

and set aside the most powerful hexes. Each was potent, she knew that, but she could not take chances; she would use four at a time. No, five. Maybe even six. She had plenty.

With delicate reverence, she set a hex on her windowsill. She set a second one beside it and sprinkled eight drops of water over it. The third she held high while turning ten times to the right and ten to the left, then set it on the floor where her right foot had stopped. The fourth she blew on until its tiny feathers were waving, then placed it on top of her dresser. The fifth she held in her cupped hands while reciting in a soft whisper the incantation written on its parchment scroll, pronouncing the syllables slowly and carefully so that each was clearly heard wherever it was supposed to be heard. Setting it on the floor beside the other one, she knelt on her window seat and whispered her prayer.

She opened the door so she could hear her mother call. She went back to her window seat and sat in the corner, watching the sun set and the sky blaze in a wash of magenta and burnt orange, and waited for the phone to ring.

The Theory of Unquestioned Beginnings

MY FATHER'S FAMILY came from Bialystok, and he likes to recite the famous names of others whose beginnings were in that once-worldly city that shifted in history between Russia and Poland but was always a center of European Jewish life. Rosa Raisa, the opera star, was one; there were Jonas Salk and Albert Sabin; there were L.L. Zamenhof, creator of Esperanto, and Andrei Vyshinsky; and there were, too, those known for their offspring, the parents of Lionel Trilling and Norbert Weiner among them. "And more," my father would say when we pressed him. "Check the encyclopedia." I did, more than one, but his list, brief as it was, exceeded theirs. The Jewish Encyclopedia did identify the city as a center of Hebrew learning before the pogroms of the late nineteenth and early twentieth century. It also noted that 39,115 Bialystok Jews were exterminated by the Nazis. Others escaped, among them those my father names.

Bialystokers crossed the ocean, wedging themselves into bulging precarious ships for rebirth as Americans; hundreds came, thousands, in the wide sweep from Russia and Eastern Europe in the last quarter of the nineteenth century and the beginning of the next—the famous, the soon-to-be famous, parents of the future famous, and those who would leave their mark in the stories told by their children. My father tells his parents' story to me; he is seventy-five years old this month, and he tells me the story as a lifelong historian-biographer whose passion is to gather loose strands of the past and weave them into a pattern through which the shape of the present emerges. It is as if he lifts his parents from one of the manila folders spread over the three sawhorse tables that, together with his long desk, form an enclosure within which he reads, analyzes, and types with two furious, flying fingers. His smile is tender, and affection softens his eyes, but his fingers are restless on the table where we have just finished lunch; he is typing the story as he tells it. I watch those fingers and measure in their urgency the fragments of Europe to which he clings, this American romantic who has created and nurtured himself as a European liberal and intellectual born, through some spatial dislocation, into a country and century in which he often feels out of place. Or it could be that his urgency is simply that of a writer coming home to a well-shaped tale.

His parents may have met in Bialystok, he says, though it is doubtful. They later discovered they were first cousins, but David, his father, probably had been born and grew up in Kletsk, just outside the Bialystok city walls, hence his name of Kletsky. (My father, upon acceptance for publication of his first biography, changed the name to a simpler pair of syllables, more Western, less Jewish, honoring a writer and intellectual he admired, yet not, he says, for either of those reasons: callow in those days, as he describes himself, he had been afraid no reviewer or reader would feel at ease shaping those foreign sounds on American tongues and so would neither review nor buy his book. Now he thinks it would not have mattered, but the adopted name is now his, and mine, the original long abandoned.)

David Kletsky's first cousin, Paula Halpern, came from a prestigious family, sophisticated and, for Jews in Russia, privileged. Her father was a lawyer, so brilliant, my father says, the Russians allowed him to practice in Moscow, a thing almost unheard of for a Jew. The tsar's ministers reminded him daily, by their professional exactitude and personal repugnance, how rare a privilege he had been granted, to be a Jew among Russians, a Bialystoker allowed to touch the hem of Moscow. He, in turn, became a Marxist, discreet but neither invisible nor mute, and soon came to the attention of the police and the tsar's personal investigators. One day he found in his desk drawers, clumsily interspersed with his own papers, revolutionary documents of a fervid and hyperbolic imagination so laden with violence and vitriol he knew they had been concocted by someone unconcerned with the possibility of judicial scrutiny. He, after all, was a man known for mild temper: a Jew in Tsarist Russia had to be compliant, deferential, compromising, smiling beneath the hoofs of degradation. His ideas of violence, so long repressed, had withered; he could not have called for the terrorist's vocabulary in the pages lying before him even had he been commanded to do so. Yet he knew they would convict him.

He looked at the papers for a long time, turning them dreamily as the early dark of Moscow's winter dulled the gleam of his desk. He took his time; he was saying farewell to Russia, his Russia, Russian law, the scaffolding of Moscow which once he had dreamt of scaling (madness) to reach ministerial level. Within a few days, he and his wife and daughter Paula, then twenty-five and unmarried, took train and carriage across Europe to reach the boat that held promise of the promised land, and promise, too, as yet unimagined, of David Kletsky, the cousin from Kletsk, the first of his family, the pioneer, to trade poverty and constriction for the vastness of America.

My father is not one to straddle ages easily. He is uncomfortable with the careless sexual volubility of our time and the indelicate camera. I have never heard him use a gratuitous obscenity, surely a record for a long-time newspaperman. No one knows better than he, recorder of human indulgences and excesses in a half dozen newspapers and seven biographies, the antics, comic and haunting, of men and women engaged in sex, politics, art, and commerce, but he has determined for himself what is proper to record, what may decently—his word—be articulated, and what is best left to silence, asterisks, or fields of white space across which modern imaginations may sprint. So he says about David and Paula, his father and mother, that they "may have been together" on the ship where they met, but he cannot be sure, since of course he never would have asked.

It was enough that from Bialystok and Kletsk these first cousins who never had crossed the breadth of the few miles separating their homes, separately had traversed a continent and an ocean, had cut themselves free of past generations and then had found each other, perhaps had 'been together' ingeniously on a ship so crowded many of the passengers never saw the ocean but made the entire crossing tucked geometrically and philosophically into their few square feet of murky storage space.

David Kletsky and Paula Halpern were married in Brooklyn after completing the rituals of entrance to the promised land (themselves constituting a kind of marriage ceremony) and, my father says in gentle, amused confirmation of his supposing them to have 'been together' on the ship, "had Annie right away." The new family found two rooms on a street that was an extension of their ship, teeming with vocal dramas in a dozen languages bonded with the tough glue of Yiddish. Husband and father, David Kletsky apprenticed and became a watchmaker. He was a good one, careful, fastidious, delicate and persistent, as a man, as a technician (these are prominent traits in his son, my father). He was harsh with errors, his own and others', proud of achievement, and, stimulated by the abrasiveness of America, zealous in the acquiring of knowledge. (My father stubbornly, assiduously, moderated the legacy of his father's harshness until, in his maturity, it disappeared entirely, but the avid search for knowledge—in him the researcher's compulsion to follow all leads that suggested origins and explanations of a world ever-expanding in scope and mystery—is a gift intact from his father.)

Paula became a dressmaker, one of hundreds, thousands who became Americans in those decades in Brooklyn, but she was faster than most, with an unexpected flair for style, and soon was providing a lift of lightness to overwhelmed, exhausted immigrant women: a brief reprieve from poverty and grinding work and children already distancing themselves through the English they soaked up seemingly overnight: sponges of assimilation.

David and Paula Kletsky, with their daughter Annie, lived without drudgery, though they were surrounded by drudgery. David redefined it by renaming America from land of promise to land of selective rewards, the most immediate and lucrative reserved for those with visible skills, and for the rest of his life he would be as relentless in the pursuit of specific skills as he was of generalized knowledge, since both set his America apart from Bialystok, and his family from the sweatshop and pushcart culture that surrounded them in the new world.

One day, working with precise fingertips on a minuscule gear, he fell ill, and within the amazed space of a few days was diagnosed as tubercular and advised of the beneficial air of Colorado. In a few weeks he was gone, making another crossing to another promised land, this one alone; Paula and

Annie were left behind.

Mother and daughter moved to New Jersey to live with Paula's family. My father knows all about Paula's father, the brilliant lawyer who fled Moscow, but nothing more of her family: she would not talk about them. He assumed they had not done well—the lawyer unable to be a lawyer in America, the mother who never learned English, the siblings who vanished into the immensity of the continent—their stories having vanished when Paula turned her back on them.

But, before that, she and Annie stayed with her parents for five years, waiting for David to send for them, Paula reading his occasional letters aloud to the child in steady tones that betrayed nothing of what she felt. No one knew what she felt. Her parents berated her for passivity, for lethargy, but she was silent on why she waited rather than following the trail west, to the return address on her husband's letters. It would not do, she had said once, and only that once, in her second or third year there. In Bialystok, her parents always had known what would not do, and she had not forgotten the secure embrace of that assuredness. She found it wonderful now that her parents had been able to move so easily from one set of injunctions to another simply by crossing an ocean. She too might change, she understood that, but now, an ersatz widow in her parents' home, she clung to what seemed at each moment understandable and possible. And then, still without explanation, sometime between her fourth and fifth year in New Jersey, she folded her clothes around the thirteen letters from her husband, and, with a bulky suitcase in one hand and Annie's clutching fingers in the other, she left New Jersey for the small town of Pueblo, in Colorado.

Sixty years earlier, Pueblo had been a trading post on

the Arkansas River, and then a Mormon settlement. It was laid out as a city in 1860, incorporated twenty-five years later, and it was flourishing with the wealth of dry, high altitude air, abundant water, timber, and coal when Paula arrived with her husband's address memorized and his face remembered only from certain angles. My father does not know if she announced her plans in advance or simply appeared on the doorstep of her husband's house and he, having mastered optometry in his five years of breathing desert air, opened wide the door, thinking her a patient come to his newly opened office. Nor does my father know what words they spoke to bridge the years and the incontrovertible evidence of David's health and financial stability amid trappings of bachelorhood, but the words, or silence, must have been adequate, for the family was rejoined and, in the next seven years, four sons were born. My father was the third.

They moved to a larger house. David was Papa to all of them, including his wife. The boys were Sebastian, called Sab, always, according to my father, Mama's favorite; Benjamin, Papa's favorite; Harry, and Leon. Outside the house, Papa was the Doctor, a Pueblo eminence, tall and spare with delicate fingers and lips, his eyes somber and his shoulders taut. He continued to educate himself with an expansive library of books ordered from New York and Europe, and made of himself, within a few years, an expert on the musculature of the eye. He became known nationally through his articles in the *Journal of Ophthalmology* and, on the invitation of physicians on the faculty, made several journeys to lecture at Columbia University in New York City and the Mayo Clinic in Rochester, Minnesota.

My father relates this with enormous pride, not simply

in his father's accomplishments and national recognition, but for the brilliance and energy, the will, that took him so far. "Not surprising," he would say with the chauvinism that grew to mythic proportions over the years, source of amusement among family and friends, "for a Bialystoker." Bialystokers had become, for my father, the apotheosis of five thousand years of Jewish endurance and upward flourishing. They represented to him the best of the leaping intellect that had ensured survival in the diaspora, and of the persistence of cultural assimilation and rootedness: anomalies that astonished even the nations that eventually expelled or exterminated them. Bialystok became for my father the funnel for those thousands of years when mind and will argued for life against daily violations; for learning against the negation of pogroms and concentration camps; for new walls, new roofs when old ones were ashes; for the exploration of foreign paths when familiar ones were barricaded or wiped out. Bialystok was the social and historical metaphor for Judaism from the giving of the tablets to settlements on the West Bank.

Does my father believe all this when he waxes historically large and lyrical? None of us is convinced, but the passion in his Bialystok exegesis soars above the dinner table and gathers us in. The romantic in us, which he fosters and rewards as it increasingly resembles his own, recognizes his need for a preserved Bialystok in a time in which he often feels out of place. While acknowledging its many benefits, my father is dubious about the modern world. He does not believe that jet planes will stay up, or tyrants down. Though his wife, my mother, moves into each decade with ease and the ability to absorb any astonishment, indeed, to ferret out those suggested but not readily apparent, my father keeps a bemused distance from the idea and the reality of satellites, expressways, and computers; from figures (of anything) in the billions; from blatant, often coarse, depictions of the human body and its functions; from the eradication of cottage industry and communal charity in favor of implacable and anonymous assembly lines and the forced gaiety of professional fund-raisers for the culturally and economically deprived.

Of course he would have been uncomfortable, too, in Bialystok, this gentle, loving man who suffers for the individual trampled by the unaware and uncaring, who reaches out wherever a supplicating hand appears, who preaches the dignity of the individual to a society entranced by examples and experiences of indignity. What would he have done in Bialystok? He would have left.

But the Bialystok my father recreates at his dinner table glows in the slanting luminous light of his late afternoon, and if he declares this a metaphor of our best, a best we gave to the world, which of us will challenge him? Our own late afternoons will come, and then what Bialystoks will we create for our own amused and loving families?

My father's love for his parents was intense, passionate, and clear-eyed. He always knew he was the favorite of neither, but across the decades that diminished in importance. He had watched his family so closely, so fiercely that, almost sixty years later, recalling them for me, he describes them still vibrant, sinews of his words: Annie, the oldest, born in New York, dashing off with friends or dancing to the radio in her room, the four boys born after the Pueblo reunion, the large house with its medical office and waiting room for patients with their own entrance on the ground floor, but mostly Papa and Mama, the brilliant domestic tyrant and the quietly smiling wife who seemed to have used up her new-world courage in tracking her husband west and was now content to be the perfect doctor's wife as the doctor defined it.

Mama rose early each morning to fire the stove, whether in Pueblo's haze of summer dust or the powdery snow of winter, and carried upstairs a cup of hot water for Papa to sip, sitting in bed, knees raised under the tent of his blanket, while she covered with a clean linen napkin the milk bottle into which he had peed upon awakening, and carried it downstairs. At the dining room table there was cream in Papa's coffee and an egg on Papa's plate, the only cream and egg at the table: evidence, my father grew up thinking, of male adulthood and dominance. Papa wore spats bought in Pueblo and Sulka ties ordered from New York City; my father and his brothers wore drawers that read "General Mills Flour" across the back, cut out and sewn by Mama. The four boys had newspaper routes, dividing their part of town into sections whose size and density corresponded to their ages and agility. Each week they pooled their earnings, placing the small stacks of coins in Papa's cupped hands, and watched them disappear into the blackness of Papa's coat pocket. The subject never was discussed. It was not a question of survival; all of them understood the family's welfare did not teeter on each week's contribution of extra cash. Rather it was a silent lesson whose meaning only Papa could explain. One week Sebastian, Mama's beloved Sab, was short his regular amount by fifty cents. A dreadful stillness settled on Papa when Sab offered silence in place of an explanation. No one knew what had happened to the money, nor did they ever find out, my father says today, not even he, closest in spirit, to whom Sab confided many secrets. This was intolerable to Papa. His voice thinned to the steel edge with which he could cut through family lightheartedness or concentration, and he announced his intention to call the juvenile judge (for whom he had fitted glasses some time since) to arrest Sab for theft. Mama fell to her knees before him and pleaded for mercy. Sab was young. He needed guidance, a firm hand, an example of tempered justice, love. She wept.

Though not one given to fable or parable, my father describes his father's rigid back and remote eyes in Talmudic terms. His Papa was searching all his life, he says, for the teleological and found only science and his imperfect children. And, too, the need to be a parent, which, he recognized, required softened moments. On rare occasions he brought home a box of candy. It would be unwrapped and admired, passed from hand to hand, until Papa or, occasionally, Mama at his gestured command, would break the mosaic of chocolate-covered caramels, nuts, and cherries by delicately lifting out a piece on the periphery. One at a time the rest of the family would follow, removing morsels with precise two-finger pincers, a few each day, always from the edge; one piece in the center remaining untouched until, a sun surrounded by hollow stars, it shone alone, magnificently desirable. It always belonged to Papa.

Rarer still, Papa would dictate a picnic. Annie and Mama would flurry to prepare food and pack it in the cardboard carton they used as a picnic basket, while the boys gathered blankets, caps, sketch- and notepads. The family would be stationed at the front door when Papa would rise from his chair, pick up his hat, and walk out to lead his forces to the field. (The picnic basket was insulated with old issues of the weekly *Pueblo Chieftain*, the local newspaper that combined reports on local events with recipes, the police blotter, weddings, births, and obituaries, filling in with rehashing of weeks past, already curiously antique. Yet it was that commingling of time past and present that made history enticing to my father, that led him to become a newspaperman, and then biographer.)

At night, Papa sat in the living room, by the fire in winter, beside an open window in the hot summers, his pipe cupped in his long fingers and cool, dry palm, playing chess against himself. My father says his father never taught the game to any of his children, or to his wife; he does not know whether a request on the one hand or an offer on the other ever was made. Nor, it seems, did his father find anyone in the town of Pueblo whom he considered a fit opponent. A mystical air surrounded Papa's chess games: each slow move had the weight of a Delphic pronouncement that, though it left much unresolved, undeniably altered the immediate world. My father would watch from a quiet corner the advance and defeat of pieces so relentless, so vanquished or victorious they seemed carved symbols of characters from his school and neighborhood: Willy Drei, immigrant from Germany, done in by local patriotism when his classmates beat him up for standing silent at the 4th of July flag ceremony (he did not know the words, he told Papa in German, and Papa gave him a transliteration that served until he memorized, before any more useful phrases, the full English text of the Star Spangled Banner); Martha Slatt, who dominated her daughter to a shadow, then asked Papa why the child (who was then twenty-nine) always squinted; Fern Nolan, who sweetly trailed after my father's brother Sab until his older brother Ben became jealous and taunted her into retreat, from which corner she wrote sad verses for the school newspaper and later became its editor-in-chief; Alden Motter, darkly handsome, who, it was whispered, shattered solid families by mesmerizing heretofore contented wives into his bed, though no one could name more than one wife—Marilee Brady, whose husband was wedded more to his hunting dogs than to her—even when Alden crashed his car into a tree beside a country road and died instantly, and everyone, assuming it was not an accident and searching for Cause, tried to list women whom he had ruined or who, better yet for Cause, had rejected his spellbinding seductions, and all they could come up with was poor Marilee Brady, weeping clear, silent tears at his funeral while her husband was in the mountains with his dogs, stalking deer.

My father peopled his Papa's chessboard with Pueblo's cast of citizens while Papa played out the whims and verdicts of his own wordless gods by the light of the winter fire or the fading arid dusk of Pueblo's slow summer evenings. On other nights Papa stayed in his book-lined study, reading from his library, the complete works of E. Phillips Oppenheim, Guizot's multivolume *History of Europe*, the sixteen-volume *Windsor Shakespeare* with marginal notes in the narrow letters and slanted lines he made with a meticulous pen, and a treasured slim volume that was an early work by the Viennese Dr. Sigmund Freud. All the books except those by Shakespeare and Dr. Freud (which my father thought had been purchased on his father's journeys to New York City) had been premiums offered with magazine subscriptions. Papa had collected them over the years as the monthly or weekly magazines arrived and, once read, were distributed by Annie and the boys to doctors' and dentists' waiting rooms, Papa's included. My father remembers the magazines, but more vividly the books as they arrived: brown-wrapped, string-tied packages delivered by the mailman whose triumphant "Here's another of the doctor's books!" announced each as if it were a royal bequest. The packages would wait unopened for Papa's emergence from his examining room, and the family waited too, for the moment he would hold them up, eyes shining (perhaps, my father thinks now, with tears) at the promise balanced on his fingertips. When, later, Mama became ill and was unable to leave her room, Papa chose, in descending order (for he thought she would recover long before he reached the least preferred) his favorite Oppenheims to take to her, and Sab and my father took turns reading them aloud, for Mama did not care to read by herself while the sounds of the family floated remotely up to her bed.

Paula Halpern Kletsky, my grandmother whom I never knew except through my father's recollections, whose memory still brings a smile to his face, died when she was fifty-four years old, a young woman who had been a vigorous wife and helpmate until a few months before her death. No one explained her illness or offered a diagnosis to her five children, but my father, remembering, thinks it probably was stomach cancer. She had excruciating pain and grew very thin.

My father then was seventeen. He loved his mother with a clarity and simplicity denied him with his Papa, and he stayed near her bed. Watching her still form, he remembered her, exactly as he does now, as she once had been, always moving, her hand on every part of the house, her imprint everywhere and on each of her children. Her small figure, round, robust, in motion, travels along his sentences as he talks of her to me (he is, at the same time, describing his wife, my mother, as both women to him are versions of the male dream of Biblical Woman, indistinguishable from the first desert-dwelling ones save for facility with gas stoves, manual shift and credit cards): in his telling, Paula cooks, cleans, sews, washes, hangs out to dry, irons, folds, neatens, comforts, even as he goes on to describe her immobile, dying, barely outlined beneath the blanket tucked to her chin, already a shadow in her shadowed room. She called for Sab, favorite of her sons, and Sab came, to hold her hand and say her name as she died. She did not know that my father had slept at the foot of her bed all the nights of her last weeks, had heard her call for Sab, and was there at the moment—it was dawn—when Sab came to help her die quietly, murmuring his name, fingers curved palely around his. Sab knew. He looked at my father, closest of all to him, and said, "But she loved us all."

Papa wept. He did not hide his face or lower his head; he sat beside his wife's bed and wept aloud, tears gleaming boldly as they followed each other's traces to his fine jaw and neat, pointed beard. At times a low wail came from the back of his throat, reverberating. My father, hearing it, visualized the Bialystok he had never seen, imagined a minyan saying Kaddish to the accompaniment, from behind a curtained section, of women's low, ritual wailing, bitter grief for the one there dead, for all the dead. My father hears it still, that wailing. He remembers crouching beside his bed, retching with unexpressed love for his mother and fury toward his Papa for such weeping, the drama of which dwarfed the legitimate pain of the sons and daughter left behind, and for that atavistic keening that engulfed the household and buried his Mama anonymously in the historical landslide of buried and unburied Jews from their beginnings to the day when Paula Halpern Kletsky died, a day that should have been her last chance to claim their full attention

But as angry as he was, my father also was awed by the despair in the low wailing that burned beneath his Papa's sobs. He tried to gather the strands of all the sounds he associated with this upright man—rare laughter on an even rarer picnic, authoritative directions to a patient, matter-of-fact dicta to his family, benevolent greetings to townspeople who bowed their heads to greet 'the Doctor,' the meditative humming of a man locked in chessboard battle with the stern opponent of himself—sounds and faces and movements of his Papa whom he loved with a longing he would recall the more vividly as, over the years, its gnawing slowly faded. "Few are the sons who attain their father's stature, and very few surpass them. Most fall short in merit." That, from Homer's *Odyssey*, is one of two epigraphs in my father's biography of an American president. The other is from *The Iliad*. "O! Jove! May he be as his father . . . live a good life and rule powerfully, and someone may say, 'And be better than his father in many things.'"

That American president was born two months after his own father's death. My father wrote his life story, and the life stories of other men of signal accomplishment who took roads far different from those of their fathers, many years after the death of his own father and his departure from Pueblo, never to return. His first biography was of a governor whose father was known as strict, given to beating his children when disobeyed. The governor would become a political power and a controversial figure much admired by my father for the lonely courage of his acts, but he was first the boy who announced to his father his intention of enrolling in high school after his return from the Civil War. His father opposed the idea; no money, food, or clothes would he provide if his son defied him. The son defied the father, attended school, moved to Chicago and later to the Illinois governors' mansion, and into the pages of my father's first book, written in tribute, in admiration, after he himself had moved to Chicago on a path divergent from his father's, and overriding his father's opposition.

After Paula's death, my father and Papa lived at home in the big house in Pueblo. Ben, Papa's favorite, went to dental college in Denver; Papa paid the bills. The doctor would have a doctor son. Annie was gone; she had married colorlessly if loudly, the adjectives that would define her life for my father, who felt as much tolerant amusement as affection for her. But as the child of that fleeting stay in Brooklyn, even to her mother Annie never seemed fully a part of the family carved from the sandstone of Pueblo; she was peripheral to that burst of sons, and she grew up slightly apart from all of them, a reminder of the babel of their first American street, as foreign to Pueblo as Bialystok to America. Sab was a pharmacist; he had married a Catholic girl—his own distancing from his father—to whom Papa was polite at all times. Leon was at home, still in high school, though usually out of the house with friends and sports. My father had graduated from high school the previous June; he had decided to be a writer and realized his enthusiasm for newspapers by going to work, immediately upon graduation, for the *Pueblo Chieftain*. In his last two years of high school, the newspaper had published a number of his articles; when he joined the staff, he already had seen his name in print.

One day a woman was murdered in the building where Papa had his new office and examining rooms. He had relocated them from home when Mama's illness began to dominate the household, and he was warmly welcomed by the merchants of Pueblo who anticipated the prestige the doctor's presence would bring to downtown. He shared the building with three medical doctors, two insurance and real estate agents, a contractor, a CPA, a law firm, an import-export company whose wares remained a mystery, and a housewife who talked to herself. She had done this since, in an odd variation on David Kletsky's departure from Brooklyn, her husband disappeared, leaving a note that said, "You'll know where to find me." She did not know, she had not an inkling, so she rented an office, filled it with topographic maps of the American West and Southwest, and spent her days searching them and her memory for clues from past conversations at breakfast, from driving home from movies, from infrequent lovemaking, that might resonate with a place name on those enormous maps and send her on a purposeful search.

These were the people who had offices in the building, and they welcomed the doctor when he opened his optometry suite and the adjoining office where he worked on the articles he continued to publish in medical and optometry journals. My father's father greeted his new neighbors with gravity; he took seriously the responsibilities of the moral, familial, and professional example he set, and he accepted the town's recognition gracefully.

The woman who was murdered was the housewife with the maps. It was discovered that she had kept a safe in her office and speculation filled the safe with money for a trip to find and bring home her errant husband. The safe was open and empty, the woman's body was nearby. The same speculation pictured a smooth-talking, self-described emissary from her husband who convinced her he could lead her to him if she had the cash for the long and difficult trip. The deluded and the eager, the townspeople sagely agreed, are easy targets.

The doctor was in his examining room when the police arrived. One of the insurance agents had seen a door ajar, had glimpsed the dead woman near her open safe. The police ordered the building cleared and the doctor and his patient, with office neighbors from every floor, descended into the street like dutiful students in a fire drill. They stood and waited for permission to return. When none came, like students, they grew restless.

"I have a manuscript," the doctor informed a policeman standing guard inside the cordoned area. "On my desk. If I could retrieve it . . . for protection . . . it would take me some time, great effort, to duplicate the valuable material if it were lost." This was his first experience as supplicant before the law, and he wavered between condescension and tremulous queries in ascending pitch and intensity. The policeman, who knew the doctor, patted his shoulder with a temerity unthinkable at any but a critical time. "No one can go inside, sir," he said, "but your office is absolutely, entirely, totally and completely safe, I assure you of that."

The press arrived to cover the story, in the person of a reporter from the *Pueblo Chieftain*, my father. Pueblo, small and rural, in one respect resembled its urban counterparts: the press was recognized. My father was ushered through the crowd of building tenants and bystanders, by now quite large, and past his father, whom he did not at first see, to the door of the building where, he would write later that day, "Tragedy struck on a quiet afternoon."

"Harry!" called the doctor to his son's back, but as quietly as he could, more urgency than desperation in his voice. "My son," he said to the officer and raised the rope before him to stoop beneath it and follow the reporter, flesh of his flesh, into the building. "Yes, sir," the officer said, firmly restraining the doctor behind the rope. "Must be proud, having a reporter in the family."

The doctor did not forget that his son did not turn back and offer him an arm to bring him into the building. He did not read my father's *Chieftain* report of the murder nor his subsequent stories as they faded away, their drama wrung to slow and mournful recall when neither the murderer nor new information was found, and the editor required new dramas to fill the paper.

Soon after the last of the stories, my father left Pueblo; he had been accepted as a freshman at the University of Chicago. Papa pushed back against the move. "There is no better school than the one in which I learned and the one in which you are learning. You have a job. You live in a town where your name means more than it can ever mean in a city of anonymous strivers. You are running from reality by indulging in more schooling." But my father had heard the siren song of the campus and a far-off major city and would not change his mind; he took the train a week before registration, to look for an apartment.

Ben returned from dental college the next day and greeted his father genially, announcing his intention to open an office in town, perhaps in the doctor's own building. "Two Doctor Kletskys in town," he said, smiling down upon his father, whom he had surpassed in height some years before.

The doctor did not return the smile. He became critical of his son, once his favorite. "You are a novice," he said. And, "You slouch; a doctor must be a model of dignity." And, "You've never worked; you cannot begin by immediately opening your own office." He suggested Ben practice elsewhere for a few years, in a town smaller yet than Pueblo; apprentice himself to an established professional; earn the right to be called 'the Doctor,' a title so lustrous in Pueblo and reserved for David Kletsky.

Ben replied harshly, perhaps more cruelly than he intended. He made reference to his mother's long illness and death: perhaps she had not had adequate care. He was caustic about 'the doctor's' image of himself when, look at him, he was frayed, his methods dated, his attitude rigid in an era of 'relating' to patients. Ben was unjust—the doctor had made himself an authority in his field and was recognized more widely and with more admiration than his dental son would achieve in a lifetime of dentistry—but Ben was fighting for a share of Pueblo (as one day, he would fight others for a share of Denver, but that was many years away), and he had been confident his father would cheerfully smooth his path. The two quarreled and for many months, while Ben built a practice in a building a block away from his father's and called himself, with a smile, "the other Pueblo doctor," they did not speak.

Sab was preoccupied with his pharmacy and his growing family. Leon cultivated the solipsism of a high school senior, often spending nights and weekends at friends' houses. The doctor was alone in his large and muffled house.

News of his father reached my father a week later. He was in Chicago, where he had rented a one-room apartment near the university, had found a part-time job on a labor newspaper, and was buying textbooks for his first term. One evening after work, he went to the library to read the latest issue of the *Denver Post* (the *Pueblo Chieftain* being unavailable) and saw an item on the second page that Doctor David Kletsky of Pueblo, the noted optometrist, had fatally shot himself in his home; the funeral would be held the next day. That same evening he received a telegram from Sab and Ben, telling him of their father's death. "Don't return," they wired. "The funeral will be over before you arrive." The next day classes began.

A Few Friends for New Year's Eve

ALL THE KURLAND'S FRIENDS had died or moved away, to Florida or Arizona, to the south of France or the Italian Riviera, seeking the sun. The Kurlands stayed put, in the house Robert had designed and built sixty-five years earlier. He and a group of friends had built their homes at the same time, and the couples remained close. There were years of picnics and hikes, evenings at the movies or theatre or concert halls, holiday excursions to Paris with banquets at Taillevent and small bistros known only to true Parisians, sailing on Lake Como, skiing at Aspen, Gstaad, and Val d'Isère, playing the tables at Monte Carlo, gliding up the Nile, bargaining in the Casbah. And birthdays! The friends loved birthdays and lavished attention on them in brilliant celebrations that were recalled in rich detail for years. Oh, what celebrations! What elegant gowns and sleek tuxedoes of those heady years! The dancing shoes, the jewels, the whiffs of exotic perfumes! With not a care to weigh them down, and still youthful enough to anticipate birthdays with pleasure, the Kurlands and their friends floated through a world of business success, growing comfort, and freedom.

And then . . . children. In an instant, it seemed, families were everywhere. The friends had become parents, awash in new routines, enveloped by infants and toddlers clamoring for attention in a maelstrom of crying, whining, laughing, teasing, clinging, loving . . . all the exploding joys and crises of raising a new generation.

But not at the Kurland's house. The Kurlands had no children. Through months and years none came, and in their bewilderment and sorrow they found themselves alone, not only because they were childless, but also because the spendthrift sharing of adventures with their friends had slowed to a few special events, and then stopped entirely. The friends were saving money for camp, for private schools and orthodontia, for family vacations, for college. And their schedules were askew: erratic mealtimes, storytelling evenings, ferrying to play dates and after-school sports, homework times, family excursions, times for quarrels and punishments, for making amends and making up. The Kurlands felt shut out; their friends' lives were unfathomable to them. In an amazingly short time, it seemed they no longer had anything in common with those with whom they had been intimate. Worse, it appeared they had not even a shared language, since, with each incremental change in child-centric homes, their friends spoke in phrases and shortcuts enjoyed only by others in that magical circle of parenthood.

The Kurland's nights were lonely, their trips solitary and infrequent. What good now the designer gowns and jewelry, the multi-course meals and vintage wines, the magnificent celebrations without friends to share them? What good wealth and freedom with no group to raise glasses in toasts to good fortune?

The days and months stretched into years, and the years passed, and then, suddenly, as if once again time compressed to a dramatic instant, the children were gone—to college, to work, to marriage. Once again the Kurlands were surrounded by friends; once again they knew unobstructed friendship, the creation and sharing of adventures, the eager smiles and happy conversations that filled their evenings (save for the display of photographs, the tales of offsprings' triumphs, the brilliance of grandchildren: moments the Kurlands endured with respectful, admiring attention before the conversation swung back to more illuminating and significant topics). Once again, the end of an evening was a time of happy reflection and anticipation of the next.

"As if we've been asleep," Eve Kurland said. "And now we're awake and everything is the way it should be."

But time slips ever faster through aging fingers, and just as the Kurlands came to accept as normal their newly busy life, just as they had almost forgotten the lonely months and years they had endured, those times returned. It happened as swiftly as a practical joke. The Kurland's friends vanished.

"You'd think some monstrous wind had come along," said Robert Kurland, "and swept them all away."

First, two couples moved to Miami for sun and sea. Then others turned their pale winter faces toward the sands and endless skies of Arizona, the palms and sun-bleached homes of Puerto Vallarta, the golden light and seemingly perpetual youth of Saint-Jean-Cap-Ferrat. A few friends remained, and that shrunken group's evenings and travels were quieter, slower: physical constrictions disconcertingly at odds with memories of those that had gone before. And then, as time slipped ever faster away, one by one those friends died.

The Kurland's telephone and doorbell were silent, their house was still. And when they looked about, they realized that not only their own world, but the world outside, was greatly changed. The neighborhood was cacophonous with exuberant young families; the corner grocery, its owners having followed their customers to sun and warmth, had been replaced by a coffee shop where students occupied the few tables, nursing drinks while scowling at laptops; new shops and clerks in the surrounding streets that once had been as familiar as a family compound were unknown and coolly distant; restaurants offered menus not easily comprehended, much less imagined on a plate. These alterations and more all but announced that the Kurlands were not welcome. Even more dismaying, leather-jacketed teenagers with relentlessly pounding music, and businessmen and briskly-suited women rushing to work, made it equally clear that they had no time for spontaneous sidewalk encounters and leisurely discussion.

Alone as before in the silence of their silent house, the Kurlands at first read voraciously, filling the evenings with the books they had stacked up during the busy years: novels, history, science, biography, travel. But after a time the books lay open in their laps as they gazed into space, avoiding clocks and watches so as not to chart the dragging hours, for neither books nor television could replace the lively presence of friends, and, after sixty years of marriage, with no children or professional days to provide anecdotes, the Kurlands had no surprises in their conversation.

"We could move somewhere," said Robert.

"Where?" asked Eve. "Our friends are in half a dozen places. The ones that are left."

They filled the days with Eve's garden and Robert's wood carving, walks in the nearby woods or along the river, but the nights . . . oh, the nights were long and dark and still, and winter came and New Year's Eve was approaching and there was no one in the world to wonder where the Kurlands were or what they were doing, if they were happy, if they were ill, if they would celebrate to welcome the new year, or if they still lived. Their house, loved for so long, took on the stifling air of—don't even think it, Robert warned silently, but Eve did—a tomb, and they ached for hands to grasp, cheeks to kiss, glances of complicity to exchange.

"How pleasant it would be if we could meet just one couple," said Eve one night. "Our age, of course, but more widely traveled than we've been lately."

Her husband agreed. "They could tell us about Annecy. I was reading recently about the lake and the town, so close to Geneva and quite pretty, but, you know, we never got there. And they could help celebrate New Year's Eve."

Together, they mused about the conversation they might have with such new friends. They gave them names—Justine and Balthazar—and endowed them with colorful backgrounds, exotic and tense. The next night they amplified, creating clever dialogue, unusual phrases, lively narratives, and in so doing discovered in Justine a wry humor they had not suspected, and in Balthazar a caustic streak that took them aback. By the end of the week their new friends had joined them for drinks and dinner, regaling them with tales of Lake Annecy and its ancient prison, and hinting at adventures in Provence, which the Kurlands remembered from past trips and Eve kept up with in the books of M.F.K. Fisher.

Once again the Kurland's faces were rosy with the joy of shared talk and laughter, their eyes alive with anticipation of each evening's visit. And then, one night when the conversation seemed in danger of flagging, Justine and Balthazar brought friends to dinner, Elizabeth and Darcy, who knew Hampshire and Bath intimately, and spoke of the vicarage and its people with whimsy and affectionate wit. Conversation at dinner was animated, though there were a few touchy moments when the newcomers betrayed their prejudices, but the Kurlands would not pass judgment or let anything spoil the newly regained excitement of a dinner party.

By the end of the month, the group at the dining room table had grown to ten: Natasha and Pierre joined them with tales of Tsarist Russia, and, from Germany came Octavian and Sophie, young, deeply in love, and blessed with such voices they led the singing at the Kurland's newly reconstituted New Year's Eve dinner.

It was a fabulous dinner, a magnificent celebration, the great teardrop chandelier glittering sparkles of light throughout the tapestried dining room. The damask-clad table glowed with candlelight reflecting off the Kurland's finest crystal and silver, the gold candles that perfectly matched the golden goblets filled with the rare port served with dessert, a Black Forest torte whose last crumbs vanished as midnight approached.

Then there was dancing until dawn. The alabaster sconces on the silk ballroom walls were dimmed to pale amber, the couples merged as dark silhouettes in their whispering intimacy. In the center of the room, Eve and Robert Kurland danced slowly, her cheek against his heart, their steps precise and elegant. They danced and danced that night, smiling at their shadowy companions but feeling no need to talk; it was enough to know that friends were there, filling the air with the soft sibilance of their turns and gliding steps, and sharing this wonderful new year, the first of many to come.

Mrs. Ellington Falls From Grace

People's memories are the fuel they burn to stay alive.
-Haruki Murakami

MRS. ELLINGTON'S LIFE is colorful, multilayered, and envied by many, and she has no reason to doubt it will continue in the same way for many years. Still, though seventy is not old by today's athletically-extended spans, she has begun to gather her memories. She files them mentally, in alphabetical order, priding herself on efficiency and a system that facilitates quick retrieval, since, even with an unlined face, firm body, and active imagination, her ability to recollect now and then falters.

Mrs. Ellington's given name is Grace, but few people know it, and memories of occasions when it was widely used are growing faint, perhaps willfully, since many are filed under M for Misalliances or E for Errors. Without husband or lovers, with no offspring or siblings, and with few intimate friends, Mrs. Ellington hears the name Grace infrequently, and if that once disturbed her, she now gives it little thought. Not being fond of it in any case, she prefaced it, effectively replacing it when she was young, with 'Mrs.,' which she found eased almost any situation in which a single woman might find herself.

She does, however, have another name, widely used: she signs her sculptures Helena, adopting the name of the celebrated fourth-century Egyptian artist renowned for her painting of Alexander defeating Darius III at the Battle of Issus. The painting was said to have been reproduced as a mosaic in Pompeii, which made her the only woman to be credited with a mosaic from those early centuries. Mrs. Ellington likes to imagine Helena's triumphs against male competitors and those who wished to dominate her at home and in society, and she has contrived an unbroken line from a long-lost Egyptian studio to her own contemporary one, from an ancient woman's lonely battle to break barriers to the fame of Grace Ellington *aka* Helena, in a modern age of acceptance and stratospheric prices.

Mrs. Ellington and Helena rarely share the same space. Helena is a sought-after guest at dinner parties, a touted presence at art openings, and a frequent speaker on art, culture, intellectual metaphors, anomie in the modern world, and other topics chosen by program directors to pique not only an audience's interest, but Helena's as well.

Mrs. Ellington spends evenings at home, reading, listening to music, especially Schubert, and visiting memories. When, inevitably, a few force their way unbidden, she struggles to crush them as a boy in her school once squashed a butterfly and she, by turns horrified and fascinated, imagined that ugliness could make time stop. But nothing stops the darkest memories: decades later, they still are tougher than she is, and all she can do is ride through them, a piece of flotsam, until finally they retreat and she can once more draw a breath.

"What a beauty you are," said her cousin Bert, on leave from his base; he was soon to be posted overseas. He draped a uniformed arm around Grace's narrow shoulders. "Sorry I missed your parents; they coming back soon?"

"An hour. Or less," she added hastily. "Probably a lot less."

"No problem, we don't mind being alone." He ran a finger along her cheek. "Time for us to get acquainted."

Grace squirmed. "You said you have to get back; you can't be late."

His arm stayed firmly in place. "So we'll move fast. Tell

me what you do all day."

Grace talked about school, her voice trailing off. Nothing interesting, she said; nothing interesting happens when you're fifteen. Almost fifteen.

"Fifteen," he said. "Fourteen. Fuck. Well, can't be helped."

He was twice her weight, ten inches taller. He told her she was beautiful and spread her legs. When he finally left, closing the front door without a sound, Grace tried to stand but fell off the couch; her parents found her on the floor.

Mrs. Ellington stirs the fire and pours a glass of wine. It will be one of the nights she cannot sleep. She picks up her book, but the words quiver and she lets it fall to her lap. She looks at the open pages and remembers a summer night.

Denver: a green park fragrant with newly mown grass, shadows on the trembling leaves, a marble pavilion, distant traffic.

Grace Ellington, eighteen years old, beautiful, sought-after, frivolous, burst onto the social scene of a provincial Denver years from being discovered by the high-tech and corporate worlds that would someday transform it. Newly arrived with parents seeking the invigorating air of the west, she studied art by day, and by night joined the square dancers in the Cheesman Park pavilion, dancing into the early hours, transported by the frenzied violin and the chant of the caller, spun and twirled by eager partners who lifted her high into the soft, summer air. One of them, taller than the others, became exclusive: handsome, dark, persistent Stuart Aaronsohn.

Two a.m. and they sat together on the front porch of Grace's home, her parents pretending to sleep above them on the second floor. The dancing had been vigorous and they had walked the few blocks from the park, their breaths slowing, sweat-glazed skin cooling. Grace's long skirt swished, luminous stars circled a crescent moon. Stuart's arm lay across the back of the swing as they drank gin and tonic with lime, their voices low. "We'll marry," he said, quietly satisfied. "It's written in the way we dance. The way we move. Perfection."

"Dancing has nothing to do with marriage," said Grace.

"It's a metaphor."

"A poor one."

"No, it's just right. The way we move together, like we know what's coming next. It's so clear: we fit each other. You feel this, too, I know it. Don't try to hide from yourself. We'll be excellent in bed."

Grace looked out, at the neat lawn, the elms in full leaf, the quiet street. "Really," she said, and, as his arm slid to her shoulders, she moved away.

Mrs. Ellington returns from shopping. She has bought groceries and wine and orchid plants for the foyer and the library where she spends most of her time. She has had a long day in the quiet of her studio, and the excursion to stores lively with after-work shoppers is a happy visit to a landscape she admires but does not join. At home, she listens to the news as she puts away her purchases and prepares dinner. The evening is mild, and she dines on her balcony with a view of glittering towers and a mercurial sky. She is at ease, her rooms are silent, she is alone.

"Helena, marry me," said William, or was it Bertrand? That was the year they both urged her to wed. But it was William, she now recalled, at a Sunday brunch. His party, to celebrate her fiftieth birthday. Guests seated at four round tables with cassoulet, a fine champagne, and bright conversation in a solarium decorated with slender junipers and tall vases of bittersweet vivid against a panorama of sparkling snow. There were toasts to Helena, to her work, her health, a successful year, and then a toast from Percival Tithe, portraitist, who tilted slightly from noon champagne as he announced that Helena, famous Helena, gorgeous Helena was known to those in the know, the knowing who knew these things, that behind her gorgeousness and well-behavedness was a professional virgin who titillated before freezing out the poor bastards idiotic or besotted enough to pursue—

"Can't remember why I invited you," said William, propelling Percival, sputtering with suddenly sober apologies, through the door. "No chance it will happen again."

Seated again, he asked Helena if she wanted him to drive her home.

She shook her head. She sat straight, with a small smile. "Let's not feed the gossip columns. Maybe it can end here."

The gossip came, and the gossip satellites, but the story soon was eclipsed by other titillations about other luminaries, and Helena sat out its brief run in her studio. Large, airy, high-ceilinged, it reflects her triumphs, as far as could be from the basement where she began, where she first knew the exhilarating freedom of molding a shapeless mass of clay to her own visions of movement and passion. Wherever she is, her hands are alive with that tactile memory: walking to the market, talking with friends, reading, her fingers move unobtrusively, curving, pinching, smoothing, searching for the shape waiting to be released.

Her basement was quiet and cool, filled with broad tables of plywood on sawhorses, her father's handiwork, and an armchair her mother had rescued from the attic. She loved to close the kitchen door at the top of the stairs and feel the quiet wrap around her, shutting out the rest of the world, and know she would be private, escaping a past that haunted and a present still scarred. Her mother bought a radio to soften the silence but Grace seldom used it: her favorite sounds were the whispering of her fingers in the clay and the scraping of her modeling knives.

No one was welcome there. Once she had had a visitor: Paula Fiske, a friend from school who had said she was interested in art, loved to look at art, loved to see art being made. Grace invited her, and soon she was almost a fixture in the privacy of the basement—"my atelier," Grace called it, rejecting the everyday name that conjured images of washing machines, scurrying insects, and jars of molding preserves.

"Definitely romantic," said Paula, who, at eighteen, was two years older than Grace and a poet, both of which elevated her in Grace's eyes. "Great work will be done here. Balzac said—"

"'—constant labor is the law of art,'" Grace finished. "You taught me that and I think—"

"Balzac said, 'Great artists, true poets, do not wait for either commissions or clients; they create today, tomorrow, ceaselessly.'"

Cowed, Grace said, "I remember. When you told me that, I made a vow to be that way."

"Then you'll be a real artist," said Paula.

"And you'll be a fabulous poet."

"And we'll host soirees in my opulent penthouse."

"What's a penthouse?" asked Grace.

"An apartment high up. Like, the top. Where rich people live."

Memories of Paula Fiske are filed under B for Broken. Mrs. Ellington recalls Paula's tall figure, the awkwardly-fitting clothes she and her mother found in thrift shops, the single braid snaking down her back, meticulously woven each morning by her father. "When I live in a penthouse," said Paula, "I'll look down on all the people thousands of feet below me. Not you. You can visit me up there. For soirees."

But a short time later, they quarreled. Grace had suggested a different ending for Paula's newest poem. "This one doesn't really fit with the beginning."

"Doesn't fit?" Paula cried. "What do you know about something fitting or not? You're totally ignorant when it comes to poetry. Or anything." She swept an arm to take in Grace's sculptures on the tables around them. "Look at this stuff." Her voice was strident. "You're an amateur, a putterer, a dilettante, an abecedarian."

"A what?" Grace managed.

Paula repeated it. "You don't even fucking know English."

Grace quailed before the brawn of Paula's words. "I do know English."

"You don't know anything." She swept her arm again. "Everything you do, everything in this whole basement is shit."

"Atelier," Grace said. "And it isn't—"

"Basement." She picked up a tall figure. "Shit. Turds."

"Turds aren't tall," Grace whispered.

But Paula was gaining steam. "Think you could be Picasso or something, no way, no fucking way you could—"

"I don't want to be Picasso, I want to be me." Grace struggled to find stronger words, but finally pushed her palms outward, straining. "Go away. I don't want you here. Go away and don't ever come back."

"Hey, that's stupid," said Paula. "We're fellow artists."

"We're not. Not anymore. Not ever. Go away. Please,

please just go away."

How young I was, Mrs. Ellington thinks, lifting her book to return to reading. How easily intimidated. But I did end it, and she did not come back. I lay awake that night thinking of clever phrases, even wounding barbs I might have flung. But when one is whiplashed, cleverness is the first fatality.

"An interesting departure, Helena," said the noted art critic at the opening of her newest show. "Intriguing." He gestured. "They hark back to your earliest work but more hard-edged, almost . . . angry, would you say?"

"I would not," Helena replied.

"Well then." He was undaunted. "Aggressive?"

"We all find our own vocabularies." She softened it with a smile.

She did not discuss her work. "It has its own voice," she said. "I would not compete with it."

Dinner that night, following the opening of her show, was in the penthouse of Penelope and Marshall Breedon, among her major collectors. "We go back a long way," said Marshall, champagne in hand. "We met . . . should I give it away?" he asked Helena, protecting, he thought, her age.

"Almost thirty years ago," she replied. "I was twenty-nine and you came to my second show."

He lifted his glass to her. "And I asked you to marry me."

There was a murmur in the group around them, and some tentative smiles. Penelope Breedon said brightly, "Marshall has impeccable taste."

"How come you didn't?" a guest asked Helena. "Or . . . did you?"

She shook her head. "Tempted though I was."

"I was divorced," said Breedon, "and I courted this

beautiful lady around the block. Even followed her to Europe—" Discomfort rippled through the guests as they glanced at Penelope, and Breedon sidestepped. "But of course it all ended happily when I met Penelope at one of Helena's famous dinner parties, and the rest, as someone no doubt said, or should have, is history."

"Marshall has logorrhea," Penelope said to Helena, who was at her right at the dinner table. "I never truly understood that word until I met him."

Helena smiled. She and Penelope were good friends. "But he knows people listen."

"They do. All the time. And quote him at parties. Occasionally annoying, but thankfully not destructive."

On Helena's right was Gilbert Thurn. "Were you really tempted?"

"Interested perhaps. Why not?"

"You told me you were tempted when I offered myself."

She nodded. "Fortunately, temptations are ephemeral."

"All of them?"

"Most of them."

"What does tempt you? Or who? Seriously."

"The work I haven't yet done."

"Helena! A toast!" Marshall Breedon raised his glass. "To a brilliant show and the splendid artist and friend who created it."

Mrs. Ellington fills her wine glass. Rain lashes her windows, and after dinner at her small kitchen table she pulls shut the drapes in her library and settles into the wing chair beside a snapping fire. Marshall Breedon, she thinks. After Penelope, my closest friend. He certainly did talk at length, but from enthusiasm, not insecurity, and he was never boring.

"Of course we will not spend the night here," said

Helena in the gallery on Michigan Avenue when he suggested it. "You're marrying Penelope in two months and you love each other."

"True, very true, but she is in New York and you are here and, as always, far more desirable than—"

"No. Stop. Not a word against Penelope."

"Dearest Helena, how could I be against Penelope, who is quite wonderful? I'm simply taking advantage, trying to take advantage, of an opportunity. How often will I have a law school reunion in Chicago just when you're here for a new show? I'm adding, not subtracting."

"You're doing neither. You are insulting Penelope. And me. And, truly, we have exhausted this subject."

"You know, one day you're going to want a lover. Or more: marriage, security, stability, predictability. You're... how old?"

"Forty-one. Quite secure. And stable."

"And content?"

"Is this a pop quiz? Believe me, I'm where I want to be."

"Are you sure you know where you want to be?"

"Don't talk like a lawyer, Marshall, and don't make this an argument. We've been good friends for a long time; don't push me into ending that."

Amid the memories of her exhibits, Mrs. Ellington recalls the first one as clearly as if it had happened the week before instead of forty-four years ago when she had just turned twenty-six. She remembers the rush of incredulity, almost intoxication, as she watched her pieces being placed in the brightly lit rooms of the gallery, and her astonishment when the few changes she tentatively suggested were honored. She had walked about, touching the sculptures, reading her name on the plaques beside them, thinking perhaps the scene was not real but only another version of the imaginary ones she had dreamed of since she first pressed a ball of clay between her hands and felt the life within it. And then the doors opened, and crowds gathered, strolling, chatting, drinking wine, kissing the air beside each other's cheeks, miraculously asking for price lists as red dots were placed beside a few of her creations, and Helena, talking to strangers, smoothly passed from one group to another, moved and spoke on the teetering edge of that intoxication so that, later, the evening blurred into one long, swelling sound, one bursting memory of faces smiling at her and her work.

That was the time she felt Helena truly come alive, a whole person, no longer the centerpiece of wistful fantasies. Several pieces sold at the show, making possible another, four years later, when Marshall Breedon bought his first two pieces. Her third show, in London, brought American, German, and Chinese buyers, and newspaper and magazine critics for reviews and interviews.

Mrs. Ellington's memories of all of Helena's shows, of her featured works at the Whitney Biennial and the Venice Biennale, are vivid and precise, nestled under T for Triumphs. She can reconstruct each gallery, the moments of increasing excitement as collectors praised her and her sculptures in equal measure, confirming her right to move assuredly through an art world critics say she is transforming with her singular vision. (At one opening, amid the throng, she saw Paula Fiske and took a reflexive step forward, but as quickly turned back to continue her conversation. When she glanced that way again, Paula was gone. Their eyes had not met.) She enjoys her new fame and wealth, and smiles at herself ironically when she recalls how quickly they became perfectly natural: those first few months of astonishment and gratitude giving way smoothly, invisibly, to acceptance and pleasure, as if gift boxes appear regularly at her front door and are welcomed without surprise.

"But I've been to Courchevel," Helena said to Walter Matheny, a Broadway actor much in demand. "I've skied in Europe and I prefer our own mountains. Especially the skiers."

"Then we'll stay local," he said, "though Courchevel is the best in the world."

Walter knew what was best in the world in every category. It amused Helena, and occasionally irritated her. She was thirty-two years old and finding new friends in politics, business, sports, entertainment. Walter brought her the world of the theater, which enchanted her even when he did not.

"I have an opening in a few weeks," she said. "Not a good time for a vacation."

"Do you use your shows as excuses?" he asked.

"For skiing?"

"For intimacy."

"Only with people who pressure me," she said lightly, and changed the subject.

They were finishing dinner at a small restaurant. "May I come up?" he asked as they walked to her apartment. "I have something to show you."

Helena laughed.

"Well, yes," he said. "A hackneyed line. I'll rephrase it. I don't want the evening to end."

Over dessert, he had been more charming than usual. "One drink," said Helena.

She served cognac. He displayed a small case nestling a sapphire and diamond ring. She shook her head. He kept his hand outstretched, balancing the case on his palm. Again she shook her head. "Thank you, Walter, I do thank you, but it would not be good for either of us."

"It would be the best, for both of us."

"No, it would not." She closed his fingers over the box. "I like you. I enjoy our times together. But you don't want permanence, you want conquests, and I'd rather not be one of them. You collect people, you know, especially famous ones, just as you keep a running total on your curtain calls. You want my name more than you want me. If I were a secretary or a salesgirl, you'd be looking past me for someone well known."

"My God, that's cruel. And crude."

"And honest."

"Which is not always a virtue."

"In your world, perhaps. In mine it is. And you would not want me any other way."

"Ah, but that shows how little you know me."

She stood up, put off by his easy acceptance of fakery, or, as he probably would say, the joys of acting. "How much better then that we're simply friends."

Mrs. Ellington spends a day away from her studio, shopping for Christmas gifts, and on a quiet evening at home wraps them and writes messages on her handmade cards. She has done this for most of her sixty years, the wrapping paper becoming more subdued each season, the cards more abstract. She has friends in many countries; they send notes and emails, cards and gifts throughout the year. She has a few close friends, all women; she enjoys the companionship of men but is intimate with none. A few times, she has tried to build on companionship, thinking she should try to breach the wall she has constructed to block off all but work, friendships, and solitude. But whenever the space between herself and another begins to narrow, when affection threatens to become tenderness, desire, even passion, she draws in, wrapping herself, even if regretfully, with irony, with coolness, with a willful shutting off of other choices. She understands what is happening, that once again she fails to bring to green and flourishing life the barren patch within her where a memory is lodged that sears what comes close. Trapped, she tries to palliate her withdrawal with a smile, a self-reproach, perhaps an overt glance of regret, before turning away.

Paula Fiske appeared at Helena's studio on a sultry August morning a few weeks after her first show. The studio was cool, with a long wall of north-facing windows; the other three walls, the ceiling and floor were white. "Good Lord, how stark," said Paula. "Blank walls. Where are the paintings? Where's the art? You'd think you'd want to liven it up."

"Where is the art." Helena glanced at the populous scene: clay and bronze sculptures, maquettes, sketches, carving tools, books, magazines, a blue coffee pot, painted mugs, ceramic vases holding small forests of pencils and sticks of charcoal. "Liven it up," she repeated with a small smile. She did not move forward to greet her visitor. Paula looked as she remembered her: tall and thin, her braid reaching halfway down her back, her eyes appraising and critical. Wandering now around the studio, picking up figures and abstract shapes, flipping pages in a notebook of drawings, squinting at sketches pinned to easels. "Busy place," she said. "How about lunch? There's a place nearby that's good. Italian."

"I don't stop for lunch." Helena straightened a sketch that Paula's finger had tilted. "Is there something you're looking for?"

"Oh, my, do I sense hostility? It can't be. Really? After all these years, you're still fuming? Still hunkered down in your basement, cradling memories? I don't believe it; we were kids, for God's sake. Here you are, the big shot artist, gallery show, the whole works, and you're still slogging through the past?"

Helena did not answer. She was embarrassed. Of course she should have moved on long ago, should have swept aside the hurt and doubt that Paula had planted in a fearful Grace Ellington who lacked not only self-confidence but a vocabulary as brutal as Paula's. Foolish to remember that now, or at any time since her first show.

"Well, I guess I was a little rough," Paula said. "More than a little, truth be told. I got carried away, said things I shouldn't have. Attacked. Like using words you probably didn't know, probably wouldn't have been allowed to use even if you did know them. I did, I admit it. You want me to apologize? Is that what you want?"

"No." It seemed beyond explanation that she had been so upset. That she still nurtured resentment, even anger. "It doesn't matter."

"Well, obviously it does. So, I shouldn't have said you were making crap, I admit that, shouldn't have said you were like a... what did I say? Something about being a little spider trying to weave a web, an *artistic* web, without knowing the first thing about it. Imaginative on my part, I must say, but I was wrong. There. I've said it. You want more? Well, I don't mind, one of us ought to act like a grown-up. So, I'm sorry. Sorry, sorry, sorry. You were just a kid, I forgot that. And so fucking serious. I shouldn't have made fun of you. You'd think I was jealous, of course I wasn't, how could I ever be jealous of you? But I did overreact when you said my poem didn't work, didn't make sense, was too broken up. I'd worked my butt off on that poem, and you weren't a poet; I don't think you even read poetry, probably hated it. So I got mad. You can understand that. And then you were sobbing all over the place, and I hated that because it made me look like a bitch. Or witch. Whatever."

Helena was silent. She had not criticized one of Paula's poems; how could she, when she was younger than Paula and in awe of her? And Paula had not made fun of her; she would have remembered that. It had been a simple quarrel; she hadn't sobbed, she'd told Paula to leave, that was all. Still, somehow rancor remained, and so she did not invite Paula to sit down.

Paula perched on the arm of a chair. "Well, what the hell. I've been busy too, you know. Lots of work running a house, like managing a corporation, toughest job ever." Into the silence, she said, "A family, you know. Or maybe you don't. A husband, three kids? Not your style, from what I hear. Two girls, twins, and a boy, a houseful of dreams and visions."

Surprised, Helena said, "You're writing?"

"God, no, who has time? I'm doing real things with real people. Poetry is for people who don't like the world they've got, so they huddle in a miasma where shadows ruminate on hexameters. People who haven't figured out love and are scared to death of responsibility. Monks. Anchorites, misanthropes, whatever. Sculptors."

Helena nodded, as if to herself. "Hostility from another quarter. You haven't changed, Paula: you still launch yourself like a missile and you muddle your words and metaphors."

"Muddle? Nope, not a bit. I'm being creative, haven't lost that. I'm just putting it to use in a better way. What I'm doing is more important, more consequential than anything you've ever done. You might admit that just once. You make little gewgaws, expensive, I admit, but they end up dead on social climbers' shelves. I wouldn't waste my time on poetry or sculpture if you paid me for it. I'm a hell of a lot better where I am, I work with the living, I make the future. I'm where divinity lies."

Helena laughed. "I have no aspirations for divinity. And now, please excuse me, but I must get back to work. The gewgaws wait."

Paula stood and held out her arms. "Sorry again. Sorry, sorry, sorry. See how good I am at saying that? So I was a little bit over the top, yes? Just like before. I get carried away sometimes; not serious, you know. And don't think I do it out of envy, God no, I'm happy where I am; I just go off the deep end now and then. Henry—my husband?—took awhile to get used to it, but now he likes it. Likes the energy. So. How about lunch in that Italian place? We could talk."

"Such a shame," said Helena. "As I said, I don't stop for lunch."

Mrs. Ellington is at home the night after her seventieth birthday, celebrated by Helena and a small group with a piano and cello recital in a private home high above the city, when Penelope Breedon calls to say that Marshall has died. A massive heart attack; he was dead in an instant. "What he wanted," she says through her tears. "Though not at that particular moment. Or any imaginable one. His goal was a hundred, at least."

"I'll be right there," says Helena.

They sit at the kitchen table and talk all night, accompanied by pots of coffee and bottles of wine. For the first time, Helena hears tales of Marshall's youth after his father died: gangs, truancies, using and selling drugs, thefts. "He was never caught," Penelope says. She measures coffee to make another pot. "And he never owned a gun. The gangs were pretty tame in those days: picking pockets, grabbing purses. Not a big take each time, but enough to buy what they wanted; they didn't aim to be royalty. But he had a weird conscience. After they divided up the money, he'd take the wallet or purse to a police station, a different one each time, say he found it on the street. The money was gone, of course, but all the credit cards were there; they were too smart to take them. And he was always thanked. Told what a good citizen he was. When he told me about it, he sounded like a race car driver remembering the Grand Prix: fast, scary, dangerous. Rapid breathing, thumping heart. I'm sure he loved every minute of it, at least in retrospect. And I think he missed it when he gave it up, at least missed it at first, gave all that up and became a high-powered lawyer. He never told you this?"

"He told me his father died when he was fifteen and he worked after school and weekends to help out at home."

Penelope laughs. "Worked." She covers Helena's hand with hers. "Thank you for being here. Thank you for being a friend to both of us. I've always been so glad by the time I met Marshall the two of you were no longer lovers."

Helena frowns.

"What?" Penelope asks.

"We were never lovers." Helena tries a smile. "Surely he didn't say we were."

"For years. Two? Three? He wasn't specific."

Helena shakes her head. "He suggested it a few times, it became something of a ritual, but nothing came of it."

"But why would he—?"

"Some kind of fantasy? I have no idea. I loved Marshall, he was a wonderful friend, but we never slept together. The last time he mentioned it was in Chicago, he was there for a law school reunion and I was setting up a new show. A couple of months before you were married. We had dinner together, that was it."

"Chicago?" Penelope frowns. "Just before we were married? But his reunion was at Stanford that year; I went with him."

"No, it was Chicago. October."

"We were in Stanford in October." Penelope brings out an album. "Our photos for that year; you're in so many of them." She turns pages. "March, Patagonia, we hiked. June, we bought an apartment. October, Stanford. Marshall gave a talk." She smiles. "On helping kids get out of neighborhood gangs." She turns more pages. "November, you took us to the Granada Jazz Festival, your wedding present. That was a marvelous time. And December, our wedding." Closing the album, she says, "He did have a reunion in Chicago, but that was at least two years after we were married. I didn't go with him that time."

She brings an iced cake to the table and cuts two wedges. "I baked; we were supposed to have a dinner party tomorrow. Oh, God, calls to make."

"I'll make them. This afternoon." Helena escapes.

There is nothing wrong with her memory of Chicago. It is perfectly clear: Marshall, sleek in a new sport coat Penelope had given him for his birthday, standing beside one of her sculptures, admiring it, suggesting a night together. A crystalline memory. And Mrs. Ellington knows her memories; they are the storehouse of who she is. She does not confuse dates or places or people. She does not misremember.

Penelope had pulled out the wrong album. She was confused; who could blame her? Marshall had just died; her life was upended. One of these days, when things calmed down, they would straighten it out.

Mrs. Ellington lingers over dinner on her balcony. It is a soft September evening, a crescent moon snagged on the spire of a nearby building, a south breeze barely rippling the air. It is the kind of evening on which she met Molly.

Penelope had introduced them. Molly had come to live with her. "My sister's child," she had told Helena. "There's a vicious divorce going on over there and they very sensibly want Molly far away until they're done. It's the one thing they agree on. There's no one else, so I said she was welcome here for as long as it took. I hope you two will be good friends. Very, very good friends."

"Meaning you want help."

"Desperately need it." Penelope, unmarried in those days, was publisher of a niche magazine. "I'm so damned busy, plus I have a social life. Plus, the biggest plus, I haven't the faintest notion how to take care of a five-year-old. Where would I even start? You're my only hope."

Helena pointed out that she was no more experienced than Penelope. She was thirty-eight years old and had never spent time with a child, never had tried to converse with one or play games or attend events. "In fact, I've never even known one."

"Right," said Penelope. "But you're wise. And calm. I thought, between the two of us we could figure it out."

The next evening Helena and Molly shook hands and Penelope served dinner in her dining room. To make conversation, she pointed out a group of sculptures on the sideboard. "And here is the artist who made them," she said.

Molly looked at Helena, then at Penelope. "May I get up?" she asked and Penelope's eyebrows rose. "Of course you can."

Molly went to the sideboard and studied the sculptures.

"They look sad."

"They are," said Helena.

"What happened to them?"

"I don't know. People have so many reasons to look sad: they're lonely, or someone hurt them, or they've failed at something important to them. Sometimes people don't know why they're sad; they just feel as if their life has gotten unbalanced somehow, out of their control."

"Or they can't be where they want to be," Molly said.

Instinctively Helena pushed back her chair and went to Molly and took her hand. "We hope you'll want to be with us right now, for a while."

They looked at each other. "Do you make a lot of those?" Molly asked, pointing to the sculptures.

"I do. Many different kinds. That's my work."

"I draw things," Molly volunteered.

"How wonderful. With pencil?"

"No, with colored chalk. Mommy gave me a box of them. I like doing it, but it gets messy."

"I know. So does charcoal."

"What's that?"

"Like colored chalk, but black. You can do wonderful things with it. I'll show you sometime if you'd like."

Helena found, oddly, that she did not want to let go of Molly's hand, but then she felt foolish and led Molly back to her chair.

Soon Molly was spending afternoons and weekends in Helena's studio, drawing with charcoal or working with clay, shoulders hunched, lips tight with concentration, reminding Helena of long ago in the basement she called her atelier, when she first felt the world slip away, leaving only the images rushing, tumbling, piling up in her mind, almost too many to contain, and the images coming to life beneath her fingers. Or Molly would stay for the weekend, and after dinner they would sit together on the balcony or in the library, making up stories with characters they would return to again and again, familiar friends or heroes or villains. And they explored the city, Molly's hand confidently reaching for Helena's as they wandered through museums or took in theater, opera, concerts, ballet. Helena cut back her hours in her studio as she filled more of each day with Molly.

"You're so good with her," said Penelope, faintly jealous though she had met Marshall Breedon and wanted nothing more than to spend uninterrupted days and nights with him.

"I'm having a good time," said Mrs. Ellington. "We're both having a good time."

But the day Mrs. Ellington came to love Molly unreservedly was the one on which Molly misbehaved in kindergarten. "I will not participate in that game," she said in the classroom, arms folded tightly across her chest. "I don't like it."

The teacher, familiar with Molly's moments, paid no attention, and in a short while Molly drifted over and joined her classmates. Later, the teacher called Penelope, who called Helena, where Molly was spending the night.

Helena laughed. "Participate."

At dinner, she drew for Molly a diagram of the school hierarchy. "You can't ignore it; you're stuck with it. Wait for the time when you make the rules; I'm absolutely sure you'll be one of the rule makers someday. But right now you don't have a choice: you're not in control."

"I don't care. I can do what I want."

In unfamiliar territory, Helena hesitated, then plowed ahead. "The thing is, you really can't. We have to work this out, Molly; your job these days is to go to school, and one of the lessons in school is learning the difference between what you want to do and what you have to do. As long as you're there, your teachers are going to tell you what they expect of you, and you're going to have to go along with what they say."

Molly was silent, her lower lip thrust out.

"Okay," said Helena. "I hate to use ploys, but I guess I have to. So let's think about your birthday party on Saturday. Penelope and I talked about this and we agreed that we'll have to cancel it if you can't deal with the system at school."

Molly's eyes widened, tears welled up. "But I have to have it! I have to turn six!"

Helena burst out laughing. She abandoned discipline and pulled Molly to her lap. Molly wailed and Helena made soothing sounds: they would talk about following rules, they would come to an agreement, Molly would have her party, and everyone would be happy. Growing up wasn't easy, it was like putting together a puzzle with pieces that seemed impossible to fit together until, suddenly, you found just the right angle, but then you had to pick up the next piece and begin the struggle all over again. But they would figure it out together and everything would be fine, there was nothing to worry about.

Mrs. Ellington had always declared she would have no children. Nor would she marry. She lived alone because it was her preference; she lived without children because it was the only way for her. Now she had a child in her arms, in her home, and she loved her.

Molly lived with Penelope and, mostly, with Helena for

ten months, until her mother came for her. The parting was terrible. "We'll visit and you'll come to us," they said to Molly's back; she would not look at them. "We can be together after school, weekends . . . as often as you say. We'll go out together, visit your favorite places, the zoo, the museums, whatever you want. We'll call you. And you can always call us." Helena put her hand on Molly's arm, but Molly, with one look over her shoulder, wrenched away, her shoulders tight, warding off touches, attempts at embrace. Her face was frozen. After a long moment, her mother shrugged helplessly. She tried to pry open Molly's clenched fist but failed, and finally held her by the wrist to lead her to the car, and they drove away.

Penelope and Helena wept as they took the elevator to Penelope's apartment.

It was easier for Penelope: she was engaged to Marshall Breedon and was looking ahead. Helena could not look beyond the present: she was caught in the web of Molly's presence, enveloping her in lingering memories of city excursions, private jokes and laughter, Molly's infectious delight in discovery, the quiet hours in Helena's studio and her library at home as she read stories aloud until Molly admitted she could read just fine, and they took turns reading to each other, looking up to exchange a smile before returning to the page.

With Molly gone, Mrs. Ellington's days felt hollowed out. Her footsteps seemed aimless, her thoughts ricocheted as in a deserted space. Work, the solid core of her life, had always been enough, but Molly arrived with an ease of loving that cracked open the core, allowing her to slip inside. Now Molly's place was empty, and often, in the middle of the night, Mrs. Ellington woke crying. She avoided places she and Molly had favored. She lengthened the hours in her studio, arriving earlier, leaving later, at midnight or beyond, coming home to dark rooms and a cold dinner. For all those expanded hours, her work did not go well; her fingers were sluggish, and she smashed more than she completed, each dogged effort seeming to mock her with what had once been natural and joyous, and now seemed lost.

She and Penelope tried to arrange times with Molly, but Molly refused to see them, even to talk to them when they called. They sent painting and drawing kits, books, games, clothes in her favorite colors, but heard nothing. Molly was unforgiving.

In time, the contours of Mrs. Ellington's days and nights returned to their former boundaries; she grew accustomed once more to silence, to solitary dinners on her balcony, to evenings in her library, reading and remembering. Helena began to accept invitations again and, in her studio, as the days merged, the clay gradually came to life, flowing into surprising shapes beneath her restless fingers.

The evening has turned cold and Mrs. Ellington comes in from her balcony, carrying her plate and wine glass. She washes them, and the pans she used in preparing dinner, and wipes clean the stove and granite counters. The kitchen gleams as brightly as the day it was installed. She pauses before turning out the lights. She struggles against a memory, but it is clutching.

She was living with her aunt and uncle while her parents were in England visiting her father's dying brother. Her aunt and uncle had gone out for the evening and she had finished drying the dinner dishes and was reaching for the light switch when Bert walked in, casually, as if he lived there. Which he did, she remembered, or he had at one time. But she had thought he was fighting a war somewhere, maybe killed in battle, gone forever. "Mission changed," he said cheerfully. "Didn't get sent over after all."

She stared at him, shrinking against the cabinets.

"And we had so much fun last time, I thought, let's do it again. Right? Right."

He was on her, engulfing her, pulling her to the living room.

She cried out, a gargled sound against the grip of his arm across her face. She bit, tasting blood. His arm jerked back. "Fucking bitch."

She screamed and tried to kick him. She screamed again. He wiped his bloody arm against her face and again clamped his arm across her mouth. She tried to say Stop, stop, please don't, please, please, but only whimpers came out, lost in his grunting as he threw her to the carpet. She cried out and he slapped her face; he pressed a hand against her throat so she gagged. "You yell again, you're dead."

The next time her aunt and uncle were out, she spent the night with a friend. Once, she went to the library and stayed until it closed; another time she sat alone in a movie theater, seeing the film twice. Still, two times he arrived before she could leave. He told her he would kill her if she told anyone. He made again as if to strangle her. "Nah, I'd use my gun. They taught me how to kill, told me I was good, a fast learner. I could pick you off a block away."

By the time her parents came home she was vomiting in the morning and had missed her period. Through a friend at school, she found a doctor and went to his house on a Friday night, to the surgery in the basement ablaze with lights and a motherly nurse who held her hand and repeated through the roiling waves of pain that it wouldn't be much longer, almost done, just another few minutes, there, see? It's all gone; you're rid of it. Now you'll be fine, good as new. You're free to live a wonderful life.

On Monday she went to school, bleeding, cramping, feverish, and was sent home. She spent the next week in bed, fending off her parents. "I don't want the doctor! I'm okay! It's just my period, sometimes it's awful, like now. I'm okay, just leave me alone."

The next Monday, she was in school, telling herself it was over, she was free to live a wonderful life.

Bert vanished. She heard he'd been sent to South Korea. The next time his name came up, her aunt and uncle were going to his wedding to a young girl just graduating from a college in Seoul. But she could not be free of him; she knew that. *I could pick you off a block away.* She never told her parents or her aunt and uncle or any friend; she never saw Bert again, though for years he lurked in the shadows, watching for a vulnerable moment.

Helena and Penelope visit the Metropolitan Museum to see the new tapestry exhibit. It is three months since Marshall Breedon died, and the two of them are often together. As they emerge from the rooms hung with huge tapestries, someone behind her says, loudly, "Grace!" Startled, it takes a moment for her to realize she is the one being addressed, and then she turns and sees Stuart Aaronsohn.

"A long time," he says, taking her hand. "And a long way from Denver. But I knew you right away, as beautiful as ever."

Helena introduces him to Penelope. "We danced together in Denver, square dancing. It was quite wonderful. Stuart and I were partners."

"We were so good," says Stuart to Penelope, "that I said

we'd get married. I still remember that, well, I remember everything about those days, even after all these years. I was crazy about this lady. I told her, from the way we danced we were a perfect fit."

Helena smiles. "On my parents' front porch. On the swing. With gin and tonic."

"Not that time," Stuart says. "That time I really fell apart. I've always wanted to apologize for that night on your porch; I behaved like a spoiled brat who couldn't get his way. But before that, when I got up the courage for a real proposal, I went all out, took you to that fancy restaurant, Celine's, remember? It's long gone, but it was Denver's best. I thought it was the perfect place for a proposal; how could I get turned down in an elegant place like that?"

"It was on the porch," Helena says. "My parents were asleep right above us. We'd walked from the park."

"Actually not," he says with a smile. "Celine's. Doesn't really matter, since you turned me down. That night on your porch, it was about a month after our dinner at Celine's, I was a total ass. So, let me make my apology right now, much delayed, but fervent. You kept talking about how hard you'd have to work to be the best artist—in the world?—I'm pretty sure that's what you said, and you said you didn't want me—not something I'd forget—and I just blew up. I said things I knew I shouldn't be saying, and I tried to kiss you, pushed you back on the swing, and you socked me in my groin. You had a most remarkable fist. Embarrassing to remember. I've tried to forget it, but it sticks: my punishment, it seems. Anyway. A long time ago and we were both young. And now here I am, never married. Not your fault, but who knows why we take the directions we take? What about you? Married with a family?"

"No." Helena is pale and Penelope breaks in. "We have to go." She takes Helena's arm. "So nice to meet you . . ." She is pulling Helena with her.

Stuart keeps pace. "Now that we're in the same city, can we get together? Dinner? Lunch, even."

"I'm in the book," says Helena. She and Penelope pick up their pace, leaving Stuart behind.

"You're not in the book," says Penelope. "You're unlisted."

"I know."

Penelope laughs. "Who is Grace?"

"Oh, a name from a long time ago. I haven't used it in years. I thought no one did anymore."

"And? What happened back there?"

They are crossing Fifth Avenue and Helena shakes her head. "Nothing important. Thank you for the rescue; I really didn't want to talk to him."

"Right, I got that. What can I do to help?"

"You've already helped." When they separate, Helena goes to her studio. She kneads a chunk of clay. "We'll marry," he had said on her parents' porch, sounding positive and satisfied. They had been sitting on the swing, with their drinks. On her parents' porch. Two in the morning. She had looked at the elm trees. From her parents' porch. He had not said anything to be ashamed of; he had not been unpleasant. Certainly she had not struck him; she had never struck anyone. He'd mixed her up with someone else. It was so long ago, he'd gotten confused. His memory is not as sharp as hers. She should have given him her phone number; by now he probably realizes he was wrong and wishes he could tell her so.

Of course he won't find her, since it is obvious he has

no inkling of who she is, what she does with her life. Which is fine. She doesn't intend to debate memories with him, and she certainly does not need his apology.

Molly came to Mrs. Ellington's apartment on a bitterly cold January evening. Mrs. Ellington was in her library, a plate of hors d'ouevres and a glass of wine on the table beside her, Beethoven piano sonatas in the background, a fire just lit, when the doorman called to say a young woman named Molly was in the lobby.

"Yes," said Mrs. Ellington. She was stunned. So many years. Molly would be . . . how old? Seventeen. She could not fit her memory of the child she had loved with an image of a young woman named Molly.

She was standing in the foyer when the elevator door opened and Molly stepped out. There was a brief pause, and Mrs. Ellington spread wide her arms. Molly flowed into them, and they held each other. "I'm sorry," Molly said at last. "I'm so sorry, it's been too long and I missed you so much, I cried every night, you wouldn't believe how long I cried, but . . ."

"You were angry." Mrs. Ellington helped her out of her coat and led her to the library. They sat before the fire, Mrs. Ellington in her usual chair, amazed to see Molly in the matching one, as if that was where she belonged. She was almost lost in it: dismayingly thin, pale even coming in from the cold, her hair strangely mussed, as if askew from pulling off her hat. "That is not your hair," Mrs. Ellington said. "No," said Molly. "I should have known an artist would notice." She stood up and leaned over to kiss Mrs. Ellington on the left cheek, the right, the left. "I learned that in Italy," she said with a laugh. Her voice was husky. "My God, it is so wonderful to see you. I should have done this years ago."

"Why didn't you?" Mrs. Ellington poured wine for both of

them and held out the silver tray of hors d'ouevres.

Molly shook her head. "Not hungry. I'm usually not. But thank you for the wine."

"You're not hungry. And you're too thin. And you're wearing a wig."

"Right. Right. I love you, you know? I've loved you since I lived with you, even more after my mother stole me from you. I hated her. After awhile we sort of got along, but I couldn't love her. Because I loved you. Penelope too, of course, but mainly you. And it just kept growing all those years I wasn't with you."

"Molly, how sick are you?"

"I knew you'd know. You always knew so much about me, what was inside me, what made me happy or sad. Or afraid. Like now, you know, I'm scared."

Mrs. Ellington leaned forward and took Molly's hand. She remembered the first time she had taken Molly's hand, when they had just met and were having dinner in Penelope's dining room. She had not wanted to let go. "Tell me."

"I kept wishing you were my mother. That's why I came. Because . . . well, the thing is, I have this . . . thing. A tumor. A glioma. It has a real name, glioblastoma, it's in my brain, and, you know, it's the worst. I mean, it kills people, nobody recovers, it grows these tentacles, and—"

In an instant, Mrs. Ellington was in Molly's chair and was holding her on her lap. "But . . . surgery? Radiation? Chemotherapy?"

"Done all that." The words were muffled; Molly's face was pressed into Mrs. Ellington's shoulder. She reached up and tore off her wig, her bald head pale and small. "Nothing left."

They talked, Molly's voice level and cold: no more tears, she said. She reeled off the names of the drugs pumped into her, the shape her life had taken: dizzy spells, headaches, double vision, rage. "Some days I feel great. Then it all comes crashing down. It's a curse." She filled in the years since her mother had taken her: schools, travel, a few brief romances, her painting. "I wanted to be an artist, like you. I don't know if I'm any good; I guess now I won't ever know. I brought you one." She took a rolled-up drawing from her large shoulder bag. Mrs. Ellington knew it was not good, but she admired it. "You need lessons in scale," she said. Molly gave a short laugh. "No time for that. Too bad."

A pale light shone through the drapes: "Dawn," said Mrs. Ellington. "You should sleep. There's a room next to mine."

But Molly was talking, almost to herself. "It's like when my mother snatched me. I knew everything was over, everything I cared about. I mean, I was five years old and I felt like I was dying, I was shrieking and crying and I remember I kicked my mother, because I couldn't stand it."

"That's what you remember?" Mrs. Ellington shook her head. "But it wasn't like that. You were absolutely silent. Frozen. You didn't say a word and you wouldn't look at us."

"That was in the car. Up to then, I fought like an animal. Trapped, you know, that's how I felt. I can still feel it, almost, how furious I was. And scared. I was scared and I was screaming—God, the noise I made—and pushing you away, remember you tried to put your arms around me and I hit you? I can't imagine ever hitting you, but that minute I hated you, and Penelope too. I thought you didn't want me anymore, you were getting rid of me. That's why I wouldn't talk to you when you called. I cried after your calls, every time. My mother said the crying would stop and then I'd love her, and she was right about it stopping, but I didn't love her and she knew it."

She drew back and put her arms around Mrs. Ellington and kissed her cheek. "I loved you. I don't think I told you that, at least not enough. I was so happy you didn't have a husband or a family so it could be just us. You know, my parents were in the middle of splitting up, so I decided you and I were my whole entire family, my only real family, and then it was all over and you weren't my family anymore and I missed you, I missed you all the time and I almost called you, but I really thought you didn't want me anymore, you'd gotten rid of me, and I was afraid to hear you say you didn't love me, maybe never loved me, maybe got tired of me, so I didn't call or write or anything." She laughed, a low laugh. "When I got older, I walked past your building once or twice a week, hoping I'd see you, but then I stopped that, too. It's so hard, you know, to remember all the beautiful things when the bad ones take up so much room, they ooze, they blot out the good stuff, the bright stuff. Anyway, I did remember my times with you, I held onto them, and they kept me going, maybe even helped me get along with my mother. Which I did; after awhile things got okay between us; I mean I did grow up, and she really tried—she bought me just about everything you could think of: clothes, trips to Europe, last year a car, all that. Everything in the world except staying alive. I guess even you can't help me with that."

Molly died three months later. She died in Mrs. Ellington's studio, wrapped in heavy blankets in the recliner Mrs. Ellington bought when Molly wanted only to stay close to her and watch her sketch and shape clay into strange, often wild shapes. In her final three months, when she was living with Mrs. Ellington, there had been no more talk of her memories of the day she was taken by her mother. Mrs. Ellington reminded herself that brain tumors probably affected memory and she would not force a sick child to relive a terrible time. The discrepancies had been disturbing, but Mrs. Ellington, fifty years old, healthy and vigorous, looking ahead to a long life, could not worry about Molly's flawed memory when she was watching her, a wraith at seventeen, slip away.

Molly was buried on a Sunday morning, clouds scudding overhead, a north wind whipping the loose dirt in whorls that skittered about the grave. Once more, Mrs. Ellington mourned, and wept. To have rediscovered Molly only to lose her again seemed more than she could bear, and she lay awake nights cataloguing the actions she might have taken over the years to bring them together, to live together, to laugh and learn together, to help Molly, if illness was inevitable, through the early days of coping with it, to the end. All futile now, she thought, and, as before, waited out the pain, waited for the time when she could accept her solitude with equanimity, even with pleasure. Only once had she shared her home with someone she loved. She would not do it again.

Helena hosts a dinner party in the private dining room of a restaurant tucked away on a sedate residential street. She will leave the next morning for her newest show in Los Angeles, and she uses the occasion to gather together artists, critics, journalists and musicians, even a novelist. At breakfast the morning of the party, Penelope chastises her. "You surround yourself with crowds; when do you have quiet times with your friends?"

"Right now," Helena says. "And all our private times together."

"Yes, but besides me. Other friends."

"Penelope, I do what pleases me."

Penelope looks up from spreading jam on her croissant. "You do have other close friends."

"I have many friends. And I'm fine."

"But intimate ones."

"I have you. Penelope, I'm sixty-five years old; might it be a little late for you to try to change how I live my life?"

Penelope laughs. "Yes indeed. Well, then, who is coming tonight? Tell me you didn't invite Percival Tithe. I know he's important, and you do admire his portraits, but after the way he attacked you at William's brunch that day, I'd think he's off your list forever."

"No, I didn't invite him, though I might, sometime. He was drunk that day—at brunch, can you believe it?—and he apologized. It was a long time ago."

"You're not saying you forgive him."

"Why not? He called me a professional virgin. Crude, and more than a little weird, but it could have been worse."

"But it—" Penelope stops. "Sorry, I didn't mean to talk about him. Let's talk about something more pleasant."

"It what? Was different? Worse? What was worse?"

"No, forget it. I'm sorry I brought it up."

"What was worse?"

"I'm not going to tell you. If you've forgotten, be thankful. Let's leave it there."

"I don't forget."

Penelope shrugs. "We all forget. It's in our genes; there's a very special one designed by some benign power to protect us from painful memories. Enjoy it; life would be intolerable if we remembered everything."

That night, William is one of Helena's guests at dinner. She asks him about Percival Tithe. "Good Lord," he says, "I thought you'd forgotten that long ago. Awful man, well, he'd probably be fine if he'd quit drinking, but there you are."

"What did he say? Do you remember?"

"Look, I don't say those words to a woman, especially one I love. In fact, I've already forgotten, so I can't help you out. Sorry. Can we change the subject?"

Some time later, after meeting Stuart Aaronsohn at the museum, Mrs. Ellington goes home and takes her dinner to the table on her balcony. The evening is hot and still, with lowering clouds. She feels hemmed in, by the sultry weather, by uncertainty, by a cacophony of voices challenging her memories.

For the first time, she forces herself to think back to the memories that have been challenged. Over time, there have been many. She lists her memories, shuffles them, organizes them by time and emotion and knows, even before formulating the thought, that they divide smoothly into two categories. Those with no discrepancies are the pleasant ones, the lighthearted and satisfying and triumphant ones. Those with stark differences in her version and those of others are memories of events that, she has been told, were filled with tension, with anger, with pain. Those, it appears, she has stripped of discord, keeping only enough to make them seem genuine, to make her believe her memory is flawless. But for the most part, she has smoothed them out.

Laundered them, sanitized and transformed them to tolerable tales supporting her image of an even-keeled and richly satisfying life.

Two memories only she has been unable to whitewash or erase. Those she lives with, their outlines jagged and wounding. Even now, a lifetime later, she cannot feel an arm across her shoulders or see a uniform, even from a distance, without recoiling. And her memories of Molly's final three months are etched and permanent; she cannot eliminate the pain without eliminating the love, and that she would not do.

For the rest, Mrs. Ellington has cleansed anger and high emotion from her life. She knows her life is indeed richly satisfying, but its absences, suddenly thrown into relief, are as vivid now as the achievements. She casts back, to isolate a memory that would contradict what, for the first time, she now sees as blank spaces she might have filled, had she admitted they were real. From her landscape of memories, she cannot find one.

Rain drives Mrs. Ellington inside, and the rain continues all the next day as Helena clears space in her studio for a new series of sculptures. She has already made sketches: androgynous, faceless figures, roughly molded in positions evocative of grief or melancholy or inwardness that, two years later, a New York critic will herald as "brilliantly emblematic of twenty-first century anomie and despair in a world where all of us, at one time or another, feel insecure, lacking clear direction or control in our lives." The show sells out amid a clamor for more of the same or, even better, different but equally devastating as metaphors for our troubled times.

Mrs. Ellington is at home a few days after Helena's celebrated opening, when Penelope calls. "I've met someone; we've gone out a few times. He's very special, I think. Come to dinner with us tonight; I want you to meet him. Actually, he says you did meet, casually, awhile back, at some dinner party."

"Who is he?"

Penelope told her and there was a small silence.

"I don't remember," Mrs. Ellington says.

An Ordinary House for Extraordinary People

SIMON AND ANTOINETTE were looking for a house. Antoinette had dreamt of this as a magical time when she and her future husband would share the search for the perfect place to shelter and sustain them when they were no longer 'he' and 'I' but 'we,' Simon-and-Antoinette: one home, one life.

But after almost a week, there was no magic, not even a spark that would illuminate this as a time to be treasured. And the day came when she had to admit that the impediment was Simon, indomitable Simon, her almost husband, her lover, mentor, and friend.

Simon brought to the search the driving persistence, the single-mindedness, and cold detachment he brought to his work, and Antoinette, most often delighted to be swept in his wake, this time let go the idea of magic (as well, she feared, as interest in the search, if not the house itself) and trailed after her beloved in silence.

There were many houses, many neighborhoods, but only one Simon, and Simon did not want an extraordinary house. "In fact, just the opposite," he said. "Why would we adopt the half-baked ideas others thought up for a home? We want a blank slate, since, obviously, any house of ours will be extraordinary."

Antoinette, not understanding but unwilling to admit it, asked if, perhaps, they should simply buy a lot and build exactly what Simon wanted.

He shook his head. "Too long; why should we wait? Any anonymous house, as soon as we make it ours, will become as extraordinary as we are."

Pleased, Antoinette slipped her hand in his. This was

when she loved him most: when he truly understood her. He had, from the time they met at a dinner party and ignored the rest of the guests to talk together the entire evening. And that was why she was here, soon to be married. All her life she had longed to be special (never daring to aspire to extraordinary) and now, beside the imposing bulk of Simon, unique Simon Lovelace, she could articulate again exactly why she needed him: he would bring her, if only in his wake, everything she wanted.

Her name was Antoinette Maloney. Rather, that had been her name as a child, until she was four years old, when her mother introduced her to a friend as Toni Maloney, and she burst into tears: that wasn't her name; it was a joke. She could not live with it, or would not, and so it had to be changed.

She would get married, she thought; that would give her a new name. But marriage was light years distant, its outlines too vague to become a goal. She asked her mother how people changed their names, and her mother talked about going to court, signing documents. She was four years old, almost five. She went to bed each night rehearsing names, syllables, sounds. And then came kindergarten, first grade, second grade: singsong chants of "Toni Baloney" trailing her across the playground. When her history class studied the Mormons, a wag loudly dubbed her "the Angel Maloney"; a fourth-grade classmate, gazing at his lunch tray, gleefully christened it "toni macaloni and cheese."

Once school had beckoned as a new life. The first morning, when she stepped into the sunny kindergarten room with lively pictures and child-size tables, she hugged her lunchbox as if hugging herself. I'm all new, she thought, buoyant and exhilarated at stepping into a world far from home, far from her parents and their friends. They were loud, the friends, and her parents became loud with them; they all slapped each other on the back and laughed at their own jokes; they called her the *cutest little thing, knock 'em dead one of these days*, and always came in the front door saying she had grown so much; *what are we going to do with you, you'll be bigger than us in no time!*

As she grew older, she learned to mention homework and grimace, so they would think she hated to leave, and escape to the silence of her room, a tiny space at the end of the upstairs hall crowded with stuffed animals and picture books later replaced by classics she found in used bookstores. She brought home books filled with paintings of elegant women in silk, and men in velvet and folded collars; mysterious forests and threatening seas with heeling sailboats; children in long dresses and knickers playing beside watchful governesses; mansions with butlers and ladies' maids and sleek cars in the driveways. She read and re-read the books, memorizing dialogue and long descriptions: vivid scenes and scenarios incalculably distant from the townhouse she shared with her parents and the neighborhood where she shied away from others her age who called her an oddball for the tales she told with animation, straight from her books but told as if hers.

Her room was her sanctuary; even her parents could not enter it. No one could comment as she colored pictures and made collages, as she learned to read and add and subtract, as she wrote her first perfectly rounded *a* and *n* and *o* and then her name. In her room, she was the heroine in her own world, in many worlds. In that private place, she became the Antoinette she wanted to be.

Her neighborhood school was something like her room: a place for making up stories, for trying out different ways of being herself, for being special. Each morning she dashed from her house and walked, almost ran, the few blocks to her classroom and her own chair with her name on it and the lessons that brought new stories to be savored and made her own.

But then the jokes began: jingles, puns on her name, the special isolation of labels. By fifth grade, she was desperate. There were ways and ways to be special, she thought, and knew she had discovered a significant truth. Ways and ways to be different. You have to discover your own; you have to make it happen your own way.

"I'm getting a new name," she announced to her parents, flush with discovery and determination. "I hate Maloney, it's awful, I'm getting a new one."

"The hell you are," said her father. "Maloney is an honorable name: name of my grandfather and his grandfather and back to ancient days in County Meath. The first Maloney came to America in 1767 and helped make this country the greatest in the world. Worked his ass off so you could have a good life. Hold your head high when you say Maloney."

Tears filled her eyes; she cried easily. She stood in the center of the living room, feet apart, arms folded, and let the tears spill over. "I hate it, I hate it. People make fun of it; they make fun of me. It's like they don't like me; they all laugh at me. I'm going to be Smith. Rita Smith is in my class and nobody laughs at her."

"You are fuck-all not going to change your name."

She did not like her father's first name, either: Connor, called by his friends Connie, which everybody knew was a woman's name, and why didn't he hate that and choose a new name? She knew why: he had no imagination. And neither did her mother, who had an awful name, too: Tina, a little name, like a baby's, that made her sound insignificant, practically invisible. Antoinette spent hours at her computer, studying names, and she knew disastrous ones when she saw them.

She had had a brother who died when he was a month old, on her second birthday, and his name vibrated in the family, a tremor that Antoinette felt in her blood, to the roots of her teeth. He had had a nice name. She'd heard it only once, but that was enough to know she liked it; she would have liked him. But her parents would not speak of him or say his name aloud.

Most people didn't understand how important names were. Names went ahead of you, like your shadow if the sun was behind you, so people saw that first. Names made people decide about you before they even met you, and what good would it do to say you weren't a baloney or a macaloni, that you were nice and got all As in school, and your teachers said you were smart and had a good imagination, if they'd already decided you were some kind of joke? People should wait until they got to know you, and then you could make them like you, no matter what you were called. But it didn't happen that way. People didn't wait; they jumped right in, and once they'd pegged you, that was it, forever.

Everybody should have a perfect name, Antoinette thought: something simple and strong that didn't surprise people or make them laugh. And things should have names, too, so nobody would be confused. Ever since she was five, she had named everything in her room: her dolls with golden hair and porcelain faces were Marietta or Isabella or Beatrice; her stuffed animals sounded kingly with names like Henry and Richard and John; her dressing table was Helen, her desk Paris, and the landscape drawings she made at school and taped on her bedroom walls were Lovers Forest and Mermaid Sea and

Mount Treacherous.

But for herself she chose Smith. She knew there was something wrong with that, since it did not fit with wanting to be special and different. But she knew, too, that a name that stood out from others and inspired jokes made a person miserable. She had no idea how to reconcile both.

So, for now, she chose Smith. It would fit in anywhere, never making her an object of ridicule. "Antoinette Smith," she said loudly to her parents. "That's my name from now on; you'll have to call me that."

Her father turned red. He launched himself upward, halted by his wife's hand, outstretched like a guard's at an intersection. "We won't change your records," her mother said to Antoinette. "Too much red tape—birth certificate, school registration, bus card, all of that. But your classmates don't see those; to them, you can be Smith."

Her father's mouth opened. Still looking at Antoinette, her mother said to him, "It's a phase."

And so was created Antoinette Smith. There never was a question about changing her first name; it was her favorite name in the world. She loved the ease of her lips on the first and last syllables and the sudden dramatic *twha* they made in the middle. She loved the foreignness of that middle syllable and the Americanness of the initial flat *A*. And Smith made it just right: straightforward, strong, easily called to mind for party invitations or an afternoon play date. She said her new name aloud, wrote it on a large piece of paper again and again with flourishes, and taped the paper to the wall beside her bed. "That's me," she said aloud. "A person nobody will laugh at. And special. How many people get to choose their own name?"

But, a few years later, Smith had faded to a bland murmur

shared by too many people who weren't smart enough to change it. Antoinette was in a private high school in Connecticut on a four-year scholarship for a minor but promising talent for drawing. She was sixteen, and coming to believe she had chosen the wrong name. The truth was, it no longer made her feel special. But then, nothing made her feel special these days. She dreamed of opportunities to do something memorable, a sterling act that would bring attention and admiration, but nothing presented itself, and she had no idea how to create one. She felt unmoored, far from the Antoinette she longed to be. Nothing had worked: the separation from her parents and their small world, the expensive school and new friends, her charcoal drawings and attempts at watercolor that she suspected would plateau, never approaching stellar. Nothing presented a scenario in which she would be noticed, looked up to, even envied.

"Everything is so boring," she said to her roommate. "We ought to be like calendars so whenever things get dull or we don't know what to do, we could flip a page to a new beginning and everything would be different. I need a new season, a new month. Well, at least a new name; that worked pretty well the last time. Something dramatic that says I'm not about to settle for being an ordinary somebody. Or nobody."

"Karamazov," said her roommate, who was studying Russian literature.

"No, that doesn't sound right; anyway, it's a man's name. But... Karenina." They looked at each other. "Beautiful and tragic. Haunting. Antoinette Karenina... romantic, bold, daring."

She wrote her new name with what she thought might be Slavic curlicues on a sheet of textured paper and tacked it to the bulletin board above her desk. "I love it. People will notice it; they'll remember it. I'm the only Antoinette Karenina in the whole school, maybe the whole world."

Through high school and into college, she kept her new name. Her friends called her Anna, which she accepted reluctantly even as she emulated Anna by wearing long skirts and lace blouses with high collars and wide sleeves (though she was not amused when a classmate, with a grin, warned her to stay away from railroad stations). She published a drawing in an obscure magazine and framed it, signed with her new name. She sent her parents a copy of her class photo, inscribed, "To Mother and Father, with love, Antoinette Karenina."

But change creates its own appetite, and years later, in graduate school, as she sat at her desk in her small apartment on Amsterdam Avenue, she pondered her name. She was twenty-four years old, pleased that she no longer resembled the confused teenager latching on to a Russian heroine, but feeling at sea over a future she could not imagine without a new name to bear her toward it.

Antoinette had grown to a woman many called striking, though she thought that an exaggeration: she approved of her dark eyes and level brows but was critical of her high forehead, thin nose, and prominent cheekbones. She had considered surgery to remake her face but rejected the idea; it was enough to change her name.

And the time had come to do that again. She acknowledged that she had become a more competent artist, but beyond that she had achieved nothing significant. Reviewing her history, she traced a progression of obvious, in fact predictable, steps, and how could she reconcile what she was today with the inchoate vision she had held close for so long: an Antoinette of whom she could say, this is my unique special self and it pleases me?

To Antoinette, most of humanity was in lockstep, and she could not bear to think of herself blending in, her progress determined by the pace of others, her body crushed by the masses impinging on her from all sides. By now she knew that a new name could not be a force for transmutation, much less a triumphal wizardry, but still a stubborn hope lingered that a new name could open the way to the creation of a new persona, compelling, empowered, fulfilled. She was sure this new name would be hers for good, even if, later, it became her middle name followed by that of an as-yet-undiscovered husband, and so she sought to combine distinctiveness with something natural, elemental, earthy. She was not the tragic heroine of a novel or a child desperate to avoid mockery: she would be a singular, real woman stepping into a future ripe with promise.

She was too old for fairy tales, but not for names with levels of meaning. She would hold fast to Antoinette—essential and now even better, since she had recently discovered it meant, in Latin, 'invaluable'—but she would adopt a new surname. She searched encyclopedias for famous people, filled small notebooks with trial names, printed them in different fonts on her computer, spoke them aloud hoping for singing tones and a shock of familiarity. And at last she became Antoinette Beaulieu, an invaluable woman in a beautiful place, the syllables foreign but not suspect. She had the initials embroidered on the cuffs of her shirts and gloves, molded into a silver belt buckle, laser-etched on her luggage. When she looked at them, she felt new and anticipatory: it seemed inevitable that, with these initials, with this name, she was embarking on a path so far never even imagined.

It took several years, but she was patient, building a

career as a midlevel executive in an advertising agency, until, at thirty-two, she met Simon Lovelace, and, in the midst of their intense courtship, found the melodic lilt of Antoinette Beaulieu Lovelace as attractive as Simon himself: a name, a person to reckon with. Perfect, she thought. Earthy but elusive, evocative and slightly mysterious.

As was Simon: tall and muscular, broad shouldered, with thighs like well-shaped tree trunks, thick reddish hair, and a neck too solid to bend to anyone. His eyes glistened; his smile was merry. He plowed through rooms, and women and men paused their conversations to watch him pass. He and Antoinette became engaged three weeks after they met, and would wed as soon as they selected a judge and witnesses, and bought a house.

Simon was destined for something magnificent. When he suggested marriage, he described his future, his gestures encompassing all of space. "Some major event which I will command, perhaps initiate. It's there; I can feel it." He was vague on details but absolute in his certainty that he would recognize the event, or its preamble, when it came, because he would be prepared. "I don't talk about it; most people wouldn't have the vaguest understanding of what I'm saying. But you would." And Antoinette was the one to share it with him. "We'll have a special life together, profoundly significant, shape shifting."

Antoinette, excited by his perception, his understanding of what she always had sought, still was baffled: she had never enjoyed ambiguities. "It sounds so exciting, so important. But if you don't know what it is, or might be, how can you possibly know—" Halted by the two deep lines creasing between his eyes (already familiar with Simon's gathering rages), she tacked seamlessly: "—that I can help you?"

His brow cleared; he enfolded her hands in his. "Never underestimate yourself, Antoinette; you are my most perfect companion. If you conform to me, I promise you an extraordinary life far beyond even the fantasies of simpler people."

She had been Smith, Karenina, Beaulieu. She had tried simplicity and found it wanting; she had turned to beauty, to the search for something distinctive and distinctively hers. Simon understood that. He understood her. Of course she would be his.

And so they looked for a house. Simon was bored and impatient. "Disgusting: tramping through the detritus of other lives." Ahead of Antoinette, he strode through brick prairie-style houses, fake Georgian houses, would-be Italian palazzos, fifties-style ranch homes. They had been searching for almost a week, and as he followed a real estate broker toward the fourth house of a long, hot Saturday afternoon, he said, "This is taking far too long; it's not as if we're looking for something extraordinary. Now this one isn't bad; what do you think?"

They stood on the front walk, hands clasped, gazing silently at the boxlike house, one of a neighborhood of similar boxes, each set back in its square of grass behind a low picket fence. A few stood out with a tree or a bed of flowers. "It's a little . . . plain," Antoinette said at last, wanting to please and to be pleased.

"But with possibilities."

She tilted her head, seeking an angle from which possibilities might appear. "Perhaps if we go inside . . ."

The rooms were square, the ceilings low. A fireplace was a dark maw faced with tin. They stumbled on the two steps from the living room to the dining room, irregularly spaced.

The bathrooms were pink. "Perfect," Simon declared.

Antoinette ran her fingers along gray Formica in the kitchen, leaving traces.

"We'll make it ours," he pressed on. "It will be extraordinary as soon as we're living in it, but of course we'll do some construction as well. And the price is ridiculously low. One does not ignore that."

"But surely we can afford—"

"We can afford anything." He turned to her. "You don't think this can be done? That we can make it extraordinary, distinctive, highly visible, so we can be found easily?"

Her eyebrows were raised, though she knew Simon disliked that. "By whom?"

"Whoever will be searching for me when I'm needed. I have no intention of living in someone's fake mansion on a street of equally fake mansions that glaze over in a scrim of anonymity. You don't see the challenge here? You don't think we are extraordinary and belong in a house we will make extraordinary?"

She looked up and saw no humor in his eyes. "I wasn't thinking of mansions, just, perhaps, a head start, to begin with at least some of the things we like."

He was silent. Simon was good at silence. At first, Antoinette had been intrigued and oddly aroused by his seeming lack of interest in prevailing in a discussion or winning a debate: he simply withdrew and let the last word go to someone else. But she soon understood that it was not lack of interest; silence was one of Simon's weapons, and, with it, he always won. It required admirable discipline, but letting a debate sputter out while he stood silent and tall on the platform of his confidence was the equivalent of letting the air out of a tire, as now, when

Antoinette's words fell flat, the discussion closed.

It was a wall, Simon's discipline. It was his armor. He walked into a room and, by virtue of size and steely possession, took command. Others watched, non-actors in his presence, as he controlled the scene. Each time, Antoinette was swept by admiration and desire and, she admitted to herself, little jolts of envy.

Simon bought the house that afternoon, and a week later they were married.

She became Antoinette Beaulieu Lovelace, added the 'L' to the initials on her clothing and luggage, and commissioned a new belt buckle. Simon hired a contractor, and their honeymoon was consumed by renovation. Early each morning they were at the house with camp stools, measuring tapes, graph paper, soft lead pencils, sandwiches and beer. Hardly extraordinary, Antoinette thought with some regret, and concluded that Simon had not been looking for a house, but a palette.

The contractor, plied with a bonus, completed the work in six months, elevating the roof five feet; transforming the pink bathrooms into temples of black and white marble; breaking out walls to construct a great room with a stainless steel kitchen at one end, a gazebo dining room, and a sweeping living room with a broad fireplace faced with gold-veined black marble. Everything was oversize, gleaming, insistent. Antoinette, who liked early American in warm woods and pastels, walked carefully, feeling she might break if she touched anything.

Simon paced the same rooms with swelling satisfaction. "Ours," he said, and drew her to him. "Extraordinary."

He had his own bathroom with an outsize tub where he lay each evening, reviewing the waning day, anticipating the new one, drying off with vigorous expectancy for what would soon summon him, the event for which he was keyed up, fully prepared. Bathed and rosy, he would stride into the bedroom with radiant certitude to escort Antoinette out for the evening, or onto their king-size bed.

He had selected the black velvet comforter for the bed, embroidered in gold tree branches, wine-colored silk on the reverse. Beneath that slippery coolness, Simon made love to Antoinette at whimsical times on the weekends and at night before sleep or in late afternoons when they arrived home from work, Antoinette from her advertising agency and Simon from the bank where, with confidence, tenacity, faint bullying, and an encyclopedic memory that gave a touch of the exotic to his work, he vastly increased other people's wealth, and thus his own.

His body was firm and massive beneath the coverlet, his hands commanding, and Antoinette responded with a passion that dismayed her: seeking equality in bed, she found instead her own ardor. When Simon lay back, flushed with triumph, she escaped to her bathroom and contemplated her image in the mirror over her dressing table. Her eyes were remote, languorous, the contours softened; she thought she looked like a woman just rising from a night of drugs and fervid, anonymous sex. After a time, she dressed and slipped quietly into the library, avoiding Simon's deep leather couch and armchairs to curl up in the one upholstered chair that was hers. There she read biographies of foreign monarchs and salon hostesses of an earlier age until Simon emerged in black tie for dining out or at home.

Six months into their marriage, Simon declared that Antoinette was to leave her job. They had finished dinner and were sitting on the leather couch in the library with espresso and cognac. The chef had left for the evening; the house was hushed, the room illuminated by a newly lit fire. It was the kind of perfect evening Antoinette could create and Simon could appreciate. "There is no need for you to work; I have more than enough for anything we would ever wish to do."

Antoinette avoided the larger issue. "How much is that? You've never told me."

He shrugged. "One doesn't bray about one's worth." He named a sum that staggered her, and she reflected for a moment on the relative weights of their total worth and, thus, perhaps inevitably, their significance, in their marriage, in the world.

"But it isn't money," she said. "I like my work. I was just named vice president; I told you that last week."

Again, he shrugged. "You spend your days gilding mundane products for gullible consumers. Unworthy even as an avocation. How much better if you spent your time honing our life together."

"You said we already have an extraordinary life."

After a long, heavy moment, he said, "You do not agree with that?"

"An extraordinary life does not need honing."

"It needs constant attention until the moment it is significantly changed." He lifted her hand and kissed it, an arousal but an annoyance, too. "I will be called upon soon to instigate or shape events few in the world could even fathom, much less share. I am prepared for this; you are not, but with me you'll learn; you're very quick. And I want you with me. This is an unbelievable chance for you, Antoinette, your only chance to make a substantial mark on the world." He examined her hand for signs of trembling. "You must feel the excitement;

I know you feel it."

In fact, she did. His voice could carry her beyond whatever doubts crept in, slyly inserting themselves in the briefest pauses between his sentences, retreating when his voice returned. Vague though it was, the outline of the panorama he flung before her obliterated any ideas she might have had for their future. And, whatever it was, she would share it. It was splendid, that vision: even unfocused, it wiped out the even less focused dreams she had pursued for so long. Simon's vision dominated, not least because he wanted her to share it. She would reach the pinnacle when he did, and there was no way she ever would reach it except as Simon's appendage. Companion, she amended quickly. Friend, fellow traveler. Wife.

"And you feel the responsibility," he was saying. "Around the world, masses of ignorant people, totally unaware, depend on us to be prepared to act. Both of us. And how will we be ready, how will we be recognized, if you diminish us by wallowing in muck like glamorizing cures for constipation or selling diapers to aging women?"

Once again, Antoinette looked to his eyes for humor, and once again found none.

"Listen to me, this you must understand," he said. "There are no limits to the life we can create; something no one has achieved before, on a grand scale beyond models: we would be making our own, forging our own, making history." He waited and Antoinette nodded. Yes, of course. She could deal with, perhaps ignore, those sly doubts. "More to the point, I've never been happy with my wife working, sending a signal that I am unable to provide for her, that what we have together is somehow lacking in sufficient stimulus to make her happy and fulfilled."

"Of course I'm happy! Of course I'm fulfilled! I love you."

This last came out in a drooping voice: words they seldom used.

"And we'll be traveling. It's past time for our honeymoon. I've made a list of places I want to see before they become irremediably westernized or melt away." He smiled, waiting for her to acknowledge his humor. "Glaciers," he said gently.

"Oh, Simon." She bit off a disconcerting exasperation at his need to make everything epic. But, again, he had shown how well he understood her: always she had wanted to see the sights illustrated in her books, romantic scenes of colorful people and places, elusive, seemingly unattainable. Gratefully, she renewed her belief in Simon's clairvoyance. Compared to that, how could her job be significant? If, later, she changed her mind and thought it important, she would go back. She was liked; she was admired; the job, or perhaps even a better one, would be hers when she returned. She could have everything she wanted, everything Simon wanted as well. "How many trips are you thinking of?"

"Planning. Three or four a year. We're young, it's the right time. It will keep me active, broadening my experience, while I wait."

"Us," she murmured. "We." The fire crackled; a log broke apart in a flurry of sparks. A few minutes later, she finished her cognac and took their glasses and espresso cups to the kitchen, and washed and dried them herself.

Their travels took them to five-star hotels in Vietnam and Cambodia, luxurious hotels in Prague and Estonia ("I told you," said Simon. "Western."), castle hotels in the wine region of Hungary, tents in the Rajasthan desert, yurts on Mongolian plains, spare rooms without hot water or electricity at the Buddhist caves of Dunhuang, elegantly rustic lodges in Patagonia, and serene ryokans in Kyoto. They became expert in packing and unpacking; mastering menus in local languages; making their way through twisted streets and narrow walkways, parks and open squares, on foot or using whatever local transportation presented itself as Antoinette discovered that Simon could read a map, find the correct subway or bus, and communicate with taxi and cyclo drivers anywhere in the world.

In thirty-one months, Antoinette was exhausted, her senses taut, overwhelmed with sights, sounds, smells, tastes. "I want to stay home for a year," she said, stretching out on the bed in their suite as they soared at 40,000 feet, fifteen hours from America. She had taken a sleeping pill. "Two years. Maybe three."

"We once discussed climbing Kilimanjaro," said Simon.

They climbed Kilimanjaro two months later, and spent two weeks on safari in Botswana, ending with a week in Cape Town. Simon's list for that swing through Africa included flying to Egypt, then Israel, and finally Petra, but Antoinette at last, definitively, balked. "You go," she said in their hotel room overlooking Cape Town's waterfront. She had a cold and a churning stomach and she went to bed every night with a headache. "I have to unwind, Simon, please, I really can't go on. I have to go home."

"And what do you plan to do if I go on alone?"

"Sleep. Read. Stare out a window. Eat oatmeal. Take walks. After awhile go back to work."

He gave a short laugh. "A pipe dream."

"I told them I was taking a leave and I'd be back. They said I could do that anytime. They like my work."

"Of course they do; whatever you do is excellent; there's damn little of that in a mediocre world. Antoinette." He put his arm about her, a rarity. "You are a special person.

We are special. You've become a superb traveler; you wring more from our trips than anyone else could dream of; it's a pleasure sharing them with you. But by now you must understand that I cannot have you attenuate what we are creating with your whims."

"We are creating a travelogue," she said.

Simon was silent. Antoinette fled to the bathroom and vomited, and they went home.

The three months Simon promised as he unlocked the door of their shuttered house slipped quietly into six, and then nine. Antoinette did not go back to work, but, for the first time, she was content to be in the house. It was still Simon's creation—overwhelming and slightly repellent (like Simon, came the sly thought)—but it was solid, unchanging, and silent: a haven. She woke each day to the lambent light of early morning, linden leaves brushing the open window, the four-note call of an unseen bird, the daily newspapers slapping the front porch, the neighbor telling his dog to shut up before he woke the whole damn neighborhood. It was as if she were eight years old again, taking pleasure in a name like Smith.

Simon was restless. He read newspapers and surfed television channels to spot the world event that would demand his intervention. Each day he walked the three miles to town and bought books he was too impatient to read. He felt stunted and warped, angrily frustrated as each day of waiting for the defining event of his life ended quietly, like any other. His destiny, the design and purpose of his life, glimmered at the horizon, a fitful glow that enticed by obscurity as much as by the brief flashes he imagined he could see if he looked away and let peripheral vision register his future. Uncertainty, elusiveness gnawed at him, sending stabbing pains through his legs, eased only by movement: walking, running, ferocious soccer practice alone on a nearby field, enraged squats in the gym. At meals or reading at night, his fingers twitched, his neck tensed, his legs danced like the limbs of puppets. Desperate for action, he fell back on travel, the complex planning that preceded it, the constant forward movement, always forward, the horizon with its intangible glow viewed from different angles. Progress, declared Simon.

"I have tickets for Egypt and Israel," he said one night at dinner, "and of course Petra: the trip we never took. From there we'll go to Turkey; you'll like that. We'll buy you leather: skirts, jackets, whatever you want. The Grand Bazaar in Istanbul, a world in itself. I bought books today; we're not leaving for three weeks, so we have time to read."

The books were piled on the dining room table, bristling with markers left by Simon so Antoinette need check out only the parts he had identified as worthwhile. Simon read rapidly, skimming, devouring a page before flipping to the next. He read standing up, sometimes pacing, sometimes leaning in their front doorway so he could look up and survey the street: construction sites with cranes and earth movers, oaks and maples turning to russet and gold, street lights coming on in the deepening violet and copper streaks of sunset.

From the doorway, two weeks before their trip, he said, "We'll sell the house; I'll call the broker tomorrow. This one is getting stale, we need something new. You've never liked it anyway."

"You just decided this?"

"Of course not. I've been thinking about it for some time."

Simon did not share his thoughts; he seemed to have no need to do so. If he did not like a restaurant, a concert, a book, he kept it to himself. Antoinette would comment, critique, admire, look to him for confirmation or a discussion, but he would say nothing. If asked directly, he might say, "I thought it was poor," or, "It was adequate," or even, "It was very good." He formulated entire debates in his mind, taking both sides of issues and resolving them. So Antoinette was not surprised that he had kept an idea to himself, but she was stunned to hear he was tired of the house.

"You said it was extraordinary," she said. "You designed it, and when we moved in you said that made it extraordinary."

He shrugged. "A word of many meanings. We've only begun to explore them."

He was entire unto himself, Antoinette thought as she prepared for bed that night. Powerful, determined, self-referential, he strode through life parting waters, seeking his destiny. And she wondered, as he lay on her, when he would begin to see her as he now saw his house: stale, requiring a replacement. Even more, she wondered why she was still here, now that the sly notes that cut across her thoughts had grown too insistent to be ignored, exposing the stark recognition that her husband was living a myth that, with the passing years, would become ever more difficult to sustain, and that would make her, inevitably, victim and villain. To that question, she had no answer.

Simon's restlessness underlay the preparations for their newest trip. Barely balanced between frustration and rage, anxiety and clinging expectation of the cataclysm that would demand his intercession, he feverishly packed and repacked; checked airline itineraries online, cursing even minor changes; called the real estate broker every day demanding explanations for the paucity of potential buyers for their house; and pushed the days away as if they were mistakes to be plowed under and forgotten. A few days before they were to leave, he worked his way through dinner, shoved his plate aside, and said to Antoinette, "I want you to change your name."

She stared at him. "Lovelace is a wonderful name. Why would I change it?"

"Good Lord, not my name. Yours."

"Mine? But I can't. It's my name. It's who I am."

"Which may be precisely the problem. It's become clear to me that the reason I haven't been called is that our life is flawed. Obviously some parameters need to be changed, weak spots that need attention. We're selling the house; next is your name. I've made a list—"

"Why don't you change yours?"

"Ridiculous. It's right for me. Yours is wrong. It doesn't—"

She shook her head.

"—belong in our life. I've made a list of a few more appropriate; the final choice is yours. We won't have time to change your passport before we leave, but we'll do it as soon as we return."

Her hands were clenched, her color high. "It's mine. It's me." And she fled, ignoring his rule that neither of them leave the other alone at the table.

He did not follow her; he kept to other rooms of the house and went to bed without her while she sat in the library wrapped in a blanket. She was shivering, though it was a warm spring night. They had been home for nine months. Long enough to have a baby, she thought, but Simon refused to consider it. Long enough for her to go back to work, but Simon had called that a pipe dream. Long enough to buy a house and furnish it this time to her taste, but Simon liked this one . . .

until suddenly he didn't. Long enough to plant a garden, buy a puppy, make friends, have intimate dinner parties. But Simon kept everything in abeyance as he waited for his momentous event. Everything in abeyance except changing her name. Changing her.

From what? From ordinary, she thought, and recoiled. No, not possible, not Antoinette Beaulieu Lovelace, not Simon's wife, his companion, his choice to share the brilliance, the greatness of his future.

The future is the point, he had said. But it receded as he searched for it. Where were they, where was she, in his driven pursuit of a nebulous extraordinary? His horizon was beyond her reach, beyond her vision, even beyond her comprehension. (And his too, came the furtive thought, but she shoved it aside: too soon, she thought, not yet.) And then she thought, I'm not what he wants. For all his work on me, the truth is, I am not extraordinary.

This time she did not reject it; she let it settle so she could contemplate it. This time, the idea was oddly pleasant, even refreshing. This time, she could think, Poor Simon: to expend so much energy, so much passion to maintain the vision of his destiny, to keep it fresh and vibrant, and then to conclude that the crucial impediment to its fulfillment is his wife. And if, as of course must happen, he comes to realize the mythology of his entire scenario, how agonizing for him to be forced to recognize that his life's vision is at best fanciful and, at worst, fiction.

It did not occur to her that he might never see mythology or contemplate fiction.

But for Antoinette, everything had a new cast. Alone the next day, she stood in her dressing room, naked before the full-length mirror, and saw Antoinette Beaulieu for the first time in many years as a singular person, not an appendage or a satellite desperate for a sun. As some materials always revert to their basic shape, no matter how stretched or twisted, Antoinette felt herself pulling back from Simon's seductive vision. She stepped forward; her reflection filled the mirror. There was no room for Simon.

She tried to remember the Antoinette of years past, who chose her own life: her name, her place, her work, her time. She had never allowed it to be enough, and how ready she was to discard it when she met Simon. How eager to believe him when he said she stood with him above everyone else, that she shared neither dreams nor desires with the millions of people who thronged the world, whom Simon casually dismissed as ordinary.

Testing herself, she repeated it. Ordinary. Ordinary Antoinette. And, as repetition often blurs fears and dislikes, soon the word lost much of its tarnish. She would never be a woman who drew all eyes when she walked into a room; she would never be singled out in a crowd. She would not be the initiator or fulcrum of earth-shaking events, nor would she be called upon to perform or even assist with spectacular deeds that would become the stuff of interminable sagas and many-versed anthems.

And thus she was the wrong wife for Simon, who would always be disappointed in discovering and rediscovering how far short of extraordinary she fell. What had happened to her that she so completely missed the baggage in the few loaded syllables of his favorite word? So naive, she thought, obsessed by lusting after a place in a spotlight, even the spillover of his.

She should not have married him, should not have been seduced by his melodious name, his size and beauty, his grandiloquence, the admiration of others, the myth that drove him.

But it was not too late. The wrong wife for Simon should move aside, clearing the way for him to find a more suitable companion. Clearing the way as well for her to make a life suitable for the woman she was. That was the clear path for both of them, a simple truth that, simply understood, they could act upon with grace and amity.

So they would separate. He would be grateful for her insights now, before there were more encumbrances, more layers to the myth of his election to greatness that would depend as much on her acquiescence as on his fantasy. He would be grateful to her for making the decision, sparing him the burden of wounding her when he came to the same conclusion, as surely he would.

She told him the next night, at dinner in a quiet neighborhood bistro. Her voice was low and pleasant, as if delivering a forecast of mild weather. But Simon reared back in his chair, his brows tight. "What are you talking about?"

She put her hand briefly on his. "I'm not the right wife for you, Simon. I'm not what you want."

"Not? Who the hell are you to tell me what I want or don't want? You don't know anything. You're ignorant until I instruct you, you're—"

"That's what I mean. You don't want an ignorant wife. You want—"

"Don't interrupt me!" He lowered his voice as others turned to look. "This is insane." He glowered at the wine bottle. "Not my Chianti. Idiots. They know which one I like."

He filled their glasses, his hand steady. "Have you read the books on Egypt? One of them in particular, of course it's a novel, which is always suspect, but—"

"Simon, listen to me, please. I want us to divorce."

"We will not." His voice was flat. "We are creating an extraordinary life, and soon some great event will make it momentous. It hasn't happened yet, but it will..."

His voice faltered. It was so abrupt, the break from supreme confidence to a flicker of doubt, that Antoinette shrank back.

"But it will, and soon." His voice was bleak. "Whenever..." He was looking across the room, across space. "I don't know why it takes so long, what more I could..."

Dismayingly, she found herself pitying him, and instinctively shied from it. She shook her head, denying the unnerving slackness of his face, her own disturbing pity, and, knowing she should say nothing that would acknowledge his unaccountable weakness, asked quietly, "Could? Could what?"

And Simon recovered. His eyes focused, the muscles of his face hardened, his back became rigid. "Be needed for some great event." He sat back. "And you will be part of it. I chose you for that. You're a beautiful woman, you learn quickly, you attract attention. You belong to me. You belong to what my life will become; you are essential to it."

"I don't know what you're talking about."

"Of course you don't. It doesn't matter. In time you will."

"And I do not belong to you."

"My love," he said as the waiter approached, "I've bought you a gift to celebrate our anniversary. One thousand four hundred and eighty days of a perfect marriage." He glanced at the waiter who had tiptoed toward them in the wash of their quarrel, but now was smiling broadly.

"Congratulations. May I bring you champagne?"

Simon glanced at the bottle on their table. "You may

bring me a good Chianti."

They held a serious, private discussion of Chianti.

Antoinette pushed back her chair, but Simon stopped her with a radiant smile. "We're ignoring you; can you forgive our rudeness? It won't happen again, I promise. I'll be with you always, always."

The waiter beamed and brought them a second basket of focaccia and a head of roasted garlic.

The next night, she heard him humming in the tub, preparing for their evening out: he had bought tickets for a film about contemporary Egypt and had made dinner reservations at a Turkish restaurant. "Two ethnicities in one night," he said merrily. "A prelude to our trip."

Antoinette had spoken to a lawyer that afternoon, but her cache of weapons was thin. "Of course incompatibility is always a possibility," the lawyer said, "but if he says you have a perfect marriage . . . and I gather you've written him little notes, for birthdays and Christmas and such, telling him essentially that?"

Antoinette nodded. Notes to convince herself as much as to please him, and she knew he saved them; he saved everything.

"Hard to prove incompatibility with a perfect marriage. If he contested the divorce, you could leave empty-handed. I gather he is a formidable presence."

"I've given him over four years of companionship, sex, homemaking . . ."

The lawyer was amused. "Maybe if it was forty. Don't misunderstand: you can leave; you can get a divorce. But with a brief marriage, no children, all those love notes, multiple trips around the world, always together . . . I think he could make a case of cruel abandonment and you would get nothing. Perhaps he'd come up with an affair: you found someone else—"

"I did not!"

"A man of means and determination could arrange to find one. He might even discover you'd cleaned out all the jewelry in the house, or the ivory netsukes."

Antoinette stood up. "This is ludicrous."

"Situations I've dealt with." He stood with her. "Of course you earned a living before you were married; you could do it again."

"Could he stop me from getting a divorce?"

"Legally, no. If you mean, could he make it so unpleasant you choose to stay, you can answer that better than I. Or if you mean, might he turn violent, you're the only one who would know that."

She had not meant it, but she had thought it.

Simon, with the optimism that came with his nightly bath, was humming Mozart. The Commendatore, thought Antoinette. *A cenar teco m'invitasti.* You invited me to dinner. How happy he is. Fully recovered from his lapse in the restaurant and once again poised for the revelation of his transformative role.

It was time to dress. An Egyptian movie and a Turkish restaurant. *I'll be with you always, always.* He would not let her divorce him. They would travel endlessly, searching for what was ever more elusive; he would pace and rage and perhaps have moments of doubt, most likely increasing as the years passed; he might, in fact, turn violent as he clung to strands of fantasy, dragging her with him to keep them from unraveling. He would find ways to keep her, because, as improbable as it seemed, he wanted her. With a different name. He should not have told me that, she thought; the idea of losing Antoinette was terrifying. She felt faint and sat down, bending forward, counting her breaths, fighting sickness.

It was time to dress; she had to pay attention. And then her thoughts diverged from her actions so that, later, she recalled them as shards of splintered moments with no sequence or order, driven by no volition. In her gleaming bathroom where silver and blue marble reflected the makeup lights, she washed her face, darkened her brows and lashes, heightened the color of her pale cheeks, wet her hair, and began to style it with her hair dryer.

Or she thought that was what she was doing. In fact, she walked a straight line into Simon's massive black and white bathroom, steamy from the hot water that filled his tub, musical from the Mozart aria he was humming. "I'm getting ready," she said to his angry eyes: he had declared he was never to be disturbed in his bathroom. She plugged in her hair dryer and turned it on. "Simon, dear Simon, I am so very sorry; I really did think you were the answer to everything." And she dropped the humming dryer into the clear, rippling water with Simon's bulk dissolving beneath its surface.

Her Striped Socks

WHEN SHE TURNED FIFTY, my mother took to wearing striped socks. I was mortified. I was about to graduate from eighth grade, and the image of my parents sitting with all the other parents in the bleachers of the gym, my mother's striped socks crossed in front of her like a pair of nocturnal creatures poking their heads out of the earth, left me breathless with agony.

But she surprised me. On my big day, she looked like all the other mothers, in fact a lot better, wearing a pale linen suit I didn't know she owned, skirt just below her knees, legs in sleek nylons, feet in white pumps with heels. Her dark hair was pulled back and fastened with some kind of glittery clip, her lips were pink, her eyes wide and black. She was very pretty, and people smiled at her as she walked by.

And then she was gone. Not the next day or the next week, but it seemed that way: after graduation, before high school. It was especially hot that summer, and the days ran together like rivulets, all identical, disappearing into the horizon, until it was the end of August and orientation for the enormous building where I'd spend the next four years was around the corner. We had shopped, my mother and I, for fall clothes—browsing the aisles of the men's department of Bloomingdale's, since it seemed I'd graduated not only from eighth grade but also from the boys' section—and a new backpack, a laptop and printer, the required books for freshmen listed on the high school website, a new seat for my bicycle, and a new cell phone so we always would be in touch. We'd had laughing lunches in sidewalk cafés separated from the traffic by tall hedges, or planters filled with flowers that attracted bees, or juniper trees in pots where customers and passers-by stubbed out cigarettes that waiters pulled out with gloved hands and dropped into green boxes that looked more suitable for birthdays than for cremated tobacco. We'd found suitcases and a duffel in the attic for class trips to Washington and New York City; we'd printed maps of the three floors of the high school so I could memorize them ahead of time; we'd bought a bus pass for days when the weather was too awful to bike. And when everything was organized, all the checklists checked off, on a Sunday afternoon I looked for her and she was gone.

It was so unfathomable I could not at first even formulate a question. She couldn't be gone; she was just here, this was where she lived, this was where she belonged, and the calendar on her desk was blank for the whole week, so there was nowhere else she could be. . .and blank for all the weeks following, a clue I at first refused to recognize. My father had not seen her since breakfast, had thought she was in the garden while he graded papers in his study. I had been out with friends, came home in late afternoon and looked for her.

"What did I do?" I asked my father. "Was she mad at me?"

I asked him that after I'd gone through the house a fifth time, looking in closets (she might have gone to get a sweater and fainted); searching the attic (she could have been looking for something and hit her head); crisscrossing the backyard, holding aside bushes to peer into the darkness and turning around in the middle of the toolshed to stare at its clutter (she maybe tripped over some garden tools and got knocked out).

"You didn't do anything," my father said. His voice was heavy and he kept looking at his hands. I wished he'd put his arm around me, the way he did on my birthday, but it seemed like that wasn't going to happen. "She's talked about leaving."

"That's not true! That's a goddamn lie!"

"Don't talk to me like that," he said, but it was automatic and flat; he didn't care how I talked, at least not then.

I assumed he was hurting inside, but it didn't show, and anyway his pain couldn't have been anywhere as bad as mine; I'd always known I was the one my mother felt closest to. She had named me Theodore after her father, whom she called a character and had loved fiercely if ambivalently. He'd died when I was nine, falling from the roof while picking apples from the tree that overhung our house, but I'd known him long enough to be familiar with his erratic life, a long, colorful graph of highs and lows.

There were short-lived periods of elation when he had bit parts in television sitcoms or commercials; longer ones when he was recording voice-overs for documentaries; and the best ones, when he'd won a respectable part in a film. But in between were empty weeks with no work, no calls from his agent, not even an autograph-seeker in the shopping mall, and that was when he'd suddenly take up flying or scuba diving, spend supine hours in his backyard watching hummingbirds at the feeder or, in a manic flurry of activity, haul out the ladder and climb the roof to pick apples.

I could not say I loved him, but my mother did, so I tried to emulate her patience and constancy, and he was a large presence in my life. And I bore his name and his blue eyes, so unlike my mother's black ones, and his straw-like hair and the narrow nose he called aristocratic, which drove home how close, in fact, we were. And of course we were close in the most important way of all: we both adored my mother. And she us.

All of which helped explain my pain, far greater than

my father's ever could be. I tried to imagine the two of us sharing our home as a refuge, shopping together, eating lunch at sidewalk cafés. No and no, but especially not the cafés. My father abhorred them: he said eating coterminous with the noise and fumes of traffic and the stares of passers-by was not a treat but an excruciating ordeal. "The music of language," he said, "when language does have music, which is too seldom these days, requires a hushed and tranquil space, or the nearest we can come to that in a cacophonous world, for us to hear all the notes."

My mother and I often were exasperated with my father's manifestos on the coarsening and steady decline of civilization, but if he noticed our reactions he never said so: he would continue until, whether from a fully developed thesis or exhaustion, he would come to a halt, nod once or twice in confirmation, and return to his study where, we knew, he was most comfortable, as we were in the kitchen or den, talking, reading together, watching television.

"She came from a small town," said my father. We'd been quiet after he'd told me not to swear at him and we'd sat for a while looking at the floor. "A speck on the map near Winnipeg."

I looked up at that. "Canada?"

"She didn't like to talk about it. Her parents were wheat farmers; they made a good living, but they identified themselves as inferior to anyone who'd gone to college and worked in an office in a city. They'd never been to Europe or, indeed, much of Canada; now and then they visited Toronto and arbitrarily picked a play or nightclub for an evening out, but that only reinforced what they saw as the imperfection of their lives. Evidently they truly loved farming and their farm and could have been content if they'd allowed themselves to be, but it seems they could not, so of course neither could their daughter, and she made sure the college she chose was a long way from Canada."

"Did she go back there?" I demanded. "Where is she?"

"I have no idea. You'll have to believe that. I'm sure she would not go back to Canada." He nodded. "She took my course in Renaissance literature her first year of college, and at the end of the year, on her eighteenth birthday, we married, very quietly; it was frowned upon for faculty and students to have relationships, much less marry." He smiled. "That is an understatement."

I was so angry I could not talk. Why had neither of them—why had she—never told me any of this?

"She wanted you to think of me as a father, not a professor," my father said, surprising me with unexpected insight into my thoughts.

"If, in a lifetime of teaching," he went on, almost to himself, "a professor finds a few students with the impassioned eyes, the craving to learn that gives him faith in his ability to shape the next generation, he is content. Or should be. Isabel was the student every professor dreams of, justification for the drudgery in too much of academia these days. My God, we did adore each other."

He stood up. He paced. He paused, frowning, head low. He slumped and looked old. He sat down. He looked to me as if he was trying out for a part on a Shakespearean stage. Anyway, I'd already rejected what he was saying; in any imagined pairing of my mother and father, I could not begin to find a place for adoration.

"I taught her everything: what to eat, which wines to drink, how to cook, how to dress. She learned to read critically and then to write, little stories that were mostly fragments, and poetry that was wild and derivative, but alive. In our first few years, she liked to read them aloud, to herself and to me, with gestures. That vitality. Of course that should have alerted me, but I was pleased and in love and not paying enough attention. It was sufficient that whatever I taught she learned, whatever I rejected she rejected . . . at least, in the beginning. Later her opinions began to diverge from mine and, again, I did not pay enough attention. By then, of course, she was obsessed with you."

Obsessed. My mother was not obsessed with me. She loved me.

This was turning into the longest speech my father ever had made to me. I knew he had a reputation for brilliance, for the breadth of his knowledge of the Renaissance, his scholarly articles and books, his talks on Florentine culture and daily life as slightly stretched metaphors for our modern age, but I knew he was dead wrong about my mother. He had no idea what she was really like; he didn't understood the first thing about her. Or me. Scholarship is fine on a campus, but it's a total failure when it comes to families.

Unless my mother really had loved him. I supposed she could have, at least in the beginning when he was the big wheel and she was just a student. But later, she woke up. Or something. Their opinions diverged. And then . . . what?

"She stopped loving me," my father went on, again as if answering my question, and I gave a little jump of surprise. I didn't want him to know what I was thinking; we'd never been close enough for that. "Most likely she grew tired of being a student. My student. Or, once given the tools, she became dissatisfied with ideas and conclusions not her own, especially mine, and it would be irrelevant that I'd spent a lifetime honing them. It was so sudden, as if between two minutes, but most likely that is simply what I want to believe: that it was a kind of revelation, a cataclysmic hormonal shift that cast everything familiar to her in a blinding, epiphanic light. You will say I should have seen it coming, and of course you would be right. Few things in life happen without a warm-up. There would have been clues, hints, scatterings of events leaving a trail to this weekend. I could go back and search for them, but why bother? She is gone. She stopped loving me. Of course"—he looked at me for the first time in his long rumination—"she loves you, but at some point that wouldn't be enough for a lusty woman. You're an exceedingly bright boy; she knows you'll be fine."

"What are you talking about?" I asked. "I'm not fine. And she's not lusty."

"Meaning?" my father asked. "What does lusty mean?" Even through his gloom he looked amused.

I was staring across the room, out the window, anywhere. "You know," I said, but it was really just a mumble. Fathers weren't supposed to broach this kind of thing with their sons unless they were looking for some kind of confession, and, at thirteen, I was short of things to confess.

"Exploding with sexual energy," he said. "Fervid, desirous, needy. You and your friends would say horny." He sighed. "And why wouldn't she be? She's young and vibrant. And beautiful."

We sat there, looking past each other. "She started wearing striped socks," I said helplessly; it was too complicated to explain.

But he got it, or seemed to, which again surprised me. For a minute I thought maybe he'd changed, come into the modern world, my world, and we could talk, maybe—though this was a stretch—have some sort of male bonding to get us through the empty landscape my mother had left behind. I knew that wasn't possible; he was getting old and people don't change that much. Still, he saw something, because he nodded and half smiled and said, "Metaphors are by definition elusive, often unfathomable." Another pause, another smile. "Absent that, there would be few if any PhD dissertations."

So I knew, since he was already making jokes, he was recovering.

But I wasn't even close to recovery. Each day seemed worse than the one before; I was curled up inside with wanting, like I was wrapped around a lead ball in my stomach that weighed me down; I felt so heavy I didn't think I'd make it to the chair or the front porch or even to school. I cried every night, like a little kid wanting his mommy. I told myself to grow up, to look ahead like my father was doing, but the tears came, the heaving sobs that tore me up so I couldn't sleep and was always tired. That was the worst. I'd go to school yawning and I'd come home yawning and I couldn't remember anything that happened in between. I kept looking around for my mother, to see her coming through a door, or driving into the garage after doing errands, or sitting next to me while we read the papers or whatever books we were absorbed in then, stopping to read a line to each other or comment on something that would lead to a discussion.

I tried to get used to doing things without her, seeing sights without grabbing her hand to share a special scene, hearing people say weird things without turning to meet her eyes in one of those perfect moments of understanding that don't come often enough in a lifetime. I decided, after awhile, that it really was impossible to get used to the absence of those things; they were part of me—and of her, too, I thought, hoping she was hurting as much as I was—and I'd just have to live with them the way I lived with the color of my hair and how tall I was.

And it was true that after about four months it did get easier—the social worker at school had been right about that—at least I wasn't crying every night and I was able to pay attention to what was happening in class. It was as if I'd split in two: I went to school and studied with friends and talked to my father, when we talked, about school or, sometimes, a war or a drought or soccer game somewhere in the world; but at the same time, everything was empty and echoing and I hated being alone, meaning without my mother, and I didn't give a damn about anything, anywhere.

My father, on the other hand, seemed to be doing fine. I couldn't believe how fast he recovered. He was withdrawn for the first few months of our bachelor existence, but I didn't hear any moaning from his bedroom, and I don't believe he missed any of his classes in that whole time. And then, less than a year after what I still called The Great Desertion, he found Georgina, a young woman at least half his age, who began making appearances at our dinner table, then in our kitchen in the late afternoons, cooking briskly and, I have to say, creatively, with my mother's pots and pans, and writing long lists for the cleaning lady of tasks we and she had overlooked or ignored. And then she moved in.

My father had given me advance notice before she cooked dinner the first time, and then gave it another twist a couple of months later, almost at the last minute: a casual throwaway. "Georgina is moving in." It was not exactly an opener for discussion. "She'll make no demands on you." Which was ridiculous; of course she would, as soon as she became mistress of the castle and sovereign over the only offspring; and, though he was not seeking advice, or even comments, I did try to make the point that he was still married, and did she know that, and was he going to divorce my mother in absentia, but my father would not be drawn; he gave vague replies until a taxi pulled up and the new Queen of the Night herself took possession, directing the driver to carry her suitcases upstairs to spare my father's back.

Of course I didn't like her; none of us had thought I would. She was pretty in a plump, blonde way; in fact, her hair was the same color as mine, which I thought unfair. She had a tinkling laugh that didn't go with her plumpness and scratched on my spine like fingernails on a blackboard, and she talked almost in a whisper so you had to lean in to hear her. Their conversations consisted almost entirely of my father's disquisitions on the Renaissance or whatever current crisis motivated him to expound, wherein he would stop to explain things ("Václav Havel was president of Czechoslovakia and a playwright," "Truman recognized the state of Israel in 1948," "Our banking system was the creation of Alexander Hamilton") and she would nod brightly, but though she remembered what he told her and could regurgitate it, I was never sure whether she was incorporating each night's cornucopia of facts into a context that would amplify or replace whatever view of the world she'd had before, or whether she was simply storing isolated bits of information she could pull out at a moment's notice when one of my father's speculations or analyses called for a response. It was not that she was stupid—in fact, she was quick and clever—but she seemed to have slept through school and bypassed books and newspapers, or maybe just never cared.

She was an excellent cook.

She was kind and paid some attention to me, but not a lot. She didn't seem to care what I thought, or whether I was watching when she gave my father these little touches that made him smile and made me uncomfortable. Neither of them, in fact, made concessions to me; sometimes my father was in such a hurry to get her upstairs he forgot to say goodnight, and, when she was aware of this, she'd give me a glancing look over her shoulder that said she was sorry, but boys would be boys, as if she and I were all of a sudden partners who found my father amusing.

I didn't like her. But I repeat myself.

My father gave her a credit card and she transformed the bedroom he'd shared with my mother and she made it nice, actually, really nice. I'll give her that: she had an eye for design, and it was like sunshine in there.

Every day she went off to her job as a tour guide on a double decker bus in the city, and in the hour my father and I had together, before I went to school and he left for his first class at the university, we downed the breakfast she'd made and gathered our things for the day, talking about this or that, but never about her.

In fact, except for that hour in the morning, we were hardly ever together. I found ways to get invited to friends' houses for dinner, or a bunch of us would go out for pizza or hamburgers after basketball or fencing practice. Now and then my father would make some comment about never seeing me, and then I'd stay home for dinner, and we'd listen to Georgina describe people she'd met that day or changes in the city she had to incorporate into her talks on the bus, or my father would go on and on about some research he was doing, and then I'd go upstairs to do homework. But we never had what people said were real family dinners with cheery smiles and deep discussions and serious questions about my growing up and what did I plan to be in my future and did I have a girlfriend. I'd answer a few questions about school, and then Georgina would tell another anecdote or my father would go back to introducing her to the Renaissance, and I'd be gone. Georgina had tried a few times to talk to me, but I didn't want to talk to her and I didn't hide it, so she gave up and concentrated on my father.

I wasn't having fun anymore, not at school, not at home, not even with friends, so one day, at the end of my sophomore year, on my fifteenth birthday, I left, to find my mother.

I'd thought about it earlier—constantly the first few months, sporadically after that—but I never could put together a plan: which way to go, where to look, how to find somebody to talk to.

I was, in this way at least, my father's son: I turned to research, to books on the search for a parent, which I now think was pathetic but, at the time, seemed reasonable. The library was full of those books: forlorn novels, poems, essays, memoirs. I remembered then that my mother had liked them; she had favored fiction and especially stories of loss or dysfunctional families. I had my own favorites, mainly Patrick O'Brian's sea adventures, but now and then I also read her choices so we could discuss them, like, which was worse: being abused as a child or losing a parent, loved or not.

Or, I could add now, being deserted.

I picked out a few books about absconding parents, but no matter what the ending--happy (reunion and joy) or desperate (reunion and resentment) or tragic (no reunion, no information)—I hated them: the few happy ones were preachy and self-congratulatory, as if the will and talents of the searcher were all it took to rehabilitate a perfect family, but most were filled with whimpering or fake bravado or wild anger at being abandoned when a parent decamped, presumably to greener acres.

That was the one I understood. Not that I was angry; I was only curious, and maybe a little peeved that I was stuck at home while my striped-socks mother had embarked upon a whole new adventure. It did not bother me that I'd been making my way mostly alone, for two years turning to my father only when absolutely necessary, for the most part growing up solo while he was immersed in his new love and the Renaissance, lately quoting from Dante and Alamanni, Rabelais and even Erasmus to illuminate contemporary politics in dinner table monologues, with Georgina chewing silently but attentively at her end of the table. I didn't need my mother, that much was clear by now: I just needed to satisfy my curiosity.

And so, the day after my fifteenth birthday, I left.

Before leaving, I did tell my father, who gazed at me for a long meditative time and finally said, "You have no money, no means of transportation, no resources. Whom do you know, anywhere, who might offer you a bed, or a meal? Will you join the ranks of the homeless young who sell themselves to survive each day?"

"Sell?" Unbelievable, looking back, that I'd not heard of homeless kids selling whatever they had, which was, of course, themselves, for food, drugs, a place to spend the night. My mother had omitted them when she taught me about sex and the world. Had she thought she would always be here to shelter me?

"Through history," said my father, "that has been the most available coinage of uprooted people of both sexes and all ages."

"I don't care about history."

"My dear boy, of course you do. Your history is that your mother abandoned you. Now you want to edit history so it comes out as you wish."

"You don't think I'll find her."

"Unlikely. She was a determined woman—"

"Is."

"—a determined woman who peopled her fantasies until they were her facts. Almost indestructible. Once she thought I had taught her enough, opened enough doors for her to make her own explorations, she rejected my corrections, even my suggestions. She grew angry. I could see it, but however much I willed myself to silence, I could not let stand comments, judgments, analyses I knew to be wrong. If not wrong, at least misguided. Our quarrels would have amused, perhaps confounded, marriage counselors: every one of them was on academics. Through it all, her self-confidence was breathtaking, her immunity unbelievable. Machiavelli, master of the fine-tuned argument, would have been defeated by your mother. As I was."

"That's mean," I said, and hated myself for not finding a better word. But it was because I wasn't used to talking to him. "I'll take care of myself and I'll find her, and you can't stop me. You don't really care if I go or not; you're just talking like you're lecturing about somebody in the Renaissance, somebody you never knew."

My father sighed and cracked his knuckles, something my mother said made her shiver. "I've not been a good father; I know that and I regret it. And I apologize. You and your mother were a unity; laughing and chattering in your room, working in the garden, cleaning up after dinner . . . I could hear you from my study. I'd stop working and listen to your voices even when the words were muffled. As an excuse, that is very weak, of course: I could have joined you at any time. And I admit it was a choice. You could say, and I'm sure you do, that your father is as weak as his excuses."

He waited, but I couldn't think of anything to say. "She sat in the front row when she took my Renaissance class," he said. "Beautiful and smart and terrible at taking tests. She froze when faced with one. I let her take oral exams at the midterm and end of the year. Then she was fine; she needed the human voice. She liked people; she was comfortable with them."

He stood and took an envelope from his desk drawer. "When you come back, perhaps you and I will find much to talk about. Not the Renaissance."

He held out the envelope, then set it on the edge of his desk nearest me. "After your mother left, I put money away to look for her. That urge—"

"You never looked for her."

"I called her friends. I called our neighbors. I called everyone in her address book, and people she barely knew. The butcher, the cheese seller, the fish vendor, her seamstress, her hairdresser. I called the police and the hospitals. And I planned a trip, several, as many, I thought, as —" He looked past me, out the window, and after a minute I wondered to whom he was speaking. "She was extraordinary, you know. Even as our life together changed, she was herself. I recognized that even as I found it difficult to find words for her. Words are the engine of my life, but with Isabel, I struggled. I would find myself, in the middle of research, of writing, looking up to stare at something—the wall, a bust, the spine of a book—caught in the effort to find precise words to pin her down. The obvious ones—needy, amiable, eager, ravenously curious—I had coasted past in the first two or three years, and the same was true of proud, stubborn, self-willed. Finally I settled on the best, though still insufficient: alive, vibrant, insatiable, open. Of course. But more. Much more."

He looked at me then. "The idea of shrinking that vibrant, elusive woman to fit a document in a detective's portfolio, an image searched for by squinting at faces on buses and trains, peering into shops, showing her photograph to salespeople, reading police reports on unidentified bodies . . . I could not do it. At first it seemed merely difficult, then obscene. She was her own person and she did not wish to be found. What right did I have to contravene that wish, to publicize her private decision? And finally it seemed comical. An old man whose wife no longer loved him, behaving like a feeble romantic, fantasizing a happy ending. Why would there be a happy ending? She left on her own; she wanted this. Why would I attempt to forestall her, to undo her own scenario? Why would you?"

I didn't know. I hated him for asking. I hated him for maybe being right. And I hated him for not offering to go with me, for staying home with his Georgina while he thought my mother was vibrant, elusive, whatever. So I shook my head, saying no to everything at once, and took the envelope. "Thanks," I said, because I did need it, and he didn't have to give it to me; I never would have known it was there. And then I said good-bye, at least I think I did; all of a sudden it was hard to talk and I felt scared, so I don't remember what I said: maybe "I'll see you" or "Take care"—something like that—and then I picked up my backpack and left.

It was summer, so I didn't need much. I'd stuffed the backpack with T-shirts and socks, one good no-iron shirt, khakis and shorts, a jacket and a couple of paperbacks. I could hear my mother's voice, so I stuck in a toothbrush. The envelope, still sealed, was in my pocket with my fake student ID saying I was eighteen, and my house keys. The keys were just habit; I didn't expect to come back. And when I left—I'm embarrassed by this now—I shut the door carefully, quietly, almost as if I were sneaking out.

My mother had taught me the major cities and capitals of all the states, and a few places she had described with happy memories. I wrote down the three I remembered and took a bus to Washington, the first on the list. We'd been there together, she and I, on my tenth birthday, eating ice cream cones from one end of the mall to the other and taking in the White House, the Capitol, and every monument and museum we read about in our guide book. My mother had a story for every sight we saw—I suspect now she made up most of them, but they were funny and she was a true storyteller, her voice calm and matter-of-fact until the punch line, delivered with drama and sometimes giggles—the tales flowing smoothly from one monument or museum or outdoor sculpture to the next, giving each an aura of historicity that enchanted me and made them unforgettable.

This time I walked the mall alone, making one ice cream cone last the distance; I visited the monuments and museums, hearing again my mother tell her stories. I stayed in a motel in Virginia, using money from my father's envelope, and as the days passed I walked in ever-widening circles with the mall as my fulcrum. For two weeks I did all the things my father had scorned: I studied faces on buses and trains and oncoming as I walked; I shamelessly peered into open doors, showed her photograph to salespeople, and sat in libraries reading obituaries online. But after a time it occurred to me she probably changed her name as soon as she walked out on us, so I didn't call hospitals or the police, because I didn't know what name to give.

The envelope from my father contained more money than I could have imagined, and with it I wandered through Santa Fe, Denver, and as much of New York and Los Angeles as I could manage, picking neighborhoods at random, studying faces, staring into windows to see if I could catch a look at people inside, showing her photograph in butcher shops, fish markets, the kind of boutiques she liked . . . and I failed everywhere. I thought I must be doing this the wrong way, but I couldn't think of anything else, so I kept going, day after day, finally just walking dozens of blocks a day, looking from one side to the other, not really expecting anything but not able to stop. I could imagine my father asking what else I'd expected. It's a huge country; my mother is one small person, and she didn't want to be found. At least, I was pretty sure by now she didn't want to be found. So I had nothing to go on, not even clues she might have tossed my way before she decamped. I couldn't think of even one. She'd told my father more than she'd told me.

Anyway, if he'd been with me I would have told him he was right: I didn't have hope anymore, I was just moving for the sake of moving. It had been over a year since I'd left home; I was lonesome and worn out, and I guess worn down. I'd taken temporary jobs whenever they didn't interfere for too long with my search, and wherever people didn't ask my age or question my student ID, washing pots and loading dishwashers in out-of-the-way restaurants; tarring roofs which I was no good at and really hated; and sitting in a roomful of people telephoning strangers to get them to take surveys or buy products, which I wasn't any good at either since I thought every time people hung up they were mad at me.

I celebrated my sixteenth birthday with a huge slice of carrot cake slippery with glutinous frosting in a bookstore coffee shop, and a soft drink that was too sweet and a cup of black coffee that was bitter, feeling abandoned by everyone, not just my mother. The police hadn't looked for me. My father had not called me on my cell phone. My friends had called, early on, but after awhile they got busy and for the first time we didn't have a lot to talk about. It was good to hear their voices, but I didn't want to hear about girlfriends and football games and weekend parties and pizza nights, and even though I tried keeping up my end, finally it all just petered out. I wasn't surprised, but it hurt anyway.

By then, I didn't have much money and I was tired of sleeping in motels on noisy highways and eating cheap fast food and getting a stiff neck from trying to sleep on cross-country buses. And I was thinking about home, the idea of home. By now it had lost its sharp edges and taken on the soft fuzziness of memory. I couldn't recall exactly what had been so awful about it. I hadn't loved my father, but I was sure I'd never hated him; we hadn't talked much, but when we did, even when we disagreed on things, I'd never felt he was trying to destroy me. It was just that he kept pushing his ideas and conclusions at me. But it wasn't just me; he pushed them onto my mother and his students, Georgina, and I suppose anybody who might cross his path, as if he had to speak and have people listen for his ideas to be worthwhile. For him to be worthwhile. I mean, what would he be, without the Renaissance? I could imagine himself wondering that, a lot, and I thought that was sad.

But then there was Georgina. I didn't like her, but the truth was, I didn't hate her either. She just wanted to make a home with somebody who loved her, and I couldn't blame her for that. You can't really blame anybody for that.

I could go back, I thought. Give up and go back. Go home. Maybe one day my mother would wake up feeling just like I do now, so lonely it hurts, so unconnected it's an ache that doesn't go away, and she'd decide to come back. And how could we be together if I wasn't there when she showed up? Plus I'd missed a huge chunk of school and was way behind, but if I really worked at it, I could make up the work and graduate with my friends. Anyway, I was so tired, and feeling invisible. Nobody gave a damn about me: everywhere I went, when I stared at people, they averted their eyes and walked faster, away from me, and when I looked into windows, whoever was inside would yell something I couldn't hear and pull shut the drapes. So I didn't see any choice but to go home.

But then I thought of San Francisco. Those sad books on the search for a missing parent often mentioned it as a magnet for people wanting a new life. I was in Los Angeles, not far away. A week in San Francisco, I thought, maybe two, a last shot, not with hope, but just to be able to say I'd tried everything I could think of, that I was putting an end to a search that was maybe a waste of time but that I had to do.

In San Francisco I did not approach corners with a faster heartbeat, as I had in other cities, but the hills brought their own kind of expectation: anyone could be walking toward me, coming up the hidden side of the crest; anyone could be anywhere on those long streets that gave vistas up or down, all the way to the top of a hill or down to the water and the horizon. I told myself to stop making up happy endings, for not learning from all the past months, but in fact those hills, each one hiding another part of the city, brought back the reason I was there, all the longing, all the hopes.

So, even when, at last, the city failed me, when I saw no one who resembled my mother, when her photograph did not bring a single wide-eyed moment of recognition, instead of turning toward home, I looked farther, looked south to the dense towns and highways of the peninsula, and finally to the green spaces of Stanford University.

My mother and I had visited the campus once, when I was really young, not even in high school but already thinking about college. We had friends nearby, so my mother thought it would be a lark to visit them and spend a day on campus, a pretend day of checking out Stanford as if I was ready to fill out an application. We'd both been enticed by the sprawling campus where students chattered in a dozen or more languages and the sun turned everything gold and copper, bright white, adobe pink and deep red. I was twelve then, tall for my age, taking advanced courses that would allow me to bypass some basics when I got to high school, and I'd felt sophisticated and worldly just being in that exalted space. My mother had waited in the library while I visited some classes and ate lunch with students who answered my questions, and in late afternoon she and I sat on a bench shaded by palm trees, looking, I thought, exactly like the couples we'd seen that day on other benches and in student lounges and the cafeteria.

In a restaurant in Palo Alto that night, we reviewed the whole special day, laughing as my mother mimicked a couple of the professors we'd seen arguing vociferously on the walks between buildings, criticizing some of the architecture, because we thought there ought to be at least something to criticize, and mapping what would be my perfect four-year program. Once I said, teasing, that when I applied to Stanford, I'd declare my intention of accepting admission only if my mother would be admitted as well.

Now, among what seemed to be the same students, the same professors, the same sun warming the tile roofs of the buildings, I found the bench where we'd sat and stretched my legs along its length so no one could join me. I thought about my mother, about the past eighteen months, and about me. I was almost seventeen years old. I'd missed my sophomore year of high school and part of my junior year, and maybe there was no way I could make it up in a year and a half, so it might take longer than I'd thought to get here, but this was the place I wanted to be. Not with my mother; I couldn't even joke about that now. She'd made sure of that.

And there it was: my epiphany. It had taken all this time for me to see it; how stupid can one person be? But now it was absolutely clear. I thought of us sitting together on this bench on that perfect day, our laughter mingled, our hands brushing as we talked about the future ... my future, it's true, but as if it were hers as well. Two lovers planning a life.

My poor mother; she would have seen it far more quickly than I, and she would have been dismayed, even terrified. To be in love with anyone not her husband would be wrenching enough, how much more so if it were with her own son, recently grown tall and, as I've been told, handsome, and always adoringly joyful in her presence? Wrenching could not even begin to describe it. And because she is an incredibly strong woman, she would have faced the truth directly, and, as always, would have thought first of me. Which would have led her, with barely a moment's hesitation over the upending of her own life, to leave. Allowing herself no time for doubt or reconsideration or weakening, she left, to save me.

A truly amazing woman. She sacrificed everything—her marriage, her home, her place in society, and above all, her son. She ditched it all, for me.

Because she loved me. That was her delight and her bitterness.

And that had been the problem with her marriage as well. No longer could I blame my father for the failures between them; how could my mother be a companion to him when she was in love with another man? She tried, I know full well she would have tried her damnedest, because that's the kind of woman she is, but she could not love two men at once; she could not be in love with her son. My father I'm sure never knew that, but he understood that she had no choice: she had to leave. *She was her own person and she did not want to be found.* Her own person, with her own love, and her husband could have no place in that love, or at her side. And, though she probably tried to find a way to make him understand, there was no way she could honor him with anything even close to the truth.

Neither, of course, could I. However I put it, he'd think it was some kind of fantasy, some sort of Oedipal fairy tale I'd dreamt up to explain what I could not otherwise understand, and to get his attention. Even if he gave it a second thought, it wouldn't change anything; his feelings about my mother by now were fixed; nothing he heard or debated would change that. He had to have settled that in his mind before he could take up with Georgina. He was content now, maybe even happy, in a life that gave him another student to be his wife, this time one who would concentrate only on him, who truly would be his. At least, I hoped that was true. And eventually, if he thought of my mother at all, he would think of her with the adjectives he had told me were insufficient: proud, stubborn, self-willed.

But I knew those words were right for my mother. She was proud and strong-willed, courageous enough to create a new life wherever she could, with whomever she chose. She would not come home.

Which left, for disposition, me.

Leading to my father's pithy quote. *You're an exceedingly smart boy; she knows you'll be fine.*

And by now I really believed it: I would be fine. There seemed to be a nice irony in that. I had to conclude that my parents were fully capable of making separate lives for themselves, before I could decide that I could, too. The genes they'd lodged in me were exceptional, of that I was sure, and at some point it seemed obvious my life would be satisfying and even adventurous.

Until then, my father and I would find ways to live together. We might not love each other—I didn't think we had a good foundation for that—but we could share a home and learn to like each other, talk together, maybe, some day, even admire each other.

The worst thing would be living there without my mother, but I'd had a year and a half of travel without her, and it had been two and a half years since she left home. The pain was still there, like a bruise inside, and I figured it never would go away, it would just become another part of me, of the person I was becoming.

As for my mother, as for Isabel, I knew she'd long for me, but she would know that she had set me on a path that would lead to success, even triumphs, in whatever I chose. That would sustain her in her new life.

So I could stop searching. In fact, I had to stop searching: if I found her now, I would destroy the hard-won contentment she'd built on the knowledge of what she'd done for me.

I pictured her in her new life, living in a cozy apartment high above some pulsing city, alone except for a cat (she had always liked cats but I was allergic to them), working at some difficult but rewarding job, going to ethnic restaurants with new friends who admired her without ever fully knowing her, having difficulty finding a new love since it would dilute her love for me. And wearing striped socks.

I smiled, and a passing student returned my smile, and I thought how simple life could be when one understood its complexities. Somewhere I had read that only poets understand the true reasons behind our actions, and so, perhaps, I was a poet. You have the soul of a poet, my mother would say, and I smiled again, because she was with me now and always would be. And when I came here as a student, I'd make a pilgrimage every day to this bench and have a conversation with her. The kind of conversation and closeness you could always count on.

His Scheherazade

WHEN KATHERINE WAS YOUNG, she and her mother spent muggy summer evenings on the fire escape, wooden steps zigzagging up the back of their three flat, identical to those throughout Chicago's South Side, platforms for gossip, recipes, ailments, taxes, world series woes, politics, impertinent salespeople, obstreperous offspring, and the outrageous state of neighborhood streets, especially for old folks. The teenagers among them hurled from building to building the insults with which they dealt with sexual tensions, jealousies, fears, and attractions; their parents and grandparents aired definitive analyses of a world beset with bad backs and lousy politicians.

Katherine was twelve when she picked up enough threads of the conversations linking the fire escapes to know they bored her. "They're banal," she told her mother.

"Fancy word," her mother said. "You don't even know what it means."

"Dull, ordinary, silly," Katherine replied. "We learned it in school."

Her mother waved it away. "You're in over your head. It means colloquial, universal, familiar. You might be more careful about slandering your mother and her friends."

"It doesn't mean those things."

"Look it up."

The next day, Katherine came back. "Those are secondary meanings. My teacher said—"

"Your teacher is ignorant."

But sitting on the fire escape, Katherine knew for sure who was in fact ignorant, and silently wrote scenarios on leaving home, turning her back forever on the neighborhood and everyone in it. Even as darkness fell and the weak bare bulbs beside each kitchen door cast pale splashes of light on the people up and down the steps, she sat with muscles tensed to escape, to take her to places where she would be on her own, successful, admired, even loved.

At the same time, she had her eye on a boy two buildings away, older and darkly handsome, probably daring, the kind of boy who would want just the future she intended for herself.

He was talking to a girl on the fire escape between him and Katherine, but Katherine was sure that more than once he looked past the girl, directly at her.

"Not for you," Katherine's mother said.

"Why not?" Katherine, as too often, wished her mother's eyes were not so sharp.

Her mother shrugged. "Boys dump a girl fast when she eyes them but won't follow through."

"Follow through?" Katherine asked.

"You know what boys want."

Katherine flushed. "That's not true. People have friends. They don't have to sleep together."

It was an oppressive September night and Mrs. Snyder, from the floor below, had brought out a third pitcher of lemonade. "Katherine? A drink?"

"Yes!" She leaped up. "I'll come down."

"Friends," her mother said, amused.

"They don't even expect it," Katherine said from a lower step.

"Listen to yourself. Ignorance speaks."

His name was Dante Abbot. He had been born Dante Abbracciavento in Sienna, a sun-washed hill town of Tuscany, but his family, setting foot on the embracing shores of the new world, even before they spoke more than a few English words, Americanized it. Dante embraced it; he knew who he was and where he belonged: within six months he was talking like an American, reciting long passages of dialogue from television sitcoms, keeping hidden his love of Italian tenors, and rocking with his friends to Prince, Public Enemy, and U2. He had celebrated his sixteenth birthday a few weeks before Katherine noticed him, and his friends were mocking him for still being a virgin. A dark-haired, good-looking girl on the fire escape two buildings from his kept looking at him, and he wondered about her.

They met a week later when he saw Katherine walking home from school and crossed the street to join her. "You keep looking at me. What about?"

Katherine stopped walking. Close up, he wasn't as handsome as she'd thought, and he didn't look as brave. She was not even sure she was interested in him. But no boy had approached her, so she said, "I thought we could be friends."

"Okay. Then what?"

"And I wanted to know your name."

"Dante."

She waited. "Oh. Well, I'm Katherine. And I wanted . . ." What did she want? To keep him interested. "I thought you might help me."

"With what? Homework?"

They were walking again, coming to her building; she had little time. "No, it's a project. Probably too small for you, but I like it. School is so dull otherwise."

He nodded. "How old are you?"

"Twelve. Oh, shit." She muttered it, but it was audible, a word her mother kept telling her never to say; boys didn't like it when girls used four-letter words. But Katherine had been mad at herself; she'd planned to say she was fifteen; people said she looked it.

He laughed. "But you'd rather be thirteen or fourteen, right? Or fifteen."

Katherine muttered something again; she felt young and a fool and opened the door to her building.

"Hold on," he said. "What's the project?"

"Oh. Well, organizing things. People, I mean. I match girls with people who need help with homework or a paper or a book they can't figure out." She shrugged. "It's little, you know, nothing you'd care about."

"How come only girls?"

"They're the smart ones."

He laughed again. "And how could I help?"

"I can't keep track of what's going on. I have notebooks, but usually I'm in a hurry and I just grab a piece of paper, whatever I can find, and write down a name and phone number and date, whatever I need, but then it's all a mess and I know that's stupid when I have a computer, but I don't know what to do with it. They keep talking about teaching it in school, but people who run schools work in slow motion, like they're afraid of cutting a new pattern."

His eyebrows rose. "Did you make that up?"

"Make up what?"

He shook his head. "Do lots of people ask for help?"

"Lots. So far, twenty. And they talk, so I'll get more."

"And they pay you?"

"Well, obviously. Otherwise, why would I do it? It's a business." She stopped. "Oh. You'd want money."

"If it's a business, you'd have a staff. They'd be salaried.

I'd be your vice president for technical affairs."

She thought he was making fun of her, but she went on doggedly. "How much would I have to pay you?"

"Not much. Five dollars an hour. But I'd be fast."

He really was laughing at her, she thought, but he was interested, and that was good. "When can you teach me?"

"Right now?"

And that was how Katherine and Dante began.

A few months later, Katherine and her mother moved away, to live in the basement of the suburban home of her mother's brother. "Too bad," her mother said. "But when the money runs out..."

"How am I going to college?" Katherine asked.

"It's a ways off. I'll find a job; we'll be fine."

Her mother found work as a waitress in three restaurants. She was fired from all of them, after informing the managers of their poor performance and the corrections she said were obvious. "Just keep your mouth shut," Katherine told her. "There's a caste system in employment and you're at the bottom."

"Truth-telling is an art," her mother replied calmly. "People like me make the world a better place. You study that; it will get you far."

"I will never study anything you tell me to."

Her mother could not keep a job. "I deserve better things; I'm way ahead of these people. Someday I'll find the right place." In the meantime, she cleaned house and did laundry for her brother and his family, who were their landlords, and for their next door neighbor. "You can't do anything," Katherine said.

"I keep a good house; it's an art," said her mother, and

when she skimmed enough from the household allowances she was given to buy each of them a new dress, Katherine knew she had no moral platform on which to stand in judgment.

At her new school, Katherine restarted her business and soon was so busy she sent an email to tell Dante about her success. She wrote once a week, not about the basement rooms in which she and her mother lived, but about school, the neighborhood, her clients, her skill with spreadsheets and QuickBooks. "Everything you taught me." Occasionally, he replied. Katherine kept writing, often asking questions about his classes, his friends, his hobbies, a new email each Wednesday, dropped into the depths of his silence. She worked on her letters with seldom-used adjectives and verbs to get his attention, expanding her vocabulary, lifting metaphors from obscure novels, now and then attaching a particularly flattering photo. When she was in her third year of high school and thinking about college, and especially a college near Dante, she went to his apartment.

It was Christmas week; he was home for the holidays. "How's the business?" he asked. They were standing in the cold hallway outside his front door.

"Fine. It's evolved." She looked at the door behind him, open a crack. "I thought we could go for a walk; is that hot chocolate place still at the corner? You know, just a place to talk."

"You know, I'd really like to. But I have a friend here."

"Oh. Well, tomorrow?"

"She's here for the holiday."

Katherine flushed. Of course he had a girlfriend; he was twenty years old, a man. "Well." She shrugged and turned to go.

"I'll call you."

She shrugged again, feeling, as years before, young and

a fool.

"Really," he said loudly, but she was three floors down, opening the door to a blast of bitter air. She wished for a swift riposte, a snapping phrase he would remember with regret, but nothing came to her. She felt, unreasonably she knew, betrayed.

But he did call, three months later, home for spring break. "How about that walk?"

They walked in the park, still winter-brown but with crocuses flowering among green shoots of daffodils. The two of them were the same height, a handsome pair drawing glances of appreciation. "Tell me about your business," he said, and Katherine, pleased that he remembered, launched into a description only slightly exaggerated, meant to impress. Growing more animated, she described her clients, almost thirty people who needed the services her small army of workers supplied: helping with homework, tutoring, getting tickets to city events, shopping, cooking, serving at parties, even, once, cleaning a house.

His eyebrows shot up, and she became defensive. "We don't, usually. I don't even list it as a service. But this was different. One of the school football players—a tight end, but actually he's pretty loose—had a party while his parents were out of town, and when everyone left the next morning the house was a total wreck. It looked like a collision between a tornado and a three-year-old throwing a tantrum. The tight end was blubbering; his parents were due back in a couple of days. Eight of us put it back together; I had to help because I didn't have enough people. It took about twelve hours. We even replaced the liquor. I charged extra for that. Because of course we're not old enough to buy it."

He was laughing. "How did you get it?"

"Older brothers. They're always ready to buy liquor for anyone who asks. They say it's God's work."

He asked if her company had a name, how many people worked for her, how much she charged her clients, how she dealt with taxes.

"Taxes? There aren't any. It's not a real business."

"It sounds like one. Shall your vice president for fiscal affairs look into it?"

"I don't have—oh. Well, yes, thank you, I guess I just never thought of it."

Five years later, upon Katherine's graduation from college, they were married on a beach in Maine. The guests were Katherine's and Dante's friends, numbering ten.

Dante taught history at a university in California. Katherine rented office space in a building near the campus while Dante found a bungalow in the hills, and they moved in on a golden fall day that promised a future as smooth and clear as the early afternoon light that streamed into their rooms.

Dante furnished his office and posted on his door his teaching and office hours. Then he and Katherine set up her two-room office suite. They shopped for used desks and bookshelves, hired student painters and carpet installers, and browsed for paintings from street artists who, amazed and grateful, added a free work to each purchase. For electronics, they borrowed from Dante's parents.

It was not an easy transaction. "They mostly don't talk to me," Dante said to Katherine as they drove home after installing the computers in her office. "Just the basics. They've not forgiven me for leaving them out of our wedding. Of course it won't last, but I apologized anyway and let them know we'd cozy up to them from now on."

"You apologized? You didn't tell me."

"It wasn't important. It was to them, but not to us."

"You know we would have made it without them."

He nodded. "Do you mind so much that they're helping us?"

"I'm going to do this on my own."

He was silent for a moment, then said, lightly, "Do I have a part in that?"

"Oh, don't be silly. Of course you do. You know what I mean."

He let it go. He had noted his wife's casual use of the first person even when talking about events that involved both of them, as if 'we' had not yet entered her vocabulary. He could imagine that causing him pain at some time in the future, but for now he let it go. They were just beginning, feeling their way through that inchoate stage when patterns had not been formed, much less settled, and their lexicon was being stretched to encompass two people instead of the singularity that had been bedrock for so long. And, Dante acknowledged, each day they took wildly separate paths, Katherine building a clientele and expanding her old business model; Dante lecturing on history and planning the scholarly articles and books he would write.

When they were more settled, he thought, calmer and more confident, it would be natural to see themselves as a couple building a life together. It would all be fine when what was strange became quotidian.

To Katherine, he said, "You'll need someone, secretary, receptionist... what do you think?"

Together they worked out a business plan and Dante suggested names for the company. But in the end Katherine settled on her own, the simple, declarative *Services, Inc.* "No limits," she said.

He offered to interview for a secretary, but Katherine shook her head. "I'll do it. I'm the one who'll be working with them."

"Them?"

"I'm thinking of two people, as a start."

It was Katherine's company, her business, her preoccupation, even, it turned out, her finances, and Dante, his disappointment moderated by relief, returned to the social and political currents of the American civil war and Reconstruction period, where he was an expert. He was young for an expert, but several universities had offered him positions, anticipating a major career following his lauded dissertation which, when published, had perched for a time on best seller lists, reaping the benefits of vivid descriptions of battles and social and sexual relationships among families riven by war. His career, it was predicted, would feature groundbreaking books and articles, generous research grants, and, though this was not required, excellent teaching. That was more than he expected of himself in those days when he was unsure of so much: the depth of his own scholarship, the extent of Katherine's devotion, and his ability to satisfy both her and the academic community to the heights they seemed to expect.

He had not always lacked confidence, in fact, growing up in his and Katherine's old neighborhood, he had been known for a certain audacity. In high school he grew tall, became the star of the swim team, developed muscles that accentuated his leanness, and excelled in his studies on the path to a prestigious university. His friendships flourished along with his studies, and others looked up to him. Girls found him attractive. Accepting his parents' predictions as realistic, in fact inevitable, he foresaw a brilliant career in law or as the CEO of a corporation in the labyrinthine world of global economics and business.

Though no clues hinted at it, his high school years were the zenith of Dante's empowerment.

It is rare, but certainly possible, that one or two discreet events can alter a belief, a blueprint, a life. But in Dante's first year at the university, against all his expectations, that was what happened.

It took less than a month for him to discover his inadequacies. He was no longer the star of anything. His classmates were swifter, smarter, more broadly prepared for the future than anyone in the neighborhood school where his path had been so smooth. They had traveled the world, triumphed on debate teams, published high school newspapers and literary magazines, acted or directed in school dramatics, fed the hungry, tutored the disadvantaged. At eighteen, Dante felt dethroned. And more than once he considered leaving school or at least trading this one for another with a student body less formidable.

He stayed because he met a girl. Her name was Miranda—"from *The Tempest*, you know," which he did not, but he looked it up—and she was everything that symbolized the campus: attractive, sharp, sophisticated. She liked him in a faintly condescending but nonetheless, to him, flattering way, and he could set his success with her against his struggles in class and his failure at attracting the friendships he knew would enhance his status on campus. He never asked her why she chose him; he happily accepted her interest, the increased visibility she brought, and the security of a hand in his and a body beside his at night. They were together for almost a year, traveling through Europe the first summer they were together (her itinerary, her money), visiting each others' homes for holidays, planning to live off campus for their third year of college.

Later, Dante recalled those months as a heady mix of fantasy and the familiar, a time when he could wait out the despair that washed over him when his work was not going well or he failed to break barriers of class, knowing that on the horizon lay a life gliding in clear progression from a perfect wife to a perfect family to brilliant heights in arcane worlds mastered by only a rarified few.

It would not be long before he was forced to recognize the level of fantasy he cultivated in those heady months, but fantasy allows little space for reality, and if he saw clues scattered along the way, he skirted or did not understand them.

He was studying for an examination in business ethics when Miranda came to tell him she had grown fond of someone else. They had had many good times together, she said, but now, for her, whatever had been between them was no longer true: she wanted something different, something more, something that was not Dante.

He knew this was madness. His reality was structured on the two of them, forever. He had managed, with her help, to keep up with his classes; he had trailed her into the social life of the campus; with her guidance, he had expanded his interests; and he had found his place in academia when she suggested he concentrate on history, particularly the Civil War and aftermath. That was when he discovered a versatility and depth of which he had not thought himself capable, a capacity for original thought and polished writing that demonstrated an expertise that was at last and truly his own.

So he fought. Battered by her words, by phrases about self-fulfillment and a natural growing apart in young couples, he flung at her a litany of memories and all she would miss by losing him. He picked up the tempo as if volume and speed could propel her backward to a time when she had loved him. But even as he knew he was strong and virtuous, he heard beneath his rant, tones plaintive and whining, at worst, a self-destructive begging.

That night his roommate said, "A college fling, happens to all of us, not a big deal; lots more out there waiting." He offered anecdotes, metaphors. "Like baseball practice: you're hot and sweaty and it feels great, but it's just a rehearsal, it's not the big game. You'll know when it's real, like you find the perfect stash, beats all the—"

But Dante was sick of metaphors, exhausted by the effort to hide what really had happened, the words flung at him when, having run out of fresh ammunition, they had begun repeating themselves. "I just don't like you anymore, I changed, you changed, whatever. There are lots of reasons. And stop asking me what they are." But he could not stop: he pressed her, and at last she threw over her shoulder as the door closed behind her, "If you really want to know, you're a lousy fuck."

Does a wound change a life? Dante, at another time, with the high-mindedness of one who had a mapped-out future, would vociferously have denied it, would have claimed that we're all vulnerable to wounds, from a pinprick to a sabre cut, but even the deep ones last only until a new pleasure heals as it reminds us of the wonders still within reach.

Later, he knew he had been mostly right, but at the

time he was shattered and for months lived the life of an outcast, convinced that everyone, with a single glance, would recognize him as fundamentally and irredeemably flawed, and in what way, and would either pity or scorn him, each equally devastating.

Katherine's pursuit—for, after her third visit to him during his senior year, he recognized it for what it was—became a singular pleasure that finally broke through, and the night she said, as they lay together, "You're a sweet boy; great in bed, too," brought him back to the world, and, irrevocably, to her. He knew she never would cause a wound that would not heal.

They were well matched, Dante thought. They accepted with equanimity the hours apart in their first year of marriage as they built separate narratives, he at the university by day, and at home evenings and weekends, researching for a book on sundered families during the Civil War; Katherine in her office days, nights and weekends, making contacts by telephone and email and training the people she had hired to satisfy the requirements of clients already signed up. When she reached home, the two of them sat down to a late dinner prepared and kept warm by Dante. They lingered at the table, finishing a bottle of wine, sharing the day's events like explorers from separate planets trading adventures, amusing each other, becoming married.

Katherine built a stable and loyal staff, and her business thrived. Dante was admiring: where had she learned all this? In her first three years in California, she doubled her staff, moved to larger offices, and opened a branch in Washington managed by a friend from college. She was direct and disarming with clients who, at her suggestion or without it, recommended her to others; her name was becoming known. Since, in her kind of work, visibility and gossip were as essential as the privacy she guaranteed to clients, she joined the boards of directors of two corporations and conscripted Dante to escort her to galas and benefits for major nonprofit organizations that were always covered by the press. If Katherine knew what a reluctant date she had at her side at those large, milling affairs where he knew no one, nor cared to, she did not address it; she needed him and he never refused.

In the fourth year of their marriage, they no longer shared wine and conversation late into the night. Now there were the large galas, or evenings at restaurants, theaters, a jazz club they favored, where Katherine was the perfect companion, as if making up for the nights when she dragooned Dante into being her escort. And if, now and then, he had the disconcerting thought that her behavior was somehow staged, that, in fact, she might have been working too hard to seem carefree, Katherine, as if uncannily in response, would laugh softly and lead him to the dance floor, or take his hand to pilot him to the bedroom, and the thought would vanish.

In rare evenings at home or on leisurely weekend walks, Katherine regaled Dante with tales of clients whose oddities she brought to vivid life. Week after week, she unrolled a panoply of characters for his amusement and delight, weaving physical descriptions, even the clothes they wore, with the issues they brought to her offices, sometimes comical, often gloomy, some potentially tragic, many so minor she gave them to people new to her staffs, a few truly challenging, her favorites, which she assigned to her top people. She never revealed clients' surnames, but their given names were so apt as metaphors for the traits she described, that once Dante asked, smiling, if she made them up, but at that she became annoyed and dismissive, as if he were a child asking foolish questions, and he did not ask again. Instead, he praised. He called her his Scheherazade and looked forward to each night's storytelling as eagerly as did King Shahryar, who, through nights of wondrous tales, came to adore his own Scheherazade.

As Dante did Katherine. He watched her stride through life, tall, dark haired, striking, bold, positive. Everywhere, it seemed, she triumphed. In another few years, with branches in four cities, her income brought them travel and luxuries far beyond any Dante had imagined in his high school days of glorious contemplation.

They had no children, which Dante regretted, but Katherine easily accepted. "You'd be a wonderful father, but I'd be a disaster as a mother, so, truly, we're better off. Certainly any putative children are."

In place of the grand accomplishments Dante had envisioned, he had and was content with newfound passions: Katherine, marriage to Katherine, her admirable success, his smaller but satisfying publications and teaching, the events of daily life that were significant because they were shared. And with his rootedness in a center of learning, he discovered a love of solitary research and writing, of knowing that his best work was done in the quiet of his office and his book-lined study at home where he spent contented hours probing the past. And if the satisfaction of those hours was subtly undercut by occasional nagging fears that his analyses were, in the end, not as trailblazing, even revolutionary, as he thought while formulating them, still he depended on them for a sense of fulfillment and for defining who he was.

The present he cheerfully left to Katherine. In his

admiration for what she had built, there was not a touch of envy. He could not imagine himself in her role, as he knew she was totally uninterested in filling his. Thus, he knew they were the perfect couple, having not the slightest wish to encroach on each other's territory, having every wish to take pleasure in each other's conquests.

Dante and Katherine celebrated their tenth anniversary with a trip to Brazil and Argentina, engulfed in cultures, sights, and sounds so removed from their lives that they truly were foreigners, bringing nothing but their preconceptions to societies that swiftly proved them in most instances wrong, confirming that this was an adventure and enhancing their delights. As strangers in strange surroundings, they were equals, and their lovemaking, dancing and dining, their swimming and long stretches of companionable reading, their languid conversations over midnight drinks on their hotel balconies all took on a semblance of fiction they did not fully recognize until they returned home.

This time, Dante returned alone, to meet his classes, while Katherine traveled to her branches in Washington, New York, and Chicago. In those days and nights without Katherine, he felt unmoored, the dark rooms of his home unfriendly, even hostile, as if they had shut themselves off from him. His movements were from habit: teaching his classes, working on his book, preparing simple meals in their sleek kitchen, reading into the night in a single pool of light surrounding his chair in his study.

He went to two dinner parties by himself, saw one movie, but for the most part spent evenings at home, and therefore was surprised when the doorbell rang on the sixth night he was alone, and he found, on the doorstep, a young woman asking for Katherine.

"Out of town," he said. "Is there something I can do?"

"Not really, well, just give her a message. I came to say good-bye."

Dante opened wide the door. "Come in."

They sat in the living room and Dante offered her a glass of wine and refilled his own. "If you'd like to write a note . . ."

"I don't have to; you could just tell her how grateful I am. She saved my life." She looked around the room, at the low fire against the evening's chill, the patterned drapes shutting out the night, paintings on the walls. "This is so nice. Does Katherine sit here a lot? I'd like to picture her here."

"She does. And how did she save your life? And I can't give her a message until you tell me your name."

"Lily. Well, not really; that's the name Katherine gave me. But she won't remember my real one; I've been with her five years and I'm sure she's forgotten. Well, you probably know all this; she probably tells you all about us."

"Not everything. She gave you a name?"

"She said mine wasn't right."

"For working in her office?"

The girl laughed. "I never go there; why would I? I have my apartment, three of us have, on the same floor, you know, Katherine keeps us in small groups; that way we have friends to talk to, and still be on our own." She smiled at Dante. "I guess I don't have to tell you how wonderful she is, and smart. I mean, she hired me after I dropped out of college and couldn't tell my parents because they're teachers and they'd never understand. So I needed a job and Katherine hired me; she turned down girls who were a lot more beautiful than me, and when I asked her why, she said men fantasize better with somebody just pretty. I think she meant men put whatever face they want on you, as long as you're like a blank canvas and not something so striking they can't get past it."

Dante concentrated on absorbing what he was hearing. He understood perfectly well the profession Lily was describing, but he fended it off. He watched the girl, certainly not beautiful, but pleasant. Her voice was light, her features regular, her hair a light brown, or perhaps dark blonde, falling straight to her shoulders. Attractive without standing out. She could be twenty-five, perhaps more; the faint beginnings of fine lines radiated from the corners of her brown (or possibly hazel) eyes.

He did not know what to say; finally he asked what Katherine paid her.

"I thought you'd know that. Because, you know, it's really the other way around; she pays for our condos and helps us out if we're short, but we pay her, you know, out of everything we make, and it's fine; I mean, how else would we get anywhere without Katherine? She's like the best big sister we could have. In the beginning she bought my clothes and matched me with these girls, they're my two closest friends now, she helped us move onto the same floor so we can talk when we get lonely or scared, like, you know, there are times when everything seems to be sort of . . . well, every job has a downside, that's kind of a given. Anyway, the three of us have each other, and it's the best family I ever had.

"Katherine, too, she's family, and she takes care of us. It's amazing that she can, you know, with her company, I mean, she has hundreds—I don't know, thousands?—of clients who have problems for her to solve, her and the people who work for her, like once she was helping somebody get out of a lease, she mentioned it one day, and, you know, she's always so busy. We're just a tiny part of all that, but you'd never know it, like, she pays attention to us, she listens if we want to talk, you know, dump on somebody when things aren't all sweet and rosy, she buys us books and magazines to read so we know what's happening if a guy wants to talk, and it's amazing how many of them do, and she keeps our kitchens full of things, you know, hors d'ouevres and champagne, whatever, since most of the action is in our condos and we need to be ready. She chooses our clients, too, so we don't have to worry about grabbers or perverts, or whatever; Katherine checks them out and keeps files on them. And she spaces them out; she doesn"t want us working every day; we have to be fresh. Besides, we go out with these guys, well, not much, but if they want an evening out, Katherine makes sure everything is ready, she buys tickets for plays and musicals, and like if a guy wants to know what's the best jazz club in town or the best bar . . . one guy even wanted a poetry slam, which I knew zip about, but Katherine actually found one. She thinks of everything; I really love her; if it wasn't for her I'd be waiting tables someplace, I mean, that's what I was doing when a friend told me to call her. I absolutely love her; she's the absolute best."

Rapt, Dante was silent. Then he asked why she was leaving.

"Getting married. Isn't that amazing? One of my clients, the poetry slam guy, in fact, he's pretty dull but he's really good to me, and you have to think of the future, you know, how you'll manage when you get older. Anyway, he lives in New Jersey so we're . . ."

Dante stopped listening. He was transfixed. Where, in all this, was the woman he had married, lived with, admired to the point of worship? In all the tales Katherine wove, regaling him with colorful characters and scenarios featuring clients who needed help with travel or difficult children or neighbors, with finding a new CEO for a floundering startup or writing applications to colleges or shadowing spouses, and dozens of other crises large and small, never had there been a hint of girls being molded as high-class escorts, or whatever they called them these days. He tried to fathom a business model created by a woman whose horizon seemed infinitely elastic, expanding as she moved toward it, stretching past whatever limits she might have felt in the days when she enlisted Dante to help run a project she said was too small to interest him.

He told himself he should be appalled. Instead, he was fascinated. Not by Lily, who chattered on, but by his wife, and he needed time to think about what he was learning. "How many girls?" he asked.

Lily stopped short. "Katherine never said. We never met any others; maybe it's just the three of us. I bet it's not, though. She thinks big."

Dante ushered her out, suggesting she write to Katherine, saying good-bye in her own words, and mail the note to her office, and then he spent what remained of the evening reflecting on his wife and his marriage. He was not one who believed marriage, by virtue of vows exchanged, brought illumination to the darkest corners of each spouse's past or transparency to every thought and fantasy and dream. In fact, he had preferred to believe in mystery, that it was crucial to keeping a marriage tantalizing and intimate. Now it seemed to him his ideas had been wanting: he had omitted or ignored questions about tolerable limits, how soon or late mysteries might safely be revealed or discovered, how large the space they occupied as a percentage of the whole.

He believed in directness, even acknowledging the likelihood of cul-de-sacs and detours. He believed in honesty while knowing there would be occasional shadings. He believed in love and sharing and support, without contention or equivocation. He was a man alone, missing his wife, pondering what they would talk about when she returned.

In fact, he realized, he felt sidelined. He envied Katherine her life, her work, her ideas; for the first time he hungered to be part of them. She was creating an environment so far removed from the one they shared, it was as if she had divided herself into two women: one who roamed freely through an exotic landscape of her own creation, guided entirely by her own compass; the other a wife and companion in a terrain constricted, quotidian, even, perhaps, shallow. In her own sphere, she created, she initiated, she accomplished. She flew, while Dante, in his hermetic office, locked to his desk and computer, regurgitated—a word he scorned but one that now seemed appropriate—the American Civil War to find nuggets of originality.

He believed fervently that what he did was worthwhile, that understanding the past and learning from it, hopeless as that often seemed, was perhaps the most important tool available to humanity. But on this night, in the silence of his house, it began to seem a vocation worthwhile but narrow, focused on individual instances easily overlooked and, in the long run, of little impact. There was, he thought, no life in it compared to the sweeping accomplishments of those who influenced the lives of others in a wide arc constantly expanding.

When Katherine arrived the next day, she brought a treasure trove of stories; it had been a week rich in actors, plots, and predicaments. Dante listened, admiring her liveliness and fluency, and not once, in their happy reunion, was the name Lily mentioned, until one night, nearing the time for her next trip, casually, she asked, "And what did you think of Lily?"

Dante listened for undertones but heard none. "I meant to tell you," he said. "I suggested she write to you herself and of course she did. And told you she'd been here. A pleasant young woman. She adores you."

"She's very sweet. Very young. She comes from a farming family, you'd hardly know it now, but when I first met her..." There followed the story of Lily's youth and mishaps, pregnant at fifteen, a miscarriage and illness that took her parents' savings, harassed when she returned to high school, stealing costume jewelry to sell at flea markets. It was a long story, colorful, detailed, sad. Dante, awed by Katherine's inventions, did not mention Lily's version or profession or impending marriage. He no longer knew what was true; he was not sure he cared.

In the week Katherine was home, they spent their days and nights together—almost a honeymoon, Dante thought with troubled irony—cramming the hours with museums, theater, opera, night clubs, art openings. Lily had no place in that frenetic schedule, except as she clung to Dante's nagging memory. And so, as soon as Katherine was gone, he did what once he would have thought unthinkable: he went to her office at night and, using the keys he found in her desk at home, began a methodical search of her files.

For the next week, he divided his time: by day at the university, writing the stories of separated families during and after the Civil War; by night riffling through Katherine's folders. He found files on people he recognized from her vivid tales—politicians, actors, bankers, chefs, even the keeper of a recalcitrant lemur in Chicago's Brookfield Zoo. The anecdotes with which she had enlivened their evenings were all there, documented in detail, with copies of contracts, fees paid, check numbers, dates. He remembered wondering if she was making them up to entertain him, but it was clear she had no need of that: the activities of her company were a compendium of drama, humor, the mundane, and occasional tragedy that had no need of embellishment or exaggeration.

On the fourth night of his excavations, he found Lily and her two friends, plus a menagerie of nine others in Chicago, Los Angeles, and Miami and, from what he could tell, Katherine was collecting income from them that matched her other top billing services. There were plans, he saw, for New York, not yet completed.

On the sixth night, he came to drugs, something he had been dreading, a file containing letters, each still in its envelope. He read the one with the earliest date: two pages referring, at first, to benzoylmethylecgonine, thereafter to 'the product.'

He sat for a long time, the file a weight in his lap, feeling helpless and angry and finally enraged. He savored the rage as a bulwark, its alternative being fear, and he could not allow himself that, knowing it would make him vulnerable when he confronted her. Because of course he would confront her as soon as he concocted a scenario.

He sat, indecisive, furious, alienated. He needed someone on whom he could dump all this so he could relax, confident that advice would be forthcoming. There was no one. No friend was close enough, no family member was an intimate, no professional could be trusted. With any other plot, he would have turned to his wife. Not now, he thought. Perhaps, not again. He was alone, seeing himself as victimized.

His watch showed midnight; he had an early meeting the next morning. He had been wavering between returning the file to its place or taking it home to have ready when Katherine returned; now he chose a third course, opening it again to read the remaining four letters. And it was then he learned that Katherine had turned down the job, no reason given, other than that she was too busy to take on another client.

She turned it down. She had drawn a line and stayed behind it. And he, her loving husband, had not trusted her to do that.

Shamed, he returned the file to its place in the cabinet and shut the drawer. He locked the drawers, he locked the door of her office behind him. There was no need to look further; the worst had been offered and rejected. He knew all he needed to know. Her escort services aside, she had done nothing he would not applaud, and however he viewed those services, he would not condemn her for them. What remained from his time in her office was contrition: she was better than he. But he had known that for a long time.

And yet. Dante was a historian. His life was built on research and further research, not stopping until all known and speculated paths had been explored. As all historians, he used fables—Pandora opening her box, Bluebeard's wife unlocking a forbidden door—as reminders to dig more deeply for layers of truths. And so he was not surprised to find himself, a month later, with Katherine on an extended trip, once again in her office, prepared for further burgling.

He found more of what he knew: the seemingly inexhaustible predicaments in which people found themselves, the demands to solve every problem, real or imagined, to untie knots and smooth rigosities. His wife was canny and persistent; she plotted action and with sure instinct matched each job with the best person from her staffs, all of whom seemed clever and content to follow her rather than strike out on their own. She inspired loyalty and rewarded it.

Dante wondered again how she had learned so much so quickly, so much that seemed arcane to him. But, reading her files, he began to see patterns, how she corresponded with clients, how she handled performance reviews with the managers of her three branch offices, how her choice of clients fell into categories, some accepted easily, others requiring several interviews, still others turned down without explanation. He began to understand her decision making, the source of her authority. Calculating the distance between Katherine's world and his secluded university office, Dante felt his envy unfold and, for the first time, wondered how long she would be content with him and the boundaries of their marriage.

In the second week of Katherine's absence, Dante's hours perusing her files became his happiest time. Each day on wakening, he already was anticipating the evenings when he would take his place in her chair in the office charged with her presence. He heard her voice as he read through documents recording negotiations, assignments, and completions, but most clearly he heard her through her letters: brisk, careful, thorough, with personal touches for each recipient. Reading them, Dante felt the warmth of her, seated just beyond his circle of lamplight, and sometimes put out his hand as if she might indeed be there, narrating the conquests of her days. His work at the university became secondary; soon he was going to Katherine's office earlier each evening: as soon as her staff and the cleaning crew left, he unlocked her door and settled in, welcoming her ghostly presence that helped bridge the time to her return, soon only three days away.

It was then that Dante came to a file with the name Ophelia, simply that. Curious, because Katherine was not an admirer of Shakespeare, he took out the slim folder of letters and began to read. These were different from those he had been reading: colder, more cryptic, almost anonymous. They spoke of two assignments carried out in separate cities and payments made, amounts not specified. They were sent to recipients at post office boxes. They included no designated task, no methods of completion, no final report. There was no mention of Ophelia.

Dante, the researcher, read through the letters again, isolating facts. Both assignments had been carried out by George Wilhelm Meltzer, one in Atlanta, the other in Detroit. One had been three years ago, the other a few months ago. In both cases, payment by the client had been made to Katherine who then paid Meltzer. The client was unnamed.

Curious, troubled, Dante stayed home the next morning and searched on his computer for George Wilhelm Meltzer, focusing on Atlanta newspapers around the time of Katherine's payment.

He was not there, which was not a surprise. When Katherine needed outside help, he thought, she would find people who knew how to stay out of newspapers or the evening news. So he searched further, retrieving Atlanta newspapers from the week bracketing the dates in Katherine's files, and skimmed them for unusual events or sudden changes or discoveries.

He found a handful of singularities. And one that stood

out.

. . . shot and killed by an unknown assailant at about ten p.m. last night. According to his neighbor, he had been at a meeting of the Atlanta Investment Group, of which he was a founder, and as he emerged from the private club where the meeting was held, he was shot at close range. No one else was injured. The assailant has not been found.

The victim was a businessman and noted amateur golfer named Hugh Staatsworth. Dante recognized the name, and he knew where he had seen it: among Katherine's clients.

Later, he would reflect on the smooth progression of his discoveries that morning and through the night when he returned to Katherine's office and tore through her files a second time. When he found the folder, he took it home, to use his own computer, and once again opened the Atlanta newspapers, where he found Hugh Staatsworth, photographed as he accepted a trophy at Pebble Beach.

The local reporter who covered that tournament wrote that Staatsworth had been predicted to finish at least two strokes behind last year's winner, but he played aggressively, while the front runner had been oddly lackadaisical, later saying he had felt unwell, some kind of stomach thing, he thought.

A stomach thing. Good timing, Dante thought. Not dangerous, not deadly; the golfer was fine in a day or two. But sufficient.

It was not an obvious connection; he knew it should be dismissed without further information. Instead, he skimmed the article again and knew he would hold onto it. Now so thoroughly immersed in Katherine's life, he could not ignore or gloss over linkages that might seem a stretch elsewhere, but in this place, at this moment, could be accepted as a logical surmise.

He told himself to slow down, back up, and go over what little he knew. It was not much: Staatsworth had won the tournament, or his main rival had lost, most likely because of illness. A leap led to the possibility that one of Katherine's employees had managed to incapacitate the rival with something mild enough to cause brief but disabling discomfort, and to accomplish it without arousing suspicion. A separate note: some time later Staatsworth was killed. Dante could see nothing to connect those two mysteries. Except, perhaps, Katherine.

He considered replacing the folder and ending his search. He could ask Katherine to explain what he had found and that would be the end of it. But he pulled back. He wanted to know more, to make discoveries on his own, not filtered through Katherine's narrative. And the story lay there, its gaps winking. He could not ignore it.

He opened another folder and found a copy of a receipt for payment by Staatsworth for an unidentified service. He made the working assumption that it was the doctoring of the golfer's food or drink; the date of payment was the day after the tournament. And on another page, dated almost three weeks after Staatsworth's murder, Dante found a payment to George Wilhelm Meltzer for 'General Services.'

He told himself, as before, that nothing was conclusive.

But, held to the light, the outlines of the scenario could not be brushed out or rearranged.

The magic of Katherine's voice in her quiet office had vanished. The warmth of Dante's pride and admiration had seeped away. Once again, he was no longer sure he knew who she was. What he did know was that he had to continue, to prove that he was wrong, or find conclusively that his wife was at the center of something monstrous.

His only key was Staatsworth's murder. That story could exonerate Katherine and end his search; he disliked the idea of her arranging the temporary sickness of a golfer, but it was Katherine and it was her business and so he could live with that. For now, all he had to go on was Staatsworth's Atlanta Investment Club and the meeting held the night he was shot. So that was where Dante began.

The Atlanta Investment Club, founded fifteen years earlier by Staatsworth and a small group of friends, had had a good run, the members investing shrewdly with a prudent amount of risk. But, after ten harmonious years, the strategy changed, skewed to higher risk. A young, eager reporter, hearing reports of acrimony, wrote a column in the business section, followed by a few stories in the next weeks of turmoil over strategy, members leaving, the chairman being forced out. When the economy shrank with Silicon Valley failures, the club's investments plunged, and where amity was required to rebuild, none remained.

The meeting at the restaurant, the reporter wrote, was to reorganize with former and new investors able to stay the course until the market rebounded.

But, the reporter wrote, quoting a member, "Staatsworth didn't have the money to invest in the new fund; he asked some of us for a loan, but nobody stepped up. He was upset, but then he said he might have a way to join in and we all wished him luck. He made a couple calls on his cell phone, then he sat around maybe half an hour, not talking, just sort of waiting. Then he left. That was when we heard the shots."

Dante shut down the computer and made sure he locked everything—the files, Katherine's office door and the outer door, and went home. He reminded himself yet again that nothing was conclusive, but already he was assembling a scenario. Suppose, he thought after checking his telephone recorder and noting that Katherine, unusually, had not called for three nights in a row, suppose Staatsworth called Katherine. Suppose he asked for a loan and she refused. Then suppose—because he might have been desperate enough—he suggested to her that he could tell the true story of the golf tournament; he could even write a bestseller about it; odder things have happened. He might have said of course he'd rather not do that; he'd prefer, as of course Katherine would, that the whole affair remain a sad episode of an upset stomach and that would be the end of it. The problem was, he needed money. This week. And he was sure Katherine could help him. With a gift, or maybe a loan if things went well, of, say . . .

Of how much? Dante wondered. What price silence, especially assuming it would be the first of many requests. He had no idea. It did not matter. What mattered was Katherine. And, if his scenario was even close to the truth, murder.

His adored wife, whom he had cherished and admired, whom he had watched with pride as she grew from raw beginner to skilled executive, whom he had envied as she built her school hobby into a multifaceted organization whose success fed greater success, whose tentacles spread ever farther, ever more prominently and prosperously.

With ever more at stake.

He sat through the night, unmoving. He always had found serenity in this, a position Katherine called his Buddha Mode, every muscle stilled, feet flat on the floor, fingers relaxed on his thighs, head resting lightly on the back of his chair. Only his thoughts would move, slowly, as ideas appeared, were discarded, reappeared in new forms to build a story that he hoped would prove useful. But tonight his thoughts had no direction or purpose. He could have said he was trying to find conclusive evidence that would calm the roiling within him, but an inner cynic taunted that he had moved beyond that, having already decided what was true. He did not need to build a story, because he already had one.

At dawn the telephone rang. Katherine, he thought. Due back tonight. He let it ring.

But his stillness was broken, and he began to pace the living room, dining room, study, kitchen, sunroom. He was possessive of his house; he had searched for it alone and purchased it alone while Katherine organized her company; he had chosen the furnishings and art works, had overseen the renovation of the kitchen where he cooked, and now was in charge of the cleaning crew and gardeners who came once a week. He wondered if other men had the same feelings about their home, wrapping it around themselves as a sanctuary, a validation, an essential embrace of rootedness and safety. He had no idea, but he saw it as a weakness in himself. Or perhaps not. He had to think about it. But not tonight.

The telephone rang again, and in the confusion of his thoughts Dante lifted the receiver. "Yes," he said.

"Oh, darling, did I wake you? I'm so sorry." Her voice was clear and buoyant, as if she were next door. When Dante was silent, she said, "Are you awake?"

"How is the trip?" he asked.

"Oh, amazing. You'd like the people here, incredibly friendly, outgoing, more than a little sly, I discovered..."

She related an anecdote about the woman she had hired

as manager for the new office, and Dante's confusion deepened; he was not prepared for even a semblance of normalcy. But then her voice changed.

"You'll know all this from a letter I just mailed describing the trip, the people, the new office, everything you need to know to keep it going, to build it. You should add it to the file I began before I left."

Dante made a sound, an audible question mark.

"The point is, darling, I'm not coming home. I thought you might have guessed that, but perhaps you didn't; you do tend to hunker down on the bright side even when everything points the other way. But, Dante, I'm sure you understand that it's better for me to be somewhere else from now on, you're smart and you see connections well enough for that. I've set it up so you won't have to worry about me or even think about me; I'll be fine, you know; you really ought to know that by now. Besides, you'll be busy: I'm giving you the company, and you won't have much time for anything else, at least not for a while. Of course you can keep teaching and writing if that's what you really want, but I think you'd have more fun dealing with real people instead of all those ghosts you spend your time with. Dante? Are you listening? Well, of course you are; historians are the best listeners. But are you still with me?"

"With you? I thought you just said—"

"I did, and you were listening. Very good. So you'll run the company—"

"Where are you?"

"I'm not going to tell you. Dante, listen—"

"God damn it, where are you? If you won't come here, I'll go there, wherever you are, but you are not going to end our marriage, end everything we've been together, without facing me and telling me what the hell is going on."

"You know perfectly well what is going on, and you know why. You know everything after reading my files these past few weeks."

Dante caught his breath. But then he thought: of course. How could he have believed she would not know? Still, he was stunned at the abruptness of it. "Spies in your office," he said.

"Oh, my darling, I don't need spies, I have a loyal staff. They protect me. When they saw it was you they didn't barge in; they just called me. You'll have to work to keep that loyalty, but I'm sure you'll do it; you're quick and lovable—"

"Stop it!" He stood and paced, his steps jagged. "Damn it, Katherine, this is insane and you know it. We built something together, it's solid and you know damn well you depend on it as much as I do. We have a history together and you are not leaving. Is that clear? You're not tossing our marriage away. You're not tossing me away. Everything you've done, everything you've made is built as much on us, on our marriage, as what you do in your office. You know this. Are you listening? You are coming home. We can talk about what's happened, what you've gotten yourself into, but I'm not going to let you throw it all away; we have a life together and I'm going to protect it if you're not."

"—quick and lovable," she went on, "and they already like you. I'm absolutely sure you'll do a splendid job: you love detail and organization, and you like people more than I do. We won't be in touch, so you can't tell me how you're getting on, but I'll know, because I know you'll be as successful as I was." She gave a short laugh. "Maybe more."

There was no strain in her voice. They could have been two colleagues engrossed in an amicable business discussion.

As, it seemed, they were. Dante slumped in his chair, suddenly helpless. This was Katherine who loved him, who slept with him and traveled with him and needed him. But if she needed him, it was not in her voice: every word was calm, measured, steady. He could almost feel her breath, she sounded so close and clear, as if they were in the same room, but the voice was disembodied; he could not read her face or gauge her body language. "Damn it," he said again, but it was weak. He stopped pacing and stood beside his chair. "I don't want your company, can you understand that? It's yours, you built it, I never had anything to do with it. I never wanted to be part of it, it was yours. Those people, your loyal people, need you, they're waiting for you. I'm waiting for you. I know you're afraid, but whatever happens we'll handle it together; we'll get through it. Tell me where you are; I can leave today, right now." He waited. "For Christ's sake, Katherine, you're being a child, you're having a tantrum, running away. Tell me where you are; if you don't, I'll use your famous company to track you down; you've told me often enough how good your people are at that. But don't make me do it, Katherine; don't make me hunt you down. We'd meet in anger and that's not what either of us wants. Tell me. Now. Tell me where you are."

"At home."

"You are not! What the hell is wrong with you? You've never run from problems before; you attacked them. You can do it again; *we'll* do it." He waited. "Christ," he muttered. He made a gesture of frustration, as if she could see him. "You don't believe me, that we can manage this, get through it, get back to where we were." He waited again. "All right, listen to me. Maybe someday, if we can't work things out, I'll let you go.

But not today or tomorrow or anytime soon. Not until we sit down together and talk about our future. There's so much we haven't even begun to talk about—"

"And we won't. You really have to stop this, Dante. Be quiet a minute and just listen. You're smarter than this; you know a quarrel will only hurt both of us, and you know perfectly well you won't get anywhere by giving me ultimatums. I've told you I am not coming back, that is final. And you will not find me. If you think my people would come after me, you don't know anything about them, and for your own sake I suggest you learn, as soon as possible. I am not coming back, Dante, you have to accept that; I'm not going to keep repeating it. I have a new home and a new business—I've been setting this up for a long time, which shouldn't surprise you—and I'm settled and satisfied, well, not completely satisfied, but as much as I can expect. Nothing you say will change any of this, and it would be easiest for both of us, especially for you, if you stop trying. When you think about it, you'll know it's best that I'm gone and that you don't know where I am or how to reach me. I'm out of your life, my darling; that's beyond discussion, and eventually it will please you. I'm saying good-bye now; you have everything you need, and we've said everything we could. I know you'll be happy and make a wonderful new life. I did like living with you; we had good times, didn't we? I'll remember them, and I hope you will, too. Good-bye, my darling; be well, be content. I love you."

Dante stood in place, the receiver dangling at his side, a recorded voice telling him to hang up. When he moved, he was sluggish, dragging through the house, trying to imagine a time when it would be natural to see each room as belonging only to him, housing only him, welcoming, at the end of the day, only him.

He could not. Katherine's voice hovered, her photograph was on his desk, her closets were full, her presence was in the chair she favored, the side of the bed that was hers, the chaise on the terrace where she read. But with all that, the night was over; the sky was brightening on what he knew would be a template for the days to come, and so he did what came automatically: he showered, shaved and dressed, and began to drive to the university.

He had driven only a few blocks when he stopped and pulled to the curb. The engine idling, he opened the windows and sat quietly, staring at the traffic, the purposeful drivers. Then, as if he had known all along this was what he would do, he pulled out, drove around the block, and headed in the opposite direction, to Katherine's, no, his office.

* * * *

Within six months, it was Dante's company. The five people who worked for Katherine had arrived early the first day he appeared, ready to welcome him and to switch loyalties, as Katherine had asked them to do. They were wary but polite and mostly deferential, because they now worked for him and they liked their jobs. And Dante, campaigning for harmony and admiration, taking charge more swiftly than he or they would have thought possible, became an executive, which he found he liked. He had feared a return to the pall of inadequacy he remembered from his college years, abandoned by a woman, out of his depth, alone with his insufficiency, but the years with Katherine and successes in his teaching and writing had given him a strength that surprised him and, almost from the first, he was having a very good time. It took only a few months for him to write in the journal he kept that the company was humming along as if there had been only a slight disruption to its pattern. By the time he finished the term at the university, sent in his resignation, and put aside his unfinished book—for the future, he thought vaguely—he had slid smoothly into his new life and rarely thought back to the one he had abandoned.

In fact, he felt liberated: absorbed, learning, on his own. His own career, his own profession, no longer viewed from the periphery. His also the suite of offices and *Services, Inc.*, the branch offices and their staffs. His house was a shell and he avoided it except to sleep. At some time he knew he would work on it to make it his, but for now he had too much to do. He had to best Katherine.

He outfitted a simple kitchen in a small storeroom next to his office and worked late each night, eating prepared meals from a neighborhood gourmet shop. He traveled to meet the managers and staffs of the branch offices and the company's major clients, and discovered that Katherine had prepared the way. A superb businesswoman, they all said, remarkable, thorough, creative. Not cozy or anything like that; none of them ever figured out how she really felt about them, but if something went wrong, they knew quick enough, and, bottom line, they were a little bit afraid of her. Not a lot; they were a team, after all, in a major enterprise, but enough to keep them on their toes. They were sure Dante would be just as sharp, just as demanding. They were glad to meet him, glad to be working with him, and of course they'd miss Katherine, but everyone needs a new direction now and then, and how clever of her to choose one while she was young and while Dante was here to take over. No one mentioned their marriage.

Gradually, Dante began to find new clients and work on new ideas, expanding into the disparate worlds of politics and the arts, challenging Katherine to tell him what was wrong with that; why she had not thought of it herself. In fact, he spoke to her day and night, at work and at home, seeking approval even as he was changing the way she had done things. He accepted the fact that she was gone, that she would not return, but he kept her close, especially as the company's income and influence grew, and he liked to envision her dismay at being surpassed.

All of it drew him in more deeply each day; each day was a discovery. He was helping people. They were grateful, they paid the excessive rates he now charged, and still they were grateful. He stood tall and bought expensive suits. A year later, when his staff saluted him with a celebratory cake and champagne, he could barely recall his life as a professor specializing in times past and, by many, forgotten. The cake was a testament, he told Katherine, the champagne a manifesto of independence and skills he was unearthing, capsizing everything he ever had thought about his own assertiveness and capabilities.

The old Dante, the historian, might have predicted a stumble, if not a fall, from such heights, but the Dante who ran *Services, Inc.* had let slip those maxims, and so was surprised, even offended, when, a few days after his one-year celebration, he received a call from the manager of the New York office, talking about "a mess, something we never thought of, a fucking, lousy—"

"What?" Dante said. It was a bark, and, more quietly, he repeated it. "What's going on?"

A fucking screw up, the manager said; a son of a bitch he'd trusted. One of his staff, Carl Ludlow, was supposed to get into this guy's house, a simple job—

"Wait," Dante said. "Get in? What the hell does that mean?"

"What it says. Get in. I know we don't do it a lot, but this was a good client and—"

"We don't do it at all."

"One of our top clients, and it was a particular problem we could help him with and it was easy, I mean we'd done it a couple times with other clients, Katherine knew—"

"What happened?" Dante's voice was rising.

"He got in fine, got the papers he was looking for, wasn't supposed to read them, but he did. I figured he might, but I never thought—"

"And?"

"Brought them back, the papers, and asked me what we oughta do with them. I didn't know what the hell he meant, like, we give them to the client, what did he think we'd do with them? But he's saying they're worth a lot of money and what did I want to do with them? Well, shit, I told him, ordered him, to hand 'em over, but all of a sudden he's talking about starting his own business and needing help to get started, and I could do that, invest in it, and when he was all set he wouldn't need these papers, he'd hand them over to me, son of a bitch, putting the screws on me after I gave him a job, trusted him . . . we vet these people, you know, the guy sings in the church choir, raises money for boy scouts, bikes on weekends with his kids, not a clue, not a hint . . ."

"Where is he?" Dante asked.

"Said he was going to his club. Waiting for my phone call."

"And the papers?"

"They're on him, he says. He doesn't trust leaving 'em anywhere. Jesus, you know, I can't fire him, what the fuck can

I do?"

Dante cut him off. "Give me a few minutes; I'll call you." He tilted his chair back and sat with his customary stillness, weighing options until the staff had left for the night. He stood then, locked the outer door, and went to the file with the Ophelia folder. He found the name and mobile number for George Wilhelm Meltzer, and, standing beside his desk, called it. His hand, he noted, was almost steady.

They had never spoken, but Meltzer knew Dante's name, and the call was brief.

"You want me to get hold of the manager?" Meltzer asked.

"No." Dante gave him Carl Ludlow's home address and the name of his club. "This is between us."

"And you want it . . . when?"

"As soon as you can get there. We can't put it off. And he'll have papers in some kind of envelope; take them with you. Let me know when you get back."

"Do you care how?"

"Up to you. Just . . ." Dante closed his eyes for a few final seconds, blotting out all that he was jettisoning. "Just take care of it," he said.

What Happens after Shoplifting

MY NAME IS BRISIA SANDOVAL. Brisia comes from Briseis, the woman loved by Achilles in *The Iliad* by Homer. I have not found anyone to love me enough to put me into a heroic poem, but I am young and I put my hopes in the unexpected and the mysterious.

(A mystery is how my mother—she who did the naming of all her children—knew anything about Homer or *The Iliad*, but only now, when I have learned so much more about her, am I asking that; earlier, I assumed someone told her the name and she liked the sound of it . . . and who knows? Perhaps that is exactly what happened.) I am twenty-three years of age, taller than average, naturally slim, and, as my mother often mentioned with a sigh, plain. (My mirror confirms this.) So plain, in fact, she directed me to concentrate on cultivating skills, arts, conversation, whatever would lead acquaintances to be so charmed or admiring they would find my face irrelevant, or, at the very least, a minor aspect of the Me they were appraising. I didn't like being plain; I thought it unfair. But there it was, and the best I could do was work around it by manipulating everything else. And, with dedication, that is what I did: from the panting precincts of a nearby exercise facility to videos on how to carry myself like a model, I perfected my body and my walk. With other videos and books I developed a pleasant but not pushy vivaciousness and lively vocabulary. Since then, men have looked at me, and looked again; women, too, though differently, which, of course, is to be expected. I enjoy being looked at—my mother said I crave it and that was probably right—and I plan each day's outfit for maximum attention.

Except when I am at work, when I wear a uniform and disappear into the woodwork, as, obviously, I am meant to do. Customers rarely look above my waist as I stand beside them to take their order; they aren't the least bit interested in what a waitress, even a classy one, looks like; they've come for fine food, perfect service, and a degree of obsequiousness, not overdone to the point of mockery, but subtle and therefore satisfying to those who expect it in everyone, everywhere, with whom they do business.

My waitressing is in the hushed, pastel dining room of an exclusive women's emporium. The room is large, with widely spaced, ivory-clothed tables and silken booths, tucked away on an upper floor behind the spacious department displaying silver, china, pewter, cut crystal, and what have you—all astronomically priced and exceedingly beautiful, as well as beyond the reach of most of humanity. In the restaurant, a hostess keeps order and sets the proper tone; the rest of us move discreetly, our midheel shoes whispering on the carpet, our smiles warm but without implications, our voices soft and neutral. We are so well trained, other dining managers come to study us and often offer us positions in their establishments. Some of us accept. Others, and I am one of them, stay. In fact, I would not leave for any increase in pay or benefits.

Why this is true of the others, I cannot say. For me, however, two reasons stand out. First, we serve only lunch, which leaves me ample time for myself. Far more important: the lunch crowd and I are a perfect fit. I study their clothes and shoes, their handbags, their jewels. I note hairstyles and hair color, and how, even minimally, they change over time. I memorize makeup, its subtle conversions, its errors. And I use my customers to build my wardrobe.

This needs some explanation. There is no way I could dress in a fashion that enhances the image I am perfecting if I had to pay for everything. First, on my salary I could not buy a fraction of what I need. Second, if I somehow did have the money, I would spend it first on a total makeover of my face, then moving from my mother's apartment to a place of my own, and, finally, shopping for the wardrobe that would fit a new face and my own living space. Since the chance of any of this happening is zero, I never had to consider how I would deal with my mother's withering comments about changing the face God gave me, or buying wildly expensive clothes, or throwing money away on rent for another apartment when the one we lived in had three bedrooms, small, but as my mother often pointed out, how many hours were we in them? My mother's voice was not loud, but it penetrated, each sentence a pronouncement. This was not true when she was worried or bewildered, as did happen, but mostly she delivered confident assessments or, less often as my brothers and I grew up, commands. I kept waiting for the day when she would stop, when I would wake one morning in a cocoon of perfect silence: the epochal life stage in which, finally, I would feel free.

Sandoval is a lofty name. It has been worn proudly by ancient rulers, Spanish politicians, artists, surgeons, baseball stars, actors, musicians . . . even a cardinal, even a creator of comic strips. My parents never would have aspired to be part of such a list had they known it existed. My father, dead now fifteen years from being in the wrong place at the wrong time—crossing 2nd Avenue at 106th street on his way to Macedonia Iglesia Pentecostal church at the same instant a geriatric driver with shriveled reflexes turned the corner and hit the brake half a minute too late—was a bricklayer, a good one, admired for his skill and speed, but that kind of accomplishment does not make the history books.

With her husband's death, my mother lost her faith. She still frequently invoked God, but as a shadowy presence with its own unfathomable itinerary, not a mover and shaker. She no longer felt protected. She did not say this in so many words, but it was clear to my brothers and me, and we followed her. No one in our family went to church after my father's funeral; no one prayed at the dinner table or at night before falling asleep. At first it was a shock, an absence that was loud in our lives, then it became routine and therefore not of note. Other people went to church; we did not. Other people prayed; we did not. No one cared; certainly not any remote mythical figure.

"*Sólo nuestra familia*," said my mother, and proclaiming faith only in her family was as close to a prayer as I ever heard from her lips.

To earn a living with four kids at home, she hooked up with two friends as a triumvirate of housemaids. The three of them had arrived in the city almost in the same week, moved to this neighborhood at about the same time, and soon declared themselves lifetime friends. Their English was whimsical but good enough, and they debated names for their company, settling on Triple Maids, which I found trite, but which amused them and made them proud. They vacuumed, mopped, scrubbed, dusted, washed and ironed their way through three apartments a day; their employers called them gems and paid them more than most cleaning women were paid, though that isn't saying much.

I had suggested to my mother that she read the contents of wastebaskets before emptying them, to find out what went on with those families—information which might prove useful in ways yet unknown—but, quite fiercely, she told me that would be wrong. My mother was good at knowing definitively the difference between right and wrong. In this case, she added, to soften the sharpness of her words, that, anyway, her reading of English was too slow; she could not take the time if she was to finish all three jobs and get home by six to make dinner for her family.

But soon that became my job. By the time I was fifteen, I was cooking for my mother and, when they were home, which was too often for my taste, my three brothers, all older than I and capable of helping out, but too macho from birth to pick up a rag or a saucepan. They did leave, however: by the time I was eighteen they had taken off in their own directions, leaving my mother and me to get along in the empty spaces they left behind.

We were not rich. In fact, we were poor. But that is an inadequate description. 'Poor' has many definitions, and one's financial position teeters on stepping stones of circumstance, from sleeping on the street to sleeping in a mansion, the latter if one has been accustomed to sleeping in a palace. 'Being poor,' is an empty phrase, not the kind that instantly explains itself, like "snow is white" or "roses can be many colors but not blue." My mother and I were not starving, and we had a place to live, cramped and gloomy from encroaching buildings but adequate as shelter. Still, most definitely we were poor, which, for me, was a condition: a weight, a fog shrouding my dreams. I hated it, hated having to debate making a purchase, weighing one desire against another, hated the constant gnawing of want that dulled the liveliness of voices, music, the sounds of the street, everything that others relished as their vivid, shimmering world.

In books and various Internet stories, I've read about poor people who live lives of dignity and good humor, who have caring friends and kind neighbors, who make the most of their lot, find ways to share, and do it with good cheer. My mother was one of them; I'll give her that. She was widely loved and admired, which amazed me, even as I was pleased to see how her friends sought her out for advice and comfort. If she'd been less intent on what I said and did, on what I was and might become, she might have been pleasant to live with.

As it was, I spent as much time as I could out of the house. After work and on Sundays I visited friends and cadged invitations to dinner, or wandered the Metropolitan Museum, getting home just in time to eat and go out again. Or, at the public library I found deep armchairs in quiet nooks and nibbled cheese and crackers when no one was around while I read histories, novels, plays, whatever gave me pointers for fitting into the worlds I aimed for. Sometimes, when the museums and libraries were closed, I even walked around our neighborhood, imagining my future while skirting the homeless. Our part of the city was home to the homeless. Like fragments from an archaeological dig, they hunched against the buildings: anonymous bundles of coats, jackets, shawls, knit caps. Propped against their knees were frantic cardboard signs scrawled in black marker, wailing about hunger, sick children, evictions, lost jobs, ailments, disabilities, hopes for a job, a new life. On the sidewalk in front of them, like supplicant baby birds with wide open beaks, were empty soup cans, the bottoms of shoe boxes, paper cups, once half a broken violin case, some seeded with a few coins or a single dollar bill. I hated all of them, helpless and defeated, not a thread of resistance or ambition in the scarecrows they'd become. I would never be like them; I would make my own way and take charge of my part of the world without begging or even asking for help.

"I hardly see you," said my mother one night when I got home late. "Once we talked."

"Years ago," I said. I was dressing to go out. "My life has changed."

"Without anymore me." It was a statement, but also a question.

It took me a minute to answer. "You're as busy as I am."

"No," she said, and turned back to her sewing.

My mother tried not to speak Spanish at home, to keep her English good for her clients, she said, and also because my brothers and I told her not to; we were Americans, our language was English. If she ever longed to slip back into it because it was easier and made her think of home, she didn't tell us; she stuck to English except for a word or phrase, depending on her mood or how tired she was. And we'd help her when she asked us to correct her mistakes, but we never had time for real lessons; she could always be understood, and we told her that was all that mattered.

The next morning, I left right after breakfast. It was Sunday, my day for checking out the collections at the department stores. Where I had mastered the art of shoplifting.

It is not easy, shoplifting. It requires skill, dexterity, dedication, control, and total attention. It is not something one can do on a whim, or to satisfy a spontaneous urge. And it is not something one can do in the same store more than once a month, since cameras record and store images of shoppers, and officious personnel with tenacious memories check them regularly.

But I was good. I had a small device, purchased on the

Internet, for removing the clumsy attachments that set off alarms if transported out of the store while still fastened to a garment. The better stores, of course, never use these; the clips ruin cashmere and fragile fabrics, impede trying on clothes, and make the garments, and the emporium itself, look cheap. I used my device for removing the attachments at large department stores where seasonal or sample sales lured weekend crowds. More sparingly, I chose finer shops, still large, but not as crowded and therefore more challenging. And I never made selections from the highest of the high end designers; the salespeople in those departments were chosen for eagle eyes, uncanny sensory perception, and swift movements. That way lay danger. Instead, I hung out with lines still too expensive for me but accessible to those who were quick and clever.

Which I was. I was not caught. I was not even stopped for questioning. I carried myself with a look of money, I was always leisurely, my designer handbag was one of the oversize ones sufficient for a weekend getaway, so I never had to carry shopping bags, a dangerous appendage. I was pleasant to salespeople but not memorably so. I was the kind of shopper high-end stores seek out and cultivate. As I said, I was good.

And I loved it, every minute from the electric anticipation of violating the rules to the moment I walked out of a store with the day's cache, by myself in a halo of misbehavior.

Still, there were problems. The immediate one was how to wear the spoils to avoid my mother's sharp eye. I had no worries about where to keep my expanding wardrobe: my mother would never go into my room, much less my closet; those were my private places, she said, and not open even to her. But wearing new clothes was another matter. A few times, with small items my mother spotted the minute I came into the room, I could say I'd had a good day in tips and found the scarf or belt or whatever on sale.

"You have good taste," she would say. "We need to buy you more things."

"I'm fine," I'd say automatically; there was no chance she could shop for me. "I don't need anything."

But I couldn't do that very often, and never with major pieces whose price tags even my mother knew were beyond the budget of restaurant tips. Finally, when I had plans for the evening, I took to changing clothes in a friend's house or restrooms in department stores, until I discovered better ones in hotel lobbies, absolutely the best, and I settled on a few select ones I could rotate over time.

I chose my excellent wardrobe for venues appropriate to the life I had mapped out for myself. I joined a high-toned church that offered, besides the saving of souls, concerts, plays, panel discussions and the like, all free and attended by people from the Upper East Side: handsome couples and a number of professional men widowed or divorced. I had splurged on a new health club and, through new acquaintances there, collected invitations to some of the city's trendy members-only bars where it is easy for even a plain woman to make friends. In all these locales I looked as if I belonged, as if I had always belonged; alert and watchful, I learned how to order drinks, how to drink them, when to stop, and when to leave, always alone. I attracted attention and was pleased to hear I generated a sense of mystery, particularly among men.

"What are you looking for?" my mother asked.

Well, actually, that was a good question.

It was a little vague, what I was looking for. Generally,

in spite of living inside that fog of poverty that kept me from feeling fully connected to people and places, I was having a pretty good time. I was meeting interesting people, taking in diverting events, frequently enjoying fine food, wine, and innovative cocktails. For many, that would be enough. But I was restless, and my mother saw that.

"A husband?" my mother asked.

Another good question.

The answer, for now, was No. Not yet. Eventually, yes of course: marriage would make life more secure, easier, hopefully more pleasant. But right now I wanted more: I wanted adventures. I wanted to conquer.

"You want to bring people down. To their knees," said my mother. That stopped me for a minute; where had that come from? My mother was not a philosophical or even a particularly thoughtful or intelligent woman.

"Meaning?" I asked.

She shrugged. "What I say. When you talk about people, you seem angry; like you don't like them. Like they're not good enough to know. What's that word? *Desprecio.*"

"Contempt," I said.

"Contempt. So. Why you don't like people? Why you are so angry?"

I was halfway across the room by then. I thought of making something up, but why bother? I told the truth, at least part of it. "You don't need a reason to be angry; sometimes you just are."

My mother nodded. "That is very sad."

"I'm late," I said, and was out the door.

I am acquainted with women who have clever mothers and are wary of them, but I was not one of them. I've always known that my mother was not smart or quick; she never set off alarms in me, except when she accidentally came out with something that sounded deeper than usual. My mother was a housemaid with no education beyond sixth grade in Mexico. She had a green card and good enough English to satisfy matrons in all those homes her trio cleans, but she never bothered to become a citizen; she was still a foreigner thinking of Mexico as home, even though, by now, it was only a vague fantasy, and most likely she knew she never would live there again. She did visit, bringing back news of cousins, aunts and uncles, dozens of photos; she even, once, had a brief romance in her hometown, but when I asked what happened, she said he insisted she live with him in his small village where there was no money and no jobs, so she turned north again and that was that. Generally, she was uninterested in anything beyond her own little world of family and friends and employers; when she read, which was not often since she fell asleep soon after dinner, she read in Spanish, easier and faster, she said, than English. My mother did not drop clues that she knew more than she let on, or saw more deeply than what was clearly in front of her, or had thoughts that were profound or insightful. She was a simple woman.

So it was a fluke, the occasional odd question and comment; nothing I needed to ponder.

"You look good," my mother said a few days later as I was getting dressed to go out. "But you wear all the time those same clothes; this weekend we look for sales and buy you new things."

A small alarm did go off that time. Was there a barb in what she said, in her smile as she watched me step into my shoes? "I'm fine," I said, as I always did. "I don't need new clothes."

"Well, but yes, I think you do," she said, still smiling.

"These things mothers know."

My mother, generally, was a happy woman. Why this was true, I do not know. She was not happy when her husband died; she lost husband and religion in one instant and was left with four noisy kids ranging from seven to twelve years old. She did menial work ten hours a day, six days a week. She was poor. She allowed herself few indulgences, not even wine or coffee, which she said did not agree with her. She lived with a daughter who was counting the days until she could move out. But she smiled a lot, my mother did. Often she sang or hummed while sewing or making her bed or cutting vegetables for dinner. She was a happy woman.

I, on the other hand, as may be obvious by now, was not especially happy. There were, of course, many reasons for this, but the main one, when it happened, was my giving up shoplifting. I had no intention of doing that; I was enjoying myself, enhancing my wardrobe, and always enough on edge to keep from being bored. But then everything fell away.

I have no idea how it happened, but almost overnight I changed. Where once I had made my carefully plotted, decisive way through predatory jungles where strategically placed watchdogs, poised for action, waited for me to make a false move, suddenly I was cautious, tense, too obviously vigilant. I walked through the aisles without my former insouciance; when I lifted an item for inspection, my hand trembled ever so slightly and I could not muster the nerve to make my usual moves: walking casually to match the item with something on another counter, perhaps another counter after that, then, with a sleight of hand, slipping it invisibly into my Coach shoulder bag. Or, on truly exhilarating occasions that happened only in winter, going into a store wearing only undergarments beneath a heavy coat, and emerging still wearing the coat but this time, beneath it, a dress, or blouse and skirt.

Now there was no opportunity for thrills or triumphs. Instead, I could sense the creatures eyeing me; on all sides I felt a heightened, more rigorous surveillance. My neck was stiff from the effort to keep from swiveling to look for threats; my legs were heavy, as if my fears had lodged there, so my confident lightness of step and bearing became sluggish and, I was sure, suspicious even to an untrained eye. This sudden failure of will might have been a brief aberration, like a sore throat or a headache, but, as soon became clear, it was not: it continued, without relief. Many days, most days, I came home exhausted without anything to show for my wanderings through those brightly lit, beckoning aisles.

This was beyond belief depressing. I began staying home on my days off, staring out a window, avoiding my mother's searching looks and her insistent probing. "You have a cold? Something happened at work? You are not fired, that cannot be; you say they always call you their best. So if you are not sick and not fired, what is wrong?"

Mostly I just shrugged and fled, to walk around the block and eventually stop at a coffee place nearby, hunching over a tall latte for hours. Even more depressing, I didn't have a clue to what was happening to me. It was like catching a disease and not knowing where it came from or how to treat it. Everything built up inside me until I was almost bursting with depression and rage and helplessness: a total mess. In this way, three weeks went by. I was furiously bored, I was tired of lattes, I hurt from all this churning inside me, I could barely talk to anyone, which made my waitressing another millstone dragging me down.

"So," said my mother on a Saturday morning as I was leaving for work, "tomorrow we shop for you."

"No." It was automatic, but she looked so surprised I tried to take it back. "I mean, you should spend your money on yourself, not on me. I'm fine; I don't need anything."

"You need," she said, nodding. "More than me."

We went shopping. I had tried to say I was busy, I didn't feel like shopping, I felt a cold coming on, but she was determined. I still lived with her; I went along.

In fact, I did more. I made her happy. We found a dress on a sale rack that actually looked okay on me. It wasn't anything like one of the designers I'd focused on in my shoplifting days, but it fit surprisingly well except across the back ("Easy to fix," said my mother. "I know how."), and much to my surprise I was okay with the way I looked in it.

"La belleza." My mother stood on tiptoe to kiss my cheek and returned home a happy lady.

The experience lacked the powerful frisson of shoplifting, but it had unexpected charms. My mother and I did not share much anymore, a lapse she noted frequently, and I had not missed it, but our Sunday morning in Bloomingdale's had been like a holiday: I hadn't once been angry, and we'd laughed at a few things together. My mother said she'd known just what I needed, and at least for those few hours she may have been right.

But, like almost everything, it had its down side. The scene had tugged at me as I tried on dresses, and it still beckoned long after we had returned home: the blazing lights that cast no shadows; the polished, bewitching display counters; the captivating merchandise laid out for the taking. I missed it, oh, I did miss it, and so the next day, my day off from the restaurant, I went back.

But nothing had changed. I had hoped, maybe expected, that my strange lapse into weakness had been cured by my enforced furlough, that I would enter the store with a resurgence of the sangfroid that in better times had brought me so much success. Instead, I was even worse. I did not glide up and down the aisles: I more or less lurched. I clutched my shoulder bag to keep it from swinging side to side, which I knew probably made me look demented. At first, I barely glanced at the merchandise, concentrating on walking a straight line, my eyes focused straight ahead rather than searching left and right for beasts of prey, my face frozen in its neutral-but-pleasant mode. This all took so much effort and attention I almost forgot why I was there.

But I did remember when I reached the entrance to the Akris boutique and immediately fell in love with a jacket, the perfect jacket for me. Rustling up a façade of my old confidence, I stood straight and tall and followed my practiced routine, browsing through the racks, focusing on jackets, choosing three to carry with me, finally circling back to the perfect one. I put it with the others and made my way to the dressing rooms.

They all looked good on me. The perfect one was perfect. I folded it over my arm and returned to the sales floor. "I'm taking this to Escada," I said to a saleswoman I had not seen before, "to try with a pair of pants I saw there." This is the part that takes real guts, and I knew I was not as good as usual, not as casual, a little too intense. But she merely nodded and went on helping another customer.

I crossed the store, took a pair of pants from a rack, and made my way to another dressing room. I did not bother trying on the pants; I knew they were the wrong size. I bent over the jacket and swiftly removed the small security device fastened to the inside, then neatly folded it and slipped it into my shoulder bag. I left the dressing room and made my way to the escalator. My heart was a jackhammer, crashing in my chest, my head, my neck, my jaw; I clenched my teeth to keep them from chattering. But I was past the second floor and walking down the escalator to the ground floor. I was fine. I was back.

I walked past the gaudy cosmetics counters and the salespeople dabbing makeup on tourists and reached the revolving door. Outside was the street, filled with sunlit, carefree shoppers. But inside, at that moment, a hand gripped my upper arm, pulling me back so that I stumbled, bumping into the hulk behind me. "Just come with me quietly," said the hulk and turned me so we were walking to the elevators, close together, like lovers.

The offices were on the top floor, past lingerie, past china and flatware and crystal winking at me under the harsh ceiling lights. We ended up in a large room that seemed full of people. My captor let go of my arm and handed my shoulder bag to a woman nearby. There was a flash and then another as someone took my picture. The woman pulled out my Akris jacket. I was feeling faint: shaky, nauseous, cold; I needed to sit down but no one was sitting, and I was in the middle of the room, far from a place to collapse. I knew I had to do something; I couldn't just stand there letting a stranger paw through my bag. And then my voice came. "It's mine," I said, and cleared my throat past the rasp I heard in it. "I brought it to try with some Escada pants. I've done that lots of times."

The woman nodded and went on looking through my

bag. In a few minutes she took something out and set the bag on the desk behind her. She opened her hand so I could see my device for removing sensors. "You came prepared," she said.

My legs crumpled and I reached out to catch myself, waving wildly in the air. The hulk, still beside me, took my arm and pushed me into a chair. But actually that was worse; I was low and little and everybody else was high and big, staring down at me, as if I was some kind of specimen. I cleared my throat again. "Look, I'm sorry. I mean, I really am sorry. I've never done this... anything like this, ever, I don't know why I did it today, I just... I don't know. But you can't tell my mother. Please, please don't tell my mother. It would break her heart. She's so good and she always knows the right thing to do and she's so proud of me and this would... this could kill her. I mean, she thinks I'm special, you know? And if she found out..."

The woman nodded. "You've never done it before, but here we are again: you came prepared."

I was trying to sit straight, to look calm and at ease and innocent, but my shoulders slumped and I knew I looked like a kid who got caught stealing loose change. Or like some kind of criminal. I tried to think of something to say, but nothing came out.

In fact, nobody said anything. There were all these people in the room and nobody talked. It was unnerving and my shaking got worse. "Please don't tell my mother," I said again, and I knew I sounded guiltier and more whining every time I opened my mouth.

The woman left the room. No one said anything. We waited. After awhile she came back. "Where did you get the Coach shoulder bag?" she asked.

"I don't know," I said, and that was the truth. "I've had it a long time."

She nodded. "Well, I think you may be a poor bet, but I'm going to let you go. I called your employer and got a rave review; it seems you're the best they've got. You should stick to that; you have a good job and you do it well; use it to make something of yourself. We'll let you go, but you can be sure we'll be watching you from now on, and that includes security in every store in the city. If you ever do this again, no one will be kind to you. Or to your mother." She took my wallet out of my bag. "You'll pay for the jacket; we can run your credit card right now."

I tried to stand up, but my legs wouldn't move. She did what she'd said: she ran the credit card and wrote in the price, an outrageous amount for a simple jacket. She held out the sales slip and I signed it. She slipped the card back in my wallet, put the wallet in my bag, and stood there, holding it, waiting. At that I did stand up, and when she handed me the bag I put it on my shoulder. "Buy a smaller purse," she said. And then: "I don't want to see you again."

"Right." It was a mumble; I was looking at the floor. And then the hulk and all the others stepped back, making way for me to walk between them, like through a gauntlet, and then I was out of there and on an elevator and on the ground floor, walking past the gaudy cosmetics counters and the same salespeople dabbing makeup on the same tourists, and finally out the revolving door to the sunlit sidewalk and the happy shoppers.

If I'd been depressed before, that was nothing to what hit me now. I had no energy or interests, nothing caught my attention. I stayed in bed. My mother brought me trays, felt my forehead, asked what had happened to me and what would make me happy. I'd called in sick at the restaurant, which was not like me. I'm never sick. The maître d' said something to that effect, and I fabricated something about a virus and told him I'd be back as soon as I wasn't contagious. A year or two from now, I thought, but in fact, and of course, I was back in three days, helping women with too much money fill their bellies, and collecting tips that always seemed minuscule but were, I was told, substantial compared to those collected by others on the wait staff. Management repeated something about me being the best, even after the witch's phone call. I don't know what she said, but I'm assuming she didn't say I was a thief; she managed somehow to keep it cool. For which I suppose I should have been grateful, but there was no way I could think kindly of that woman for anything.

A couple of weeks later, dragging around the house on my day off, feeling like a failure and a weakling and thinking others would see me as a total loss system, which meant I couldn't go anymore to the private clubs and bars where I'd spent my evenings in better times, where women looked at me and, because of what I was wearing, knew I was worth knowing, which meant no future for me beyond waiting on tables and smiling nicely to make sure of tips, I saw a small box on the dining room table. It had not been there at breakfast. My name was on it, in my mother's sprawling handwriting. I left it there.

"What is this?" I asked when she came home from the last cleaning job of the day.

"What is it? A present! You didn't open it? Why not? It is for you. Your name is there."

"It isn't my birthday, it isn't Christmas, it isn't anything."

"*Madre de dios*, you are so hard. It is a day for a present.

Are you going to open it?"

I opened the box. It was a necklace of cheap imitation pearls alternating with metal beads. It was something I never in a thousand years would wear. But my mother was smiling and waiting and I still lived in her apartment. "Wow," I said and held it up. "Where did you find it?"

"Costco had a special. Pearls make me think of you. It will go with everything, yes? Pearls go with everything."

"Right." I leaned down and gave her a quick kiss on her cheek. "Thanks."

"Put it on," she said. "See how it looks on you."

"I'm wearing a sweatshirt."

"So? Pearls go with everything."

And they did. This particular strand of off-color plastic went fine with a sweatshirt.

"*Bueno*," my mother said, but it was sad; she was no longer beaming. "Maybe with the dress, the one we bought together..."

I did not answer and after a minute she said, "*Bien, la cena...*" and went to the kitchen.

I should have made dinner while she was at work. I knew that. But I hadn't been able to get up the energy to walk into the kitchen, much less cook. All I wanted to do was sleep, but I was slept out so even that was denied me. Actually it was better at work; I didn't have to think about anything but getting the food to the tables and smiling, always smiling, and since none of the customers gave a damn about me, they never looked closely enough to note that maybe all was not chipper in my life, that maybe I actually had a life like a real human being. Like, maybe, them.

But my mother knew, and she was not happy. A few days later, when we were finishing dinner, she said, "I know you have better jewelry. I'm sorry about the necklace."

I waved it away. "Not worth thinking about. It's fine."

"No," she said, and stood up to clear the dishes. She didn't look at me, but I knew what she was thinking, so I hauled myself out of my chair and we did the dishes together for the first time since the catastrophe.

Sometimes I feel almost envious of my mother. Of course that's the wrong word; there is absolutely nothing in my mother for me to envy, but now and then something hits me, and so far I haven't found a better word for it. Things are so clear to her: sharp-edged, easy to define. From the time she came here with her husband, with her first son inside her, she had a definite goal. They would get green cards and jobs and they would have children, American children. And however many they were blessed with, they would save enough money to buy all of them college educations and see them into the world as successful, prosperous citizens in a country where they could be anything they wanted.

My mother saw all this distinctly and luminously, and I must say she achieved most of it. My brothers all went to college; I chose not to, but money was not the reason. It's true there wasn't much left by the time it was my turn, but to tell the truth I couldn't imagine four years living even tighter than we already were while studying and taking tests on things I'd never use. My mother said I was crazy, but she didn't dwell on it; she'd been worried about where the money would come from, and she was proud of her sons and what she'd accomplished. She knew, we all knew, she'd done it by herself without ever going on about how hard life was: I never heard her whine or complain about anything, not even her back, which I knew was bad because I could hear her taking pills. She wasn't a saint: she didn't get all syrupy about how great everything was, which even she knew wouldn't have made sense, but she always managed to celebrate a piece of good news and beam when something went well, like the time I tried on that dress she bought me and it fit, while bypassing the difficult parts, like her sons leaving home and not calling or coming to dinner or bringing her birthday presents or whatever, and my not being the loving daughter she probably dreamed about when, after three males, she finally got me.

So when I thought about these things, this odd feeling crept up on me, not really envy, but a sense that she knew lots of things I didn't know, that her life had a direction I was missing out on: not having that clarity, not being able to ignore or minimize whatever was painful, not even trying to stop complaining or longing for something else. I had no idea what my mother longed for, but I figured there had to be something since my own list was so long.

I was truly in a funk and, when I had the energy, I tried to think of ways to get some excitement in my life, work out a plan to replace my most stellar experiences in spiriting away designer clothes from exclusive shops, but that was a tough one.

I thought of picking it up again, the whole shoplifting bit, traveling to stores in different cities, but the fact was, I knew I'd lost my confidence and there was no way I could see myself sashaying up and down aisles as if I wasn't thinking about anything but looking at gorgeous stuff and deciding what to buy. Every time I imagined it, I could feel that hand on my arm, feel that smothering group of people looking down at me, knowing they could do anything with me they wanted.

After awhile, what the hell, I thought, I wouldn't go back

to it: it's really not my kind of thing. If you thought about it, shoplifting was nothing more than a hobby for amateurs: clumsy, time consuming, chancy. There had to be better ways, and a clever person ought to be able to figure them out.

I dreamed up a scenario where I'd copy numbers from the credit cards of diners I served, then wait awhile, like a couple of months, before using them to buy whatever I wanted online and have them delivered to a friend of mine. I thought this was clever and foolproof until it occurred to me that when the owner of the credit card reported a transaction she hadn't made, a fraud expert in a bank would check the address where the items were delivered, which would be a straight line to me. That was the end of what I knew was a pathetic scenario to begin with.

I thought of searching the cloak room of the restaurant where I worked, removing purchases that were my size and taste, but it took less than a minute for me to realize how feeble that was: it was embarrassing to think I'd even thought it up.

As before, I stayed home at night. I wasn't going to clubs or bars. I wasn't taking walks around the neighborhood. I wasn't window shopping; those days were over. I wasn't reading or watching television: nothing in a book or magazine or on the screen distracted me from my misery. At first my mother was pleased that I was spending evenings with her, but soon she zeroed in on worrying about me, and when that happened she reverted to the same questions she always asked, her complete store of possible reasons for my behavior. "You are not well?" "Too many customers, and you are tired?" "The customers were rude and you are angry?" "Your boss did not give you a raise?" "*Madre de dios*"—she said that often as my mood blackened—"you have an illness you are not telling me about? *El càncer?*" That one she whispered.

"I'm fine," I said and repeated it, like an endless loop. "I'm fine, don't keep asking me. I'm fine."

But of course that didn't satisfy her. She had to have a cause in order to mount a campaign to correct a fault or a flaw or a lapse. Only an act of God would she accept as beyond her ability to mend. "We could go shopping again," she said. "That would be good." But she sounded so doubtful, my reply already hung in the air.

"I don't need anything. I'm—"

"Fine. Yes. Many times you say so. But . . ." She shook her head. She was sewing, replacing buttons on an ancient blouse of mine, I suppose to make it look newer, dressier, whatever, and she bent over it, looking suddenly small and old.

Do you know how you feel when you know you're doing something wrong or did something wrong yesterday or the day before, but there's no way you can do anything about it? I was getting angry; my mother was making me feel I was not being nice, I was making her unhappy. But I can't make you happy, I thought, as if she could hear me. Because you can't make me happy. We're poor. We live in a dingy apartment with windows that look into brick walls or other people's windows. I spend my days smiling at people who don't know me and don't want to; I serve them food and drinks, still smiling, smiling, smiling, while they chatter away and don't look up as I slide their plates in front of them, or, rarely but once in a while, when I make a mistake and give the crepes and the salade nicoise to the wrong women, they frown in my general direction while I apologize and switch the plates.

You work your ass off cleaning up other people's messes, I silently tell my mother; you take pride in it, but you shouldn't;

you should be raging at having to scrub their toilets and wash their underwear and semen-stained bed sheets; you should be as enraged as I am at the deal you've got with no way to get out from under. Look at us: we don't take vacations; we don't travel anywhere for any reason, not even simple trips like Niagara Falls or a Broadway show; we don't buy frivolous things; we don't sit around deciding what pleasure to indulge in next. Other people do; lots of people do. Who the hell decided that? Who makes the rules? Not us, for sure. It's infuriating, and the fact that you don't even think about it being infuriating is what makes me turn my back on you and treat you like a fool, like a doormat, because that's what you are.

"So angry," my mother said, more to herself than to me. "*Furioso. Siempre furioso.*" She looked up from her sewing. "You want. So much you want."

A few days later I found a gift-wrapped box on my bed when I came home from work, and others followed, one a week. The wrapping paper was cheap, but what was inside was not. A gold David Yurman Renaissance bracelet. A silk blouse, Armani. A pair of Manolo high-heeled shoes.

"What the hell is going on?" I shouted at my mother. "Where are you getting these things?"

"Do not curse," my mother said automatically. "You do not like them? They're for you. They should make you happy."

That last was mostly a question, and all I could do was shrug. I had no idea what would make me happy anymore. "How are you getting them? What am I supposed to do with them?"

"*Ay dios!* Wear them, use them, go out at night, wherever you used to go, with people, with friends. Smile sometimes. This would hurt you? You like having a face dragged down like a wet blanket?"

Soon the gifts slowed down to every other week, but they kept coming. I asked my mother, more than once, where they came from, and she just shrugged, like it wasn't worth talking about. So pretty soon I stopped asking. In fact, I began to take them for granted, and that made it easy to wear them. I loved wearing them; I felt almost like me again.

My evenings opened up, as if someone raised a window blind and the whole city came into view. I went back to the clubs and bars where I'd once hung out, I looked good and smiled, not because I had to but because I felt like it. I rediscovered small talk, remembered how to be bright and witty, how to toss around facts from theater and musicals, from gossip, even politics I knew nothing about but memorized from newspapers and television. I filled my nights. It wasn't the same as before—it was not my own cleverness that had accumulated everything I was wearing, which dulled my pleasure slightly, and also I was pricked by annoyance at not knowing what my mother was up to—but none of that kept me from enjoying myself. I met some women I recognized from society pages who were friendly in a casual way, and a couple of men who were pleasantly attentive. I was eating and drinking in a style I'd come to believe was essential to an acceptable life. It did not take long for me to feel I was back where I belonged.

Somewhere beneath all this, I knew it was insane that I did not press my mother to tell me how she was pulling off this stunt, but at the same time it made an odd kind of sense, since I knew without a doubt whatever she was doing had to be illegal. I mean, maybe she found a bundle in the street one day and couldn't wait to spend it all on me, or she came across a stash absentmindedly left in an ATM, or, right in front of her on

5th Avenue, a money-clipped stack of thousand-dollar bills fell out of the pocket of a sprinter trying to beat someone else to a cab, or some such miracle, but the fact was, I didn't believe in miracles. It had to be illegal, was how I saw it, and I'd narrowed it down to shoplifting—like daughter like mother, though the idea of my mother as a criminal was hard to swallow—and if that's what she was doing, in fact whatever she might be doing, the thought came to me that, if I actually knew for sure what she was risking, I might not feel comfortable accepting any more of her gifts. I wasn't sure of that—I did like what she was choosing for me; how did she learn to have such good taste?—but I had enough doubts that it was better for peace in the family just to let it go.

In any event, we weren't talking much: we'd gone back to our old ways, sharing an apartment and now and then a dinner, but mostly living like roommates who didn't have much of anything in common. Except, of course, for the gifts. I thanked my mother for each one, and she nodded to show she'd heard me, but since I'd stopped asking how she got them, there was no conversation. I dressed at home now, and she always told me how nice I looked, but that was it. Definitely our apartment now featured mostly conversation stoppers.

I'd assumed the gifts would stop at some point, but they kept coming, one every other week, and after nearly four months it had become easy to think this was the new normal, and why should it change? But it was not the new normal, and so it changed.

This is hard to talk about, even to think about, but here is what happened.

I came home from work one evening and found on my bed not another brightly wrapped package but a thick envelope with my name on it. Inside, carefully folded, were several sheets of paper torn from the pad my mother kept by the kitchen telephone for shopping lists. Her looping handwriting filled both sides of the sheets.

"*Mi querida hija. Esto no es fácil, pero tiene que ser.*"

"My dear daughter. This is not easy, but it has to be."

I translate as I read. I am an American; I think in English.

"*You are a good girl and I am proud of you. You work hard and you make yourself pretty and I wish all good things for you. But they cannot come from me, I do not know how to make you happy. I thought I knew and I tried, we bought you a dress and then I gave you presents, but still you do not smile and we do not laugh together, so I know I am not good at being your mother. I do not understand you and that is hard for me. You asked me where the presents come from and now I will tell you. I did a terrible thing. I took them from the people who pay me to clean their houses. They are very nice, these people, they are good to me. But I stole from them to give you presents. The first time, I took a bracelet. The lady had so many, and I took one that was almost the same exactly as another one in her jewelry drawer, so maybe she did not notice. To now she has not said anything so I think she has not noticed. The next week, with a different lady, I took a blouse. I said to her there was an accident, I spilled furniture polish on it and it was ruined. I said she should take money from my salary, but she said no, it was not my fault and I need the money. This is how it was with all the ladies I work for. Eighteen, we clean eighteen apartments and when I have done this in all the apartments I think I can stop. It would be good to stop, but first I need to bring you nice things. So every week, sometimes two weeks when I find something good for you, I do this. Never twice with the same lady, each time a different* one, so each lady thinks it happens only one time. Two times the people are in Europe so I just took. The other ladies always say it is not my fault, they will not take money from my salary, I need it. It was easy, I did not know it could be easy, soon it was like habit, like shopping for food in the market, my ladies like me and they trust me. They are good people. But I am not. I am criminal. All those things you wear and they are good on you, you look nice and I think maybe you are happy wearing them even when you do not look happy. But I cannot do this anymore. Last time and the time before I feel sick when I tell the lie to the lady I work for and when I wrap your present I throw up, last week this happened and this week too and I think it is not me stealing and lying. I do not know me and when I think about this my head hurts like it will split open and I cannot look in the mirror because I did these things and they were easy and now I am not me. So I go away. A long time ago I thought this would be a great sin. But now I know there are worse sins and I cannot live with these sins. I am sorry. I love you and I am sorry."*

The telephone rings as I'm halfway through the letter a second time. I'm having trouble with the letter, my mother doing these things, being somebody I don't recognize, and I barely notice the ringing, but then I pick it up and a nurse from Lenox Hill Hospital says my mother has been brought in, she fell from a high balcony in an apartment building on the East Side, and she is dead and can I come immediately.

A great sin.

A worse sin.

It's like there's a hole under me and I'm falling, but I can't move. I stand there with the telephone in my hand and feel the floor give way beneath me, but I'm in the same place. I can hear myself breathing. I say my mother's name but there's no sound. Nothing makes sense, nothing in the letter, nothing in the telephone call. This is not me, this is not my mother, this is not happening. And now I'm not sure who I am.

I go to the hospital. I take a taxi; I remember the taxi but not much else except the Pakistani driver asking if I'm all right because I'm crying and he doesn't want me to pass out or something in his taxi. At the hospital there are two policemen. One of them tells me my mother came to a building where she worked; the doorman said she greeted him, and of course he knew her, he knew she had keys to the apartment where she worked. They said a few words about the weather, and then my mother went back to the freight elevator which all the maids used and he didn't see her again. The doorman said the owners of the apartment she went to are in Europe. The policeman says they figured my mother was cleaning the balcony, she had a bucket of soapy water and sponges and a broom, and somehow, maybe climbing up to reach something, she went over the railing. She fell forty-eight floors.

The nurse is listening; she asks if I want to see my mother and I say yes, but I can only take a look, a quick awful look, because it isn't her anymore, and then I sign a lot of papers they keep sliding in front of me, and finally I go home.

But it isn't home anymore. It's a cave, cold and dark; my footsteps are loud. Not my mother's home, not mine. My mother is dead.

But she can't be dead. She was just here, her voice is still here. No, not here. There is no voice here. The rooms are silent, so silent it is like a voice itself.

But that was what I wanted... right? I remember waiting for the day my mother would stop talking, how I longed for the time when I would wake one morning in a cocoon of perfect silence. I called that freedom.

It is not freedom. I don't know what it is, but no way can I call it freedom.

I listen for her even while telling myself how stupid that is. She isn't here. But a little while ago she was. She was here this morning, making breakfast, quiet, but she is always quiet in the morning. Was. Was quiet in the morning. My mother is dead. She is not here; she won't be here. Ever. Ever again.

Her letter is on the kitchen counter where I'd left it. Standing there, I read it again. And again and again. I don't know how many times I read it, but at some point I fall asleep on the couch and when I wake up the letter is crumpled in my hand.

I wake up to a nightmare, angry, furious. Damn it, she had no right to do this to me. She never thought of how I'd feel. Thought of herself, always herself. Stealing things. Who the hell asked her to do that? She probably got a kick out of it—it was easy—then all of a sudden decided she shouldn't be doing it so she killed herself. Stupid. Stupid and selfish and mean.

All morning I'm angry, and then it's gone. I read the letter again, flattening out the crumpled sheets. The Spanish sentences bring back her voice; I can hear her, see her. Standing at the kitchen sink, her back to me as she makes dinner. Sitting on the couch, watching television, her back to me as I dress to go out. Scrunched into an armchair, sewing, her face lowered over a new button. I see her, but I cannot see her face. I try to remember her face, but I can't see it. Damn, damn, damn, why can't I see her? This woman who threw away everything she was and wanted to be for a crazy reason, why can't I see her anymore?

I run through the apartment, room to room, looking for a picture of her, but there is none. There is not one picture of my mother in the apartment. On her bedroom dresser is a picture of my father and pictures of my brothers and me, but nowhere is there a picture of my mother.

Her eyes were brown, I think. I'm sure they were brown. She was light-skinned. All of us are. A tinge of color, no more. Her hair was black—all of us have black hair—but hers was turning gray, gray streaks like ribbons, and she wore it in a bun. I never saw her with her hair down; I don't even know how long it was before she wrapped it up.

"I don't know how long it was," I say out loud. The words fall to the floor and dry up like spatters of rain.

I'm walking through the apartment, back and forth, with nowhere to go. She's gone, I tell myself. She won't be back.

The next minute I'm running again. I can't explain what I do next; I do it without thinking. I'm sort of humming to myself, at least I'm making sounds that seem strange to me, and I run into my bedroom and open the dresser drawers and the closet doors and grab all the gorgeous things I stole over the years, and then the ones my mother stole, and I stuff them into one of those big black garbage bags and haul it down the stairs to the street.

I swing the bag over my shoulder like Santa Claus and I run. The bag is heavy and I have trouble running, but I manage to keep going, and in a few minutes I come to the homeless. I stop in front of a man with his head on his knees; I drop the bag and reach inside to grab a cashmere sweater. "Take it," I say and throw it in his lap. "Take it!"

I'm turning away, but he yells at me. "Hey, stop! Take it back!" His voice is hoarse. "Shit, you ain't sticking me with no stolen stuff . . . take it back!" He flings the sweater at me, but I shake my head and run, his voice following me. I come to a woman with a faded paisley shawl over her head; I pull a silk blouse out of the bag. "Here!" I say and shove it into the open box at her feet, and then I'm gone, to the next shapeless person and the next and the next, throwing silks and satins, cashmere, lace, leather at their feet.

"Where will I wear it?" one woman screams at me. Another woman yells, "What the fuck I do with a pair of spiky shoes?" "Sell them!" I shout; my voice is a screech I don't recognize. One man grabs the amber necklace I drop in front of him and runs it through his fingers, saying, like a prayer, "Holy Christ." A woman snatches up the skirt I throw at her and says, "God, maybe for Susie," and I almost stop because she sounds like my mother, but I go on, I have to go on, the bag is still heavy on my shoulder; I keep taking things out but it doesn't get any lighter, it still feels as heavy as when I started, and I have to get rid of everything in it, I can't stop until I've gotten rid of all of it, and when I come to the end I'm a long way from home, but I keep walking and then, in a minute, I'm exhausted and out of breath and can't go another step, so I sit on the curb to rest and a policeman comes up and asks me what I'm doing. "Resting," I say, and then I'm angry. "Is there a law against sitting here? I'm tired, and as soon as I've rested I'll go home, but until then I'll damn well sit here and rest."

"No kidding; you're a smart ass, aren't you?" He stands there looking at me. He looks at my empty garbage bag. "You sure you got a home?"

I tell him the address. My anger is gone and I start to cry. "My mother just died, died, she died, and I'm so tired."

"Jesus," he says. "Your mother, that's the worst." He stands there while I cry. "You're a long way from home. You want a ride?"

I just stare at him; I'm not used to nice things happening.

"Let's go," he says and grabs my arm and pulls me up from the curb.

We don't talk in his car; I sit next to him and I can't stop crying. In front of my building I don't even say good-bye; I try to say Thank You but I'm crying too hard, so I just nod and then I can't stop nodding, like I'm spastic or something. I drag myself upstairs, pulling on the banister, and walk into our apartment—my apartment I guess, but then I think maybe I can't afford it. I don't even know what the rent is or what bills there are; my mother took care of everything. I think probably I'll have to get another job, work more hours, earn enough to live on, try to do what she did.

I have to call my brothers, I think. They could help me. They ought to help me; they owe it to me.

But that thought disappears before it's even finished. I don't want them to help me. They never offered to help my mother; they left her, and me too; they never come to see us; they call once in a while, but we never have much to say.

I have to do this on my own. My mother would be proud of me for that. Find another restaurant where they serve dinner. Lunch where I am now, dinner somewhere else. Find something for Sundays. Earn money, pay bills, figure out how to live. I hate the idea: I never had to do it or even think about it. All the times I was waiting to get my own place to live, I never thought about what it would really be like.

"Well, here it is," I say aloud. But the sound of my voice scares me and I shut up. I can't do this now, I think. I'll figure it out tomorrow. So many things to figure out. I have to bury my mother. I don't know how to do that. I have to look for more work. Find a smaller apartment. Tomorrow after work I'll make decisions. Right now I'm too tired. I'll do it tomorrow.

I think about food, about dinner, but I'm not hungry. All I want to do is sleep. But before I go to bed I go to my dresser, to my jewelry drawer, empty now except for the fake pearls my mother bought at Costco. I put them on over my sweatshirt. "Pearls go with everything," my mother says.

Acknowledgments

This collection owes much to Cynthia Barnard and Len Grossman, whose generous gifts of expertise, attention, care and time made possible its being born as a real book. Andrew Sharpe, equally generous with technical ingenuity and hours of endruns around Microsoft Word's eccentricities, made possible a manuscript with which a publisher could work. Larry and Carolyn Zaroff's eager reading and warm encouragement helped speed the manuscript to completion and kept the author's self-confidence on an even keel. And Michael Fain's tolerance of the ill-temper to which authorial frustrations occasionally give rise has been admirable and always appreciated, even if silently. My love and gratitude to all of them.

CPSIA information can be obtained
at www.ICGtesting.com
Printed in the USA
FFOW01n2336090116
20188FF